THE GIRL ON THE RETREAT

A.J. RIVERS

The Girl on the Retreat
Copyright © 2023 by A.J. Rivers

All rights reserved. Without limiting the rights under copyright reserved above, no part of this publication may be reproduced, stored in or introduced into retrieval system, or transmitted, in any form, or by any means (electronic, mechanical, photocopying, recording, or otherwise) without the prior written permission of both the copyright owner and the above publisher of this book.

This is a work of fiction. Names, characters, places, brands, media, and incidents are either the products of the author's imagination or are used fictitiously. The author acknowledges the trademarked status and trademark owners of various products referenced in this work of fiction, which have been used without permission. The publication/use of these trademarks is not authorized, associated with, or sponsored by the trademark owners.

PROLOGUE

Jacob couldn't breathe.

It felt like his lungs were collapsing in on themselves, devoid of air, the pain crushing in his chest.

But he kept going.

All he could think about was the point ahead. He couldn't see it yet, but he knew it was there. Somewhere in the distance, hopefully not too far, was the end point he'd been focused on since the moment his feet first started pounding into the ground.

His body was struggling. He could feel his muscles giving out and his heart beating erratically, not able to keep up with pumping enough blood to fuel him. But he pushed forward. He couldn't let himself stop. Not even for a second. He had to get to that goal ahead. He couldn't let anything stand in his way. Not now. Not this time.

Rather than letting the pain stop him, he used it as motivation to keep him going. That pain meant he could still feel something. It meant he still had presence in his body and could make it do what he wanted it to do. It meant he was still alive.

Even when his joints felt like they were going to break apart and his muscles weakened until his legs sagged and he nearly hit the ground, Jacob forced himself on. He wouldn't let himself think about anything but covering the space beneath his feet. He couldn't think of anything else around him. He didn't want to get distracted or to let his thoughts get taken over.

Instead, he pushed harder. He ran harder. He gritted his teeth against the pain and kept going.

Finally, ahead of him, it came into view. He almost sobbed with relief. It was so close. If he could just get there, he would be done. At least with this part. He could find a place to rest. He could refill his lungs and give his heart a chance to catch up. If he could get there, he might make it.

As he got closer, the fragmented hope that had started to come together in the hollow of his chest faded. There was a fence. He should have expected it, but he hadn't. He should have known that it wouldn't be so easy. He wanted it to be. He'd earned this. He'd done what he needed to do. He'd come this far. It should have been easy. He should have been able to just run past the edge of the crumbling, forgotten pavement and belong to himself again.

But that wasn't how it was. The fence stood between him and everything. Between him and life.

Somewhere inside him, a voice told Jacob to just stop. To give up. It didn't matter anymore. He'd done what he could, and it wasn't enough. He could just let the weight in his muscles pull him down and not worry about any of it anymore.

He wanted to listen to it. He was exhausted. He felt delirious and frantic. But he couldn't. He'd come this far.

He ran for the fence, ready to leap onto it and climb to the top. He couldn't see any barbed wire or razors on the top designed to make the passage over it even more difficult. It was just a fence, chain-link like when he was a child. Jacob had climbed over plenty of those in his early years. Sometimes to get into places. Sometimes to get out. All he had to do was stuff his toe into one of the holes, launch himself over the top, and drop down on the other side. He could do it again. His body would remember.

When he was within a couple feet of the fence, Jacob used all the energy he had to launch himself onto it, his hands outstretched, ready to grab on and pull him over the top.

THE GIRL ON THE RETREAT

As soon as his hands touched the metal, a hot, intense pain rushed through him, accompanied by a high, snapping buzz. He dropped immediately and crumpled to the damp grass, writhing from the lingering pain running along his nerve endings and stinging in his bones.

He needed to get up but he didn't have the time. The shadow touched his face before he saw anything else. It blotted out the stars and the dark blue rim around the moon. In the next instant, he saw the figure come down over him. Jacob wished he could see his face. If only for a second, he wanted to be able to trace the features of the person capable of doing this.

Instead, he saw the knife.

Jacob tried to crawl away. He managed to get himself to his hands and knees, but the electricity rendered his muscles almost worthless. He couldn't get away. The first thrust of the knife slammed him down onto the ground on his stomach, stealing what little breath had found its way back into him. The next went through his shoulder and pinned him down. Something—a foot or a knee—crushed down into his spine to hold him down as the man wrenched the knife out of his body.

He could feel the sinew within his body clutch the blade and resist it moving out of him. He could hear the suction of the wound and feel the blood rolling down his skin. Jacob dug his fingers into the ground and tried to pull himself away, but the man flipped him onto his back and brought the knife down into the center of his chest. It came out and sliced back through his flesh, chipping his ribs, piercing his heart.

His lungs collapsed, depriving him of air.

The weight of the man crushed his chest.

But the knife kept going.

Jacob stopped breathing.

CHAPTER ONE

H E CAN'T BREATHE.
His chest is heaving like he can't get control of his breaths.
But he keeps going.

His eyes are locked ahead of him like they're frozen. They aren't moving. Nothing around him is taking his attention. He's focused only on the goal ahead. He knows where he's going. The question is whether he's going to get there.

He's struggling. He doesn't want anyone to know it, and he's doing his best not to show it, but his gait is getting more awkward and his pace is uneven. He's not going to let himself stop. He has to get to the end. It's all he's been thinking about. He has to get there. Even if his body gives out on the way.

Which is why I'm jogging beside him.

"Xavier? You sure you're okay?" I ask.

His jaw is set and his eyes don't move, but he gives a sharp nod. He swerves a little bit, but Dean is on the other side of him, so we act

THE GIRL ON THE RETREAT

as bumpers to keep him on his own path so he doesn't drift into the way of the other runners coming up around him. I haven't looked back recently, but I have a feeling there aren't too many of those other runners left. At this point, the only ones passing us are men in designer jogging suits with gleaming white shoes that have never touched pavement. They stop every few feet to chat with one of the observers or do a quick interview on camera.

"Buddy, shoot me a thumbs up if you think you're going to make it to the end," Dean says.

We both look down at Xavier's hands clenched tightly at his sides, pumping in a textbook jogging motion that makes me worry for his future ability to straighten his elbows. It takes a second, but one thumb pops up from his fist.

"Alright. Let's do this," I say. "You're not far from the finish. Just a little longer."

I happen to know exactly how far he is from the finish because I've already been there. I got to within a few feet of the big balloon arch over the finish line and realized neither Xavier nor Dean were still with me. We'd started the run together and they assured me they were going to be able to keep up. After all, we've been training together for the last couple of months. And it isn't like we're attempting a marathon. Just a 5K. But apparently that is approximately a K and a half too long, because that's about where I lost them.

To his credit, Xavier really has been working hard to get to this point from his philosophy of running only if there was an active serial killer situation occurring in his immediate vicinity. That caveat is much further away from abstract than most people would like to believe.

The reality is, effort or not, athleticism is not Xavier's strong point. He has done some power walks around the block with me in the predawn hours, he will play the hell out of some mini golf, and he's been known to get very expressive on the trampoline in his backyard. But the real picture is that he actually should have been jogging. When he goes into the gym Sam built in the spare room, he's usually dangling upside down over a Swiss ball or doing bicep curls with a one-pound weight. Sam once bench-pressed him, but we don't speak of that. I've also heard he can headbutt grown men into oblivion, but I haven't personally seen that in action. I'll take Ava's word for it, though.

I won't pretend I didn't have my reservations when Xavier volunteered to join me for this run. When I first agreed to be a part of it, I thought it would be something Dean might like to do with me. Sam has been doing well with his recovery from the gunshot wounds he sustained over the summer and is largely back to normal, but I'm not so keen on him running multiple miles over a paved course just yet. I'm probably being too protective and a massive hypocrite considering everything my own body has been through, but I told him I'd rather have him rooting us along on the sidelines and to be there to celebrate with me at the finish line. So, that's where he is.

He cheered for me when he first saw me approaching the line, then I watched his expression go to confusion and his applause slow to him essentially just holding his own hand as I waved at him and turned back around to go find Dean and Xavier. The other runners were less than thrilled at me making my way against the current, but fortunately there aren't many here who are truly serious about the outcome of the race and the vast majority of those who are, finished well before I did.

I spend my fair share of time working out and don't have the luxury of not having running be a part of my regular life, but I'm not a speed runner. I can keep up with people I am chasing and generally get away from those chasing me, but you'll never catch me frequenting podiums with medals around my neck. I just don't have that particular love of the sport.

Xavier's gaze is still focused unwaveringly in front of him and the red color of his face is climbing to a somewhat frightening shade, but I know well enough not to try to stop him. If he has this in his head, he's going to do it no matter what. It's just up to Dean and me to make sure he's still upright when he gets there.

"You're doing great, X," Dean encourages him. "Just remember why we're doing this."

The goal of the run is to raise awareness and funds for initiatives designed to put more focus on solving cold cases and reignite searches for missing persons. The brainchild of a collective of high-powered philanthropists known as the Omnia Foundation, the run is just one of several events they've organized in their push to provide additional funding for private investigation into cases that have gone unsolved, searches for people who have been missing for years with no leads, and increased community programming to help increase personal safety and social activism geared toward decreasing crime and holding criminals accountable.

I'm not as swept up by the generosity of the whole thing the way the media has been. I know full well they aren't doing this just because they are magnanimous. Not that I am jaded enough to think the group of wealthy businessmen are only supporting these efforts for their own benefit. And there is something to say for the power of persuasion and influence when it comes to encouraging the community to contribute to causes. But I also can't just pretend I believe they aren't aware of the good reputation that will come from this.

That's on them. What really matters to me is that the money will go to causes close to my heart. I don't particularly care if the organization is only going through the motions of all this to look good, as long as they do good work. The man who contacted me and asked me to be involved, Dan Vreeland, doesn't strike me that way. I think he cares more about the cause itself than the reputation that comes from it. The fact that he confided in me that he is personally the biggest anonymous donor to the organization's efforts just underscores that for me. He wants to support what's happening, not be recognized for it.

That was enough to get me to agree to come be a part of this run. Not only did my entry, as well as Dean and Xavier's, come with donations from us, but also the prestige attached to my name. They splashed it all over promotional materials and I heard it over the radio. It's surreal to think there are people who put more credence into the efforts of the group because of my involvement, or would want to be involved themselves so they could be a part of something alongside me, but there it is.

There was a time when I was bothered by people recognizing my name or even my face. The whole concept of my career holding any sort of celebrity was uncomfortable and I did everything I could to resist it. My career is extremely important to me and I take it very seriously. The thought that it's somehow entertaining to people turning on their TVs at night or scouring newspapers and magazines for mention of my newest pursuit felt wrong. I didn't want to be anybody's poster child or glamorize any element of crime, including its investigation and bringing criminals to justice. It is intense, grueling, and often painful work, physically and mentally, and I had no interest in somehow turning that into a public persona.

It took some time for me to realize it didn't take away from what I do as long as I don't let it. Gone are the days when I wasted thought and energy trying not to be out in front of the public. It took away my ability to effectively go undercover, but it isn't like I can't walk down the street without people flocking to me to ask for my autograph. One of my cases did end up as a movie, but it was about the victim of the crime, not about me. That's about as close a brush with true fame as I've had, and I'm fine with leaving it that way. But when the opportunity comes up for my name to mean something beneficial, I'm willing to share it.

That's the goal today. At this moment it's ranking just below the goal of getting Xavier over the finish line. After that, I'll work on everything else again.

CHAPTER TWO

"He's looking a little pale, isn't he?" Dean asks. My eyes slide over to my cousin as we both jog sideways beside Xavier so we can simultaneously keep our eyes on him and encourage him along.

"He always looks pale," I say.

"But, like, particularly so. Maybe he's dehydrated. Why hasn't there been another water station?" Dean asks.

"Because we're only about a tenth of a mile from the finish line," I point out. "There's water and food just past the medical tent."

"Maybe he needs the medical tent," Dean says.

"Have you met him? What do you think is going to happen if one of those people in an obnoxiously neon t-shirt comes at him with a blood pressure cuff and an ice pack?"

Dean's expression tells me he knows exactly what would happen and he does not want to be a part of it. He turns to Xavier with an encouraging look. "Come on, buddy. We're almost there. You can do it."

The bright spot of the situation is that because this is a charity fundraising run rather than an actual race, the pacesetting car is very forgiving. It's in place to make sure that traffic doesn't come in and take out the lingering runners rather than ensuring that those runners keep up with a specific speed and hold to an acceptable finish time. I've been in the cheering squad to support other agents during several runs before and I've witnessed those crews sweeping through and gathering up the stragglers to deliver them past the finish line. It's not a great moment.

I can hear Sam cheering as we get closer to the finish. His voice rises up above everybody else's as he roots us on. We finally pass under the banner at the finish and I turn to grin at Sam as Dean stops and bends down to draw in a breath. When I look back, I notice Xavier isn't with him. He's still running straight past the finish line.

"X, you're done!" Dean calls as we catch up to him. "You did it."

He shakes his head slightly and I realize he's on his way to the refreshment tent.

A few minutes later he's stretched out on his back, his arms and legs spread out around him like a starfish, empty sports drink bottles around him and a bottle of water gripped in each hand. A volunteer came by and placed a snack box on his chest and it's still sitting there. Dean stands beside him, staring down at him as I walk back up from going to get Sam. He glances down at Xavier.

"Can you get drunk off of electrolytes?" he asks.

"I don't think so," I say. I watch him for a few seconds. "I hope not."

"Agent Griffin?"

I turn around to see Dan Vreeland standing behind me.

"Mr. Vreeland," I say, extending my hand to shake his. "It's good to see you."

"Please, call me Dan."

"And I'm Emma. This is my husband, Sam Johnson," I say, gesturing to Sam. "And my cousin, Dean Steele." The men shake hands and I glance behind me to Xavier. "That's Xavier Renton."

"Nice to meet you, Xavier," Dan calls over us. He looks at me with concern. "Is he alright?"

"Oh…" I look over again. "Yeah. He just dug deep for that run." Xavier lifts one of the bottles of water into the air by way of greeting. "See? He's good."

Dan is smiling when I turn back to him.

"Did you enjoy your run?" he asks.

"It was great," I say. "Beautiful weather for it."

THE GIRL ON THE RETREAT

"It really is. Thank you again so much for being willing to participate. Adding your name got us a big boost in signups."

"Well, I'm not so sure about that, but I'm glad it was a success. I appreciate you inviting me," I tell him.

"You're too modest," Dan says.

"Always," Sam agrees, nudging me with his hip.

"Are you hanging around for a little bit? If you're not in a hurry to head out, I'd love to introduce you to some of the other supporters," Dan says.

"Absolutely," I nod.

He grins and gestures at me to follow him. I look over at Dean, who is already waving me away.

"I'll stay with Xavier. He's twitching a little. I think he's going to sit up soon. We'll find you," he says.

"Okay. I'll see you in a bit."

Sam and I follow Dan past other runners celebrating their accomplishment, posing for pictures, stretching, and gathering in clusters to chat. A couple look like they aren't too far away from joining Xavier, but many others look like they leveraged their frequent tennis games and golf meetings to lightly jog their way through and finish in pristine condition. They're here for the photo ops rather than the finish time.

Dan leads me directly toward one of them, a tall man with a big laugh and something about him charismatic enough to cause a small group to flock around him. He acts like he's playing out the pages of a leadership book, making eye contact with each of the people near him, casually tossing out first names as he talks, and keeping his body language closely monitored to appear both in control and approachable. He catches sight of us when we're a couple steps away.

The people in front of him part as he turns his wide chest toward Dan in acknowledgement.

"Agent Emma Griffin," Dan starts, holding his hand out toward him. "This is Kyle Harris, my colleague and friend. Kyle, this is Agent Emma Griffin."

"FBI," Harris finishes for him, reaching out for my hand. "Of course. As soon as I saw that you'd agreed to be a part of this, I told Dan I just *had* to meet you. We really appreciate what you're doing for us."

I shake my head. "I'm not doing anything."

"The people who suddenly signed up after the announcement of your involvement went out would probably argue that," he points out. "There are a lot of true crime buffs around here."

"Well, I guess that's to be expected considering the purpose of this whole thing," I admit, waving my hands around as I swing back and forth slightly to indicate the entire event. "And I've noticed digging into crime is one thing that seems to cross all kinds of boundaries. A couple of my cases have brought me into contact with amateur detectives and they've covered all sexes, ages, socioeconomic groups, education levels, careers… basically any type of person you can think of. Something draws people to it."

"The puzzle can be intriguing," Dan agrees. "Everybody wants to think they can figure it out."

"That's encouraging, though, isn't it?" Harris asks. We both look at him questioningly and his eyes flash back and forth between us. "I mean, all these non-professionals wanting to find out what happened to other people? It means they're worried about people they don't even know. They want to find justice because they care so much. It's kind of beautiful, from a certain perspective."

His eyebrows are raised hopefully and the positive energy in him is almost tangible.

"I like that way of looking at it," I finally say.

"There are some other people I want to introduce Emma to," Dan says by way of making sure the conversation doesn't continue.

I shake Harris' hand. "It was good to meet you," I tell him.

"You, too. Any time you want to chat true crime, you let me know."

I give a polite chuckle and follow Dan away from the group. We pass by the medical tent and make our way toward two tents beyond it. One has tables of refreshments set up for the runners, visible through open panels on the sides of the tent. The other tent is fully closed and a small sign out front declares this area the domain of un-defined "VIPs." I feel like I should have some sort of special credentials as we walk to the flap of the tent, but Dan walks us right through without hesitation. I suppose being with one of the organizers of the event makes me legit no matter where I am.

And considering I'm starting to feel like part of the race entertainment rather than just a participant, I think I likely qualify as a VIP anyway. At least, that's my argument if anyone decides to question my presence in the tent.

I take a fresh bottle of water from the table to the side as soon as we walk in and sip on it as Dan guides me through. He's looking around obviously trying to find someone and his steps pick up as he notices them. We walk up to a small, round table where four people are enjoying plates of snacks far more impressive than what I imagine is in the boxes over at the regular refreshment tent. A woman comes up behind one of the men, resting her hand on his shoulder, and for a moment the tableau looks like a throwback game of poker.

They glance up from their conversation as Dan approaches.

"Hello, Dan," one of them says, standing and extending a hand for a friendly shake of greeting. "How did you enjoy the run?"

"It was great," Dan says. "I made better time than I thought. How about you, Tom?"

"Can't complain," the man says, looking over at me. "Hi."

Dan puts a hand in the center of my back in a gesture that's not quite a hug but something broaching it.

"I wanted you to meet someone important. Emma, this is Gary Nielsen, Cory Mellon, Brad Carver, and Tom Murphy. They, along with Kyle who you just met, make up the primary core of the organization. Guys, this is Agent Emma Griffin."

The men stand and shake my hand in turn.

"Gary. It's fantastic to meet you. Thank you for coming."

"Brad. Great to have you be a part of this. We appreciate your support, Agent Griffin."

The third man isn't quite as enthusiastic as the first two. He gives me a somewhat apologetic look as he shakes my hand.

"I'm Cory. I'm so sorry, but I'm not familiar with your name," he says.

Beside me, Dan cringes like he's embarrassed the man would say anything like that. Before he can say anything, Tom gives a slight shrug.

"I have to admit, I'm in the same boat," he adds. "I'm sorry. I'm sure I should know considering how much Dan pushed for your involvement, but I can't place your name."

Dan's hand returns to my back like he's supporting me through the blow of the two men not knowing who I am.

"Gentlemen, this is Emma Griffin, preeminent FBI agent. You know? She took down Leviathan? She solved the crimes of Salvador Marini?"

Their faces remain blank.

"Emma's been responsible for solving some of the most difficult cases of our time and has put away dangerous murders no one has been able to touch."

"It's alright," I say as he takes a breath like he's taking a second to gather up some more lavish descriptions for my career he can use to try to shame them into recognition. "It's really fine. FBI agents aren't exactly known for our full publicity schedules. It's nice to meet all of you. Thanks for having me be a part of this."

I feel like I've gone through the same rotating collection of words a dozen times this morning and I'm not sure what I actually mean by them anymore. It's a weird little quirk of the language I didn't notice much before Xavier came along and taught me the very specific joy that is trying to understand what he's saying and why he's saying it. Sometimes he rattles off phrases or bandies back and forth in canned conversations that feel nothing short of rehearsed. It took me a little while to learn that that's because they are.

You ask how someone is doing when you first encounter them not because you actually want to know but because it's the expected social engagement. You tell people it was nice to meet them not because it was any sort of actual pleasure or you even cared about meeting them but because it leaves future social interaction open. What he likes to refer to as the on-ramp to friendship or at least the merge-point to comfortable casual acquaintance. Fairly flagrant traffic analogy usage for someone who doesn't drive. But accurate.

"She's the agent who solved that bus station bombing in Richmond," Dale adds. "And took out that trafficker. The one who was operating out of that resort."

The men look like they are searching for the name of the criminal, but I hope they don't find it. I don't want to hear it. I know exactly who and what he's talking about, and I don't want to think about it anymore. I especially don't want any of them to get a sudden spark of fascination and ask me to tell them about it.

I smile and try to throw them off their concentration by detouring the conversation.

"That's right. But I'm actually really interested in hearing more about your organization and what it does," I say.

"Great," Cory says. "Why don't you grab something to eat and join us?"

CHAPTER THREE

THE DOORBELL BREAKS MY CONCENTRATION. I'M SURPRISED AT the sound, thinking it's still the predawn hours when I got out of bed to dig through the case file of an extremely slippery art thief who may also be linked to a large human trafficking ring, but a glance at my clock says that it's mid-morning already. I must have completely lost track of time. I've been working the case for the last few months, trying to find the piece of evidence that would prove the beliefs I have about him.

That's one of the things about my career that gets to me the most. Knowing who is responsible for something but not being able to prove it. I've stared into the eyes of men who I know have slaughtered a dozen or more people but who are only being brought up on charges of drug trafficking or assault. They know what they've done. They know I know what they've done. Yet, the evidence isn't there to actually hold them accountable. It pushes me to my limits—and has, at times, pushed me over the edge. All I can do is dig deeper. All I can do is try harder and make sure I can find every bit of detail that will ensure they are forced to face responsibility for everything they've done.

But burying myself that deep into these investigations can quickly make time disappear, which means I often find myself losing track of the time of day or things like eating and sleeping. This morning I climbed out of bed carefully to avoid waking Sam up and went into my office to look through my notes in search of something that woke me up. Something one of the witnesses I interviewed said came back into my mind while I was sleeping; I woke up with the words echoing through the back of my thoughts, but I'm not sure what about it is bothering me.

Apparently that rabbit hole took much longer than I thought. Sam must have left for work already. I have some vague recollection of hearing him call out that he was leaving and that he loved me, and calling back that I love him, too. Most likely that's accurate. He doesn't leave without saying goodbye to me unless there's an emergency call and he can't find me. Even then, he usually shouts as he rushes out the front door.

I walk out of my office and smell coffee lingering in the air. It brings a smile to my lips. He got me a new coffeemaker for Christmas that has a timer on it so he's able to make coffee for me even when he's not actually in the house. It's a nice little touch when I'm so piled with work that I barely come up for air and we only end up crossing paths for a few moments each morning and evening rather than actually spending time together.

Promising myself a visit to the kitchen after I open the door, I go through the living room to peek out at the front porch. A delivery driver is standing close to the door holding what looks like a large basket. I open the door slightly and peek out, immediately recognizing the young man now that I'm seeing his face and not just the brim of his hat.

"Hey, Joe," I say. "How are you doing today?"

He smiles at me with one of those kinds of smiles that look like men hold onto them from the time they are born. Boyish and charming, earning them plenty of admirers at every junction of life. Sam has that kind of smile. I fell in love with it when I was seven years old and haven't gotten enough of it yet.

"Hi, Mrs. Johnson," he says, using the married name that sets apart my regular life in Sherwood from the time that's dedicated to the Bureau. "I'm doing okay. I've got a delivery for you."

"I see that," I say. "I didn't know you were doing deliveries. I didn't see you over the Christmas season."

THE GIRL ON THE RETREAT

"Well, a lot of the people who signed up for the holidays quit after Christmas so there were openings. I'm saving up for college next year, so it seemed like a good idea," Joe says.

"Good for you."

"Thanks," he says, then holds the basket out toward me. "Here you go."

"Thank you," I reply, taking it from him. I look at as much of it as I can see around the large puff of cellophane and flowing gold ribbons. "I wonder who this is from?"

He shrugs. "Doesn't say."

"Give me a second." I set the basket to the side and go for my bag to take out some folded bills to give him as a tip. He grins when I present them. "It's cold out there today. Stay warm. And good luck with your savings."

"Thank you. I will. Have a good day," Joe says and scurries off the porch and back toward his van.

He's not working for one of the large national companies but a small local company that does courier work and deliveries for businesses in Sherwood. Other than some packages and legal paperwork, a lot of its business comes from older people and those who are sick or otherwise stuck in the house ordering grocery deliveries or items from other stores on Main Street. I'm sure they will keep Joe plenty busy and that smile of his will make sure the tips keep coming.

I close the door and pick the basket back up to carry it into the kitchen with me. Setting it on the table, I go to the coffeemaker and pour a cup from the full carafe. Sipping the dark roast, I go back to the table and pull the end of the ribbon on the front of the cellophane. The thick plastic crackles as I move it away in search of a note. Finally, I find an envelope tucked in among various packages of chocolates, cookies, and crackers.

Inside the envelope is a plain dark blue card. As I open it, a couple of photographs slide out. I catch them and see that they are of me from various points on the course from the run a few days ago. At the bottom of the stack is one of Dean and me helping Xavier over the finish line.

The sound of the front door opening makes me lift my head and a few seconds later, Sam comes into the kitchen carrying a bouquet of yellow flowers.

"Hey, babe," he says. "You found your coffee."

"I did. Thank you. Were those outside?" I ask, looking at the flowers. "I thought Joe handed me everything."

Sam gives me a questioning look. "Joe?"

"The Harper boy. You know the one who used to get you called out all the time because he played basketball in the street and his neighbor hated the sound of it," I tell him.

"Ah," Sam says. "Yes. The horror of a teenage boy getting fresh air and wholesome competition ten yards from his own front door. I don't know how our town survived it."

I chuckle. "Well, now he has taken his menacing of society to a new level and is saving up to go to college in the fall."

"How dare he?" Sam says.

"I know. He's working with the delivery company. He brought this just a little bit ago." I gesture at the basket sitting on the table.

"Who's it from?" he asks.

I look at the card. "Dan Vreeland. Thanking me for being a part of the run. It sounds like they raised even more than they were expecting. I still don't think that has anything to do with me, but he thinks it does."

"What are those?" Sam asks, gesturing at the pictures in my hand.

"They were in the card. I guess there were photographers along the course." I pull one of the pictures out and show it to him. "That one's particularly flattering."

Sam laughs. "That had to have been right after you got some water. You look like you're either yelling at the woman in front of you or trying to eat her."

"Motivation. Helping her run faster," I say.

"Oh, that's a good one of Xavier," Sam chuckles, pointing out the one at the finish line.

"We should get one of those little buttons you can push so it plays inspirational music every time we look at it."

"I think he'd like that. Wait… who is this?"

I look at the picture in Sam's hand. It's one that I hadn't gotten to yet when he came into the kitchen. At first glance the picture looks like it's of me. Taken from behind, it shows a thick blonde ponytail and a racerback tank top just like the one I was wearing during the run, but there's something about the positioning of the runner's body that doesn't look right, and her head is tilted toward a person beside her like they're having a conversation, but I don't recognize the other runner. I didn't spend any of my time out on the course chatting with anyone I didn't know, so I don't know who it might be.

"Look, whoever it is was wearing red pants. Mine were green. It's definitely not me," I say. I bring the picture closer. "Definitely looks like me, though. That's weird."

"I wonder if she got any pictures of you," Sam shrugs.

THE GIRL ON THE RETREAT

I laugh. "Maybe she got one of both of us heading for the finish line. One from when she actually finished and one from when I almost got there and then went back to find Dean and Xavier."

"If they took it from the front, then they would know for sure it was a different person because no one out there looked as pretty as you," Sam says.

I scrunch my face at him and stick out my tongue. "You know that flattery gets you nowhere with me, mister."

"Mhm. Sure," he replies sarcastically. "Anything good in here?"

He makes like he's coming in for a kiss but then abruptly swoops his head away to poke through the contents of the basket and snag a couple chocolates. My mouth drops open from the deception and I shoo him away. "Get your own!" I say through laughter.

"Well, maybe I can make it up to you. These are not from Dan. These are from me," he says, holding out the flowers to me again with a wink. The man sure knows how to melt my heart.

"Oh, really?" I ask, taking the bouquet and bringing them to my nose to breathe in their sweet fragrance. "What's the occasion?"

"I don't need a reason to bring my wife flowers," he says. I give him a look and he pops one of the chocolates into his mouth. "But this time I do. Valentine's Day."

I don't need to look at the calendar hanging on the wall beside the back door to know that today is not actually Valentine's Day. It's not until this weekend, and even then, Sam and I don't have plans. At least, not ones that I know about. Most women would probably be thrilled to hear that their husband started Valentine's Day celebrations well in advance of the actual holiday. I'm not exactly there.

It isn't that I don't love and appreciate Sam. I just have complicated feelings about the holiday itself. It's never been one that I've been eager to celebrate. I was never the girl who waited on pins and needles to see which tiny Valentine's Day card I would get from my classmates, or pranced through the hallways of school displaying armfuls of roses and balloons like it had direct correlation to my worth. If I did have a date for the holiday, I always tried to avoid restaurants at all costs and would much rather do something creative or just stay at home.

Likewise, I was never the type to rage against Valentine's Day or make a big deal out of hating what it represented. My best friend Bellamy often said we were each other's valentine, but that was more so neither of us ate the entire bag of conversation hearts and because we conveniently dislike the flavors of chocolate the other likes so we can mix and match easily.

I don't have a problem with Valentine's Day and I've been known to throw on something red and sparkly for a night out on occasion. My issues are far more recent. The holiday is attached to some bad memories for me that I would rather just avoid altogether. That has resulted in me avoiding the holiday for the last several years. A couple of times Sam and I have tried to do something, but it always feels like we're making plans because other people expect us to rather than us actually wanting to. I don't need a specific day on the calendar or a dog and pony show of gifts to know my husband loves me or to prove something about our relationship to everybody else. So, we don't. Or we order pizza and give each other silly gifts.

This year, though, apparently something else is going on.

"Valentine's Day?" I ask.

"I know," he says. "And if it makes you feel any better, I didn't actually plan it originally for Valentine's Day, but it just worked out that way and I thought it would be good for us."

"What would?" I ask.

"Seth is letting us use his lake cabin for the weekend," he tells me, his face lighting up.

There's that little boy smile.

It's been about a year and a half since Seth, one of the men in the sheriff's department, inherited the lake house from his grandmother and told Sam he could use it whenever he wanted. He knows how much Sam loves the outdoors, especially anything involving the woods or the mountains, and is eager to do him the favor. We just haven't had the chance to actually use it.

We've planned to a couple of times, but each time, something has gotten in the way. I'll openly admit the majority of those obstacles have been because of my work, with cases getting complicated or court dates coming up and we needed to rearrange our schedule. But the last time we planned to go was actually cancelled because Sam got shot and was stuck in the hospital—but technically that was also because of a case I was investigating, so it's on me. Which means I'm happy to take any opportunity I can to give him the getaway he's been wanting so much.

And maybe, just maybe, the fact that it's only a couple of days away will mean we'll actually make it this time.

CHAPTER FOUR

WE DIDN'T GET EXACTLY THE EARLY START ON OUR VALENTINE'S Day getaway as we wanted to and I'm doing my best not to think about the sound of the phone ringing behind me as I closed the front door before our drive. This weekend isn't about work. Leaving Sherwood means leaving my office, my files, and my phone behind. I have my pager, but I've promised to leave it on the kitchen counter and only check it if I happen to go by it during the day. Not that it's going to make that much of a difference because there's no phone at the cabin. If someone does page me, I'll be able to see it, but that's about it.

If there's a serious emergency, I'll have to drive down the mountain to the nearest ranger station to find a phone. Not ideal for a variety of reasons. I've already spoken with Xavier and made sure he understands what constitutes an emergency in this situation and what doesn't. I've also made sure he has a plentiful supply of cereal. Dean is working in town this weekend, so that should keep things better under control.

The sun is just starting to set when we pull up to the side of the cabin. It's adorable tucked into the pine trees on the top of a hill overlooking the lake. The flush of red and pink light splashed across the rippling surface of the water makes the surroundings look like a postcard. Even in the first seconds stepping out of the car, I know this is somewhere I would like to spend more time. Particularly in the summer when the breeze coming up off the water doesn't feel like it's carrying tiny particles of ice. Small pockets of snow nestled at the base of some of the trees are picturesque, but there's something to be said for being able to spread a blanket out on the shore and stare up at the stars through the night in velvety summer heat.

"It's beautiful up here," I say, brushing my hair away from my face as I turn to watch Sam start to unload our bags. "I'm surprised Seth didn't want to bring his girlfriend for the weekend."

Sam chuckles as he sets down one of the bags and reaches in for another. "Seth has a lot of really good memories up here with his grandma and his cousins and everything, but he's not exactly an outdoors person. He told me the last time he came out here was five years ago for a family reunion and after that his grandmother was too sick to make the trip. Without her, he doesn't have a lot of motivation to be without a TV or phone."

"And around all this fresh air and nature?" I ask.

"That about sums it up. And I've only met Stephanie one time, but I get the distinct impression she shares his view on getting out into the wilderness."

"Seems like it's a waste for him to inherit the cabin, then. Why didn't she leave it to one of the cousins he used to come here with?" I ask.

Sam flings one of the bags over his shoulder, tucks another under his arm, and picks up the third. "Apparently he was the one who came here the most to see their grandmother and when they weren't here, he talked about his memories a lot, so she thought he loved it and would be devastated if he didn't get it."

"Good job, Seth's grandma," I snicker. "Way to be perceptive."

"Well, it turns out the rest of the cousins all had the same plan to just sell it if they were the ones to inherit it, so at least this way it stays in the family," Sam says.

"So that when Seth is a grandfather he can force another generation into summers of family memory-making in order to select the one of them he'll hoist it off on when he hits his deathbed?" I ask.

"Something like that. Of course, by then it might have been reclaimed by nature." Sam looks up at the small structure and lets out a sigh, then snaps his eyes back to me. "But before that happens, let's enjoy it. Come on."

I laugh and take one of the bags from him to carry up a narrow, multi-level flight of wooden steps far more grand than the cabin itself. The small building has been well cared for even without frequent visitors. It's pretty basic but still looks like the perfect spot for a relaxing weekend. It seems isolated in its little spot among the trees, but I know there are plenty of other cabins and larger homes studding the mountain, with a beautiful view of the lake. I'm sure that during the summer months the lake fills with families and groups of friends. It would seem like the cousins would love that kind of socialization, especially when they were teenagers.

Of course, Seth is a good decade younger than me, so maybe my idea of an ideal teen summer aren't the same as his.

We get everything into the cabin and unpack before poking around a bit to see if there is anything we need. Seth told us his grandmother had hired a neighbor, a man who lived full-time on the mountain to be the caretaker for the property when she stopped visiting and he'd asked him to make sure it was ready for them to stay in.

As we look around, it's obvious he'd taken the request very seriously. The cabin is as spotlessly clean as a log cabin in the middle of the woods can be, the linens on the bed and handmade blankets draped over the back of the couch smell freshly laundered, and there are a few basic groceries in the kitchen. A note on the counter gives us the neighbor's name and contact information in case we need anything. I don't know how I feel about that. It's one thing to have someone be willing to stop by and make sure everything is in good condition and there aren't any major problems that need to be handled. It's another to treat a neighbor like a resort concierge. I'll have to do some prodding to find out how this man is compensated and thank him myself.

"How do you feel about hot dogs over the fire tonight?" Sam asks.

"Sounds perfect to me."

He smiles and goes outside to get the large firepit going while I collect what we'll need to cook and eat outside. Grabbing a couple of the blankets, I carry everything out and down to the pit where it's located several yards down the hill toward the lake. Sam has already gotten the flames started, but it will be a little while before the fire is hot enough for us to actually cook any food over it. I leave everything on one of the cut logs positioned around the fire as seating and wrap one of the blankets around myself to ward off the added chill that came along with the sun disappearing since we went inside.

Dropping a kiss to the top of Sam's head as he crouches by the fire and prods the center to help it grow, I take a kerosene lantern and carry it with me down toward the lake. The water calls to me. It always has. As I've gotten into adulthood and learned more about the childhood and youth that was foggy for so long, I've found out that I wasn't born near the water and most of my life wasn't spent anywhere near it. But many of my most treasured memories are of the times my family spent in Florida when I was young.

There are still a lot of questions about why we lived in the house that we did and why it was available to us whenever we needed it. Or what it was that kept bringing us back to that same spot. They are questions I'm probably never going to ask. I met the daughter of the owner of the house years ago and found in her pieces of the puzzle of my life that had been hidden away from me for decades. I revisited the house and found more pieces of myself. Along the way I learned about my father's work and why he was so often away, and the realities of what the incredible woman my mother was and why she was there the night she was murdered. It's enough for me. I used to think I needed to know all the answers, but I've learned I really don't. Those answers aren't going to do anything for me.

What matters now is that my mother's grave is there. Eli's grave is there. The waterpark where I used to lie on the lounge chairs with my father and brave the sizzle on the bottoms of my feet from the sun-baked cement to get paper boats of golden, salty French fries is there. The beach where I built sandcastles and buried my feet and screamed into the ocean is there. The theme park where I watched families living out dreams while I walked familiar sidewalks and waited for magic is there.

It's all there. And I frequently long for it.

That's not home. It never really was. No matter how much it meant to me and how many good memories I have of it, Florida isn't my home. That's Sherwood, with its quiet, sleepy neighborhoods and quaint town green and everybody in everybody else's business under the banner of community. It has its drawbacks, but it's still where I have my comfort and happiness.

But despite Florida not being home, it still has a tight hold on me. I haven't been back as frequently as I used to over the last few years, but that pull doesn't really go away. It always gets stronger when I'm near water. I'm not a person who is going to wake up before the sun and relish hours of swimming laps, but I am drawn to the water. I love to sit in

THE GIRL ON THE RETREAT

the quiet and stare into it. There's something about it that both soothes and excites me.

I walk out onto the soft sandy bank around the lake and snuggle down deeper into the blanket wrapped around me. The sand is too damp and chilly to sit down on right now, so I just stand a couple of feet from where the water washes up from soft ripples across the surface. The air smells clean and heavy here, filled with the plants and rich soil beneath the water.

A few minutes later I feel Sam's arms loop around my waist and he presses a kiss to the side of my neck. I'm thankful for the peaceful calm that comes over me with him there. Not just the feeling itself but my ability to feel it. It still doesn't feel too long ago that any kind of touch like that would have immediately put me on edge. Rather than relaxing back into his arms, every muscle of my body would have gone tense in preparation of fighting back.

Instead, I just breathe in my husband's embrace and stare out over the water. There are plenty of dark memories revolving around water that linger in the edges of my mind. If I let them, horrific images of the beach and the waves will take over. But I don't let them. The water is mine. It's one thing I won't share.

CHAPTER FIVE

Him

THE PRISTINE BLACK SURFACE OF THE TABLE WAS THE IDEAL backdrop for the photographs spread across it. He scrutinized each of them, occasionally pulling one of them out of the line and setting it aside. There were details he looked for in the images. He needed them to be perfect.

He slid two images out of their rows and brought them closer so he could compare them more intently. To most, they would likely look identical, but he could clearly see the differences. He would accept nothing less.

The woman's dark hair was swept around one shoulder to trail down her chest and pool on her stomach. In one of the photos, a breeze had picked up several strands and carried them across her face so they marred the pale expanse of her cheek. One clinging to the edge of her lip made him want to reach into the photograph and brush the strands away.

He selected the one with her hair lying in place and brushed the other to the far corner of the table to sit among others that had been rejected.

The next comparison was among a series of five. These were less similar, showing the same woman from slightly different angles. It should have been difficult to choose. Each one was so close to perfect. He should have had to think more about it, take his time to choose. But he didn't. This wasn't the first time he'd stood in front of this table and looked over rows of images. It wasn't the first time he'd scrutinized to the tiniest detail.

He knew what he wanted. He knew what *they* wanted. He had standards.

Three of the photos didn't fit those standards. They went to the corner with the others.

The look in the woman's eyes made him pause when he compared the next set of images. They gazed out like pools of rainwater. The slight change of angle in the next picture created a darkening in one of her eyes. A closer look revealed the reflection of him holding up his camera. It completely blocked his face, and even if it didn't, the reflection was far too small to clearly identify any of his features. But it was still there. He pushed it aside. Even that tiny indication ruined it. They didn't want him. They wanted her.

He carried on until he'd gotten through all of the images he'd spread across the table. They were now divided into two stacks. One went to the top of the table to be laid out again and divided up to fill the envelopes waiting on another table to the side of the room. The rest he brought to a smaller table a few steps away and, one by one, put them through a shredder.

CHAPTER SIX

"**A**GENT GRIFFIN? EMMA?"

I adjust the phone on my shoulder and twirl around so I can walk back up to the grocery bag sitting on the kitchen table without wrapping the telephone cord around myself. The cordless phone that is Bellamy's current obsession isn't my cup of tea with its short range and tendency to snap and crackle more than a bowl of rice cereal during phone calls, but in moments like this, I can see the appeal. Even if it only lets you walk ten feet from the dock, at least there's no twisty rubber coil to get tangled in.

"Yes?" I ask, starting to unpack the groceries Sam and I bought this morning after getting home to a nearly empty kitchen last night.

"It's Dan. Vreeland."

"Oh! Dan. Hello. How are you?" I ask.

The pantry is just too far for the phone cord to reach without sincere risk of the handset slipping from my grasp and snapping into the wall, so I collect those groceries in one area of the table rather than trying to put them away. I can get to the refrigerator and start filling the vegetable crisper.

"I've been better," he responds.

"I'm sorry to hear that," I say.

"It's nothing serious. Just stress, really. And it's actually the reason I called you."

He can't see the quizzical look that comes over my face as I stuff the remaining produce into the refrigerator and head back to the bags.

"What can I do for you?" I ask.

"I'm glad you put it that way because I need a massive favor. It's something I think you will be interested in and would enjoy participating in. At least, I hope," Dan says.

"Is it another run?" I ask. "A bike-a-thon?"

Dan laughs like this is far funnier than it actually is.

"It's a true crime seminar."

I'm not even sure how to react to this.

"A true crime seminar?" I ask.

"Yes. It's another event that we've put together for this weekend. We've been planning it for over a year. True crime enthusiasts are coming together to discuss cases, learn about forensics, get tips on personal safety and self-protection. It should be really amazing," he says.

"It sounds like it," I agree. "It also sounds like a lot of work went into it."

"Yes. It did. But apparently not quite enough. One of our presenters withdrew. He was supposed to lead at least two seminars and workshops during the event as well as participate in some of the other activities. Now he's not going to be there at all. He's leaving a massive gap in the programming and the only person I could think of who could possibly fill a gap like that is you."

He says it with a slight lilt at the end of the sentence like he's hoping to sound endearing. Like maybe I won't stop and think about what he's saying and just agree.

"You want me to take his place?" I ask.

I don't tell him that I don't exactly feel prepared for that kind of undertaking, standing here barefoot in my kitchen gripping a box of bottle of orange juice and trying to remember if I have a tray of cinnamon rolls frozen or if I need to bake them fresh.

"I was hoping. I know it's asking a lot, but I really do think that you would be incredible. You saw the reaction of the people at the run. They were thrilled to have you there. And most of those were just investors and business connections. Imagine the reaction we would get from those who are invested in the true crime world," he gushes.

"I still don't have my head fully wrapped around this whole true crime obsession," I admit. "I spend a lot of time wading through cases. I see things I can't imagine anyone would ever want to see."

"It's a fascination for them. Like any other hobby, I suppose. You told me your husband enjoys baseball. And your friend Xavier likes…"

Everything. And nothing.

He continues to try to sell me on the idea as I tangle and untangle myself from the cord putting away the rest of the groceries. Sam headed to the office for a while to check how everything went while we were gone and he'll be home soon. There's not going to be a fabulous dinner waiting for him on the table, but I could probably throw something together.

"I'm looking forward to giving them something that they'll enjoy, but the part I'd like to think is the most important goes back to the original goal of the foundation: to help," Dan says. "I want to help keep people safe and provide support for victims of crimes. Some of this retreat is about trying their hand at being detectives or learning about cases from real law enforcement, but that's not all of it. The self-defense and safety skills workshops are the parts that are the most important focus for me. And I know that's something you care about as well."

"I do. Let me talk this over with my husband and I'll get back with you. You said it's this weekend?" I ask.

"The event officially starts Saturday, but all the presenters are coming Thursday to get settled in," he says. "It's being held in Merrywether."

The town is about an hour outside of Sherwood, so not too far to travel.

"Alright. I'll give you a call back," I tell him.

"Thank you, Emma. I look forward to hearing from you."

It takes me a second to get unraveled and get the phone back on the cradle. I sort out the ingredients for dinner and get everything else put away while I think about the possibility of doing the event. It sounds beneficial, I have to admit. My passion for justice doesn't just begin and end with solving cases. I also want to help people stay safer in a world progressively getting more dangerous.

I'm still thinking about it when Sam gets home. He finds me staring down into the pot of chili I'm stirring slowly.

"Are the kidney beans threatening to revolt?" he asks.

"They're like that," I say. "I can't ever be too careful."

I kiss him hello as he passes to get a drink from the refrigerator.

THE GIRL ON THE RETREAT

"Speaking of like that, Ben Cathers called four times while we were gone," Sam says.

"Locked himself out again?" I ask.

"Twice. The other two were because his cat got stuck in a tree in the front yard."

"Isn't the only tree in his front yard a dogwood he planted two years ago?" I ask.

"Yep. James was off duty so he went up there and got the cat both times. He didn't even have to reach all the way above his head."

"James is four inches shorter than Ben," I point out.

"And now you understand why I'm seriously questioning the idea of this whole community helpline at the station," Sam says.

"But if he didn't have it, he'd be calling 911."

"True. I guess this is a better alternative." Sam took a long swig from his can of pineapple Slice. "What about you? Was it really the kidney beans or was there something else that got you staring at the chili?"

"I got a call from Dan Vreeland," I tell him, then proceed to sum up his invitation. "I didn't commit to anything yet. I told him I needed to talk it over with you. What do you think about it?"

"What matters is what you think about it," Sam says.

"I'd still like your input," I say.

"I think it's an interesting opportunity. And it sounds like an honor that they thought of you."

"As a last-minute replacement," I counter.

"Sure, but you said yourself that they've been working on this thing for a really long time. Longer than you've even known Dan Vreeland. Which means they booked the guy you replaced back then."

"That's true."

"How about other than that?" Sam asks.

"From the very beginning of my career, what made me want to go into the Academy was wanting to help people. After everything that happened with my parents, I wanted to do anything I possibly could to protect people and stop criminals. That's more than just the fieldwork as an agent. This sounds like something that fits with that."

"It does," Sam nods. "In a way, it's like your own community hotline. You can reach out to these people and help them keep themselves safer. Or know how to help others stay safe. You really can make that difference."

I sigh. "But my schedule is really tight right now. Eric has me consulting on three cases and I'm still working on that missing person. I feel like I'm close with the other case. I have so much going on I can't even wrap my head around the thought of trying to prepare seminars and workshops in just a few days, not to mention actually taking that time off."

"Is the retreat being held in the middle of the woods?" Sam asks.

I give him a questioning look as I take a pan of cornbread out of the oven.

"What?"

"Is it some sort of isolation retreat? They're going to cut you off from the rest of society for the duration of the event?" Sam asks.

"I'm not questioning Dan's ability to theme the hell out of an event, but I don't think it's strictly necessary to put people immersing themselves in crime stories out in the middle of nowhere. It's probably not the best choice," I say.

"Right. Which means you'll have access to a phone," Sam explains. "You're not being asked to speak all day for the entire event. And I've been to some conferences and things in my day. Generally they wrap up in the early evening. If you're really that concerned about not getting anything done, you could bring your files with you and work on your downtime. If you need to talk to Eric about something, you can call him."

I think about this for a few seconds. "It does seem like something that could be really important."

"Then I think you should do it. And don't worry about putting together what you're going to say. It's just a couple of presentations. You talk about your work all the time. How much could you actually need to do over a weekend?"

It turns out, I don't need to worry about what I'm going to present over the course of a weekend. Because when I call Dan after dinner to tell him I'll do it, it turns out he conveniently forgot to specify the event is a weeklong retreat at a luxury resort. And I have the distinct feeling there are some woods involved.

CHAPTER SEVEN

DAN SLIPPED THE DETAIL THAT THE EVENT WILL STRETCH ON well past the end of the weekend into the conversation like it wasn't a big deal. Just a casual mention that I'd just agreed to spending ten days at an event that seems to be in argument with itself about whether it's a true crime convention or an extended personal safety seminar.

By the time it sank in, I'd already committed to filling in for the guy who dropped them and Dan sounded both relieved and excited. Even though I was frustrated I'd been a bit misinformed at the beginning of the conversation, I couldn't bring myself to rescind my agreement. It still sounds like it could be valuable and, much like agreeing to go out and do the run with Dean and Xavier, if I can utilize my notoriety for good, as strange as it might seem to me, I'm going to do what I can.

Sam isn't as much on board with me being a part of this whole thing now that he knows it isn't just the weekend, but I told him I'd already given my word and am going to do it. I spent the last few days trying to put together the seminars and workshops I'll be leading throughout the week. It was a daunting idea when I first hung up the phone with Dan, but once I got started, it was easier than I'd expected it to be. I'm not finished as I drive toward the resort. I have enough of a framework to make me confident for the first couple of days, but I'll be chasing the other days. I tell myself I'll build them based on the days as I get through them and that will make each more effective.

Or I'll fly by the seat of my pants and hope for the best. Either way, it will be better than not having someone there.

At least, that's what I'm trying to tell myself. Let's be honest, I'm not really feeling good about that. I don't do mediocre well. I'll probably just check in and spend the rest of today perfecting the first two days of presentations, then work on the rest.

The resort isn't far from Sherwood, but the drive sends me in a direction I don't usually go, and it feels much farther away than it actually is. It brings me through a tiny old town that makes Sherwood look almost metropolitan, then skirts just a few miles away from the main road leading to a large tourist complex. When I first heard the event was being held in Merryweather, I assumed that was the most likely venue.

Instead, I find myself weaving up a long driveway toward a resort that looks like it was either built on the skeleton of an old hotel and modernized, or designed with that aesthetic in mind. Perched on the top of a hill, the sprawling white building has a deep wraparound front porch with stately columns, a large balcony on the front, and many tall windows. The driveway leads up alongside the building and around to the back, not providing any parking in the front. It's almost as if the owners of the venue didn't want to mar the visual of the space with vehicles.

I go to the back and follow along the drive that dips down and to a fork, where I follow the small wooden sign that shows where parking is. Eventually, I come out to a large stone carriage house sitting at the mouth of the parking lot, the creative angle blocking much of the sightline so the cars parked there aren't visible for someone just walking near the house.

There's no one waiting to direct me, so I park and grab my bags. Hauling them away from the lot isn't the most energizing start to the retreat. As I approach the building, wondering if I'm supposed to go all the way around to the front and into the main door or if there's an entrance at the back, Dan Vreeland suddenly appears. He's distracted as he wipes his hands off on the front of his shirt, but when he sees me, his face breaks out in a smile.

"Emma! You're here! It's great to see you," he says, coming toward me.

"Good to see you, too," I say. I gesture vaguely behind me. "I parked back there. Is that right?"

I don't see any other parking area or a garage, but the paved drive does continue along ahead without any indication of what might be there, so it's possible where I parked is for guests and there's a staff location elsewhere. But Dan nods.

"You found it!" He reaches for one of my suitcases. "Here, let me help you with that."

"Is there enough space in that lot for everybody coming to the retreat? It doesn't look very big."

My real thought isn't for the parking situation but the attendance at this event. The way Dan characterized it made me think this was going to be a fairly large audience, but that lot isn't big enough to hold more than thirty or so cars and a handful of them are already full.

"We've arranged for offsite parking for the guests and shuttles to get them here," Dan explains. "It's a space consideration, of course, and it's nice to have everyone's complete focus because there's nowhere for them to go. But I have to admit it's also a selfish endeavor to a degree. All the guests were given their choice of three different arrival slots and had to select one while registering for the event. That way we know when everybody is coming and have control over their arrival. I'm sure we'll be ready to hit the ground running, but if something was to happen that delayed us, having the offsite parking and shuttles controls who is here and allows us to keep them from arriving until everything is ready and in place."

"I can appreciate a bit of manufactured crowd control," I say.

Dan grins. "Thank you again for doing this. You have no idea how happy I am to have you. And everyone we've told has been thrilled."

"Everyone you've told?" I ask.

It seems like a strange qualification for my presence.

"I talked it over with members of the board, of course, and a couple of the guests who were personally invited rather than just registering. But for the rest of the guests, you being here is going to be a surprise. I can't wait to see how excited they are," I say.

"If they're expecting the other person, won't they be disappointed?" I ask.

"I doubt it," Dan tells me. "Maybe a couple of them would have wanted to hear him speak, but that's what he does most of his life, so if there are any actual fans, which, again, I doubt, they will have heard him already."

"Who is he, anyway?" I ask.

Dan is walking me toward the back of the building rather than to the front as he talks.

"Lucas Bremmer. The true crime writer. You know, those books that are somewhere between non-fiction and fiction. Leaning toward the non. Anyway, his writing means he's done really extensive research into a lot of murders, kidnappings, and even some organized crime. He does talks about the cases and the work he's done with the police and other investigation organizations to get the details right, especially for the crimes that are still unsolved."

"Cold cases?" I ask. "Not a very common subject for these types."

Dan nods, juggling the bag he's holding to open the door so we can go in. I would have just opened the door for myself, but he's kept himself positioned in just the right awkward space I haven't been able to take a full-length step or reach around him.

"Mmm-hmmm. He said he got interested in them when he came across a news clipping about a murder in his hometown and realized it was never solved. Eventually he gathered up so much information that he thought to release it in a book. So, he did. And it was wildly successful."

"At least he found something he enjoys," I say.

"And is exceptional at, if you listen to him," Dan says with a laugh. "In all honesty, I think he's disappointed he only writes. He'd rather be a detective actually solving the crimes, not just writing about them when no one else can figure them out."

I nod. "I can see where that would be frustrating."

The door we go through leads us into an airy sunroom that stretches nearly the entire length of the back of the house. We pass through into what I'm assuming is considered the lobby. It has the soaring ceiling of an atrium in the center but stretches on either side into alcoves and open spaces with arrangements of furniture like they're encouraging people to gather here. There's no one in any of them and I'm not sure how inclined people staying in a place like this would be to lounging around in the lobby.

But perhaps I'm wrong. This could be the kind of place where people like to collect, make connections, sit next to a fire and read in public. I guess I'll find out over the week.

"This is the main floor," Dan explains as if he could hear my thoughts. "It has the lobby, public gathering areas, the dining room, a coffee lounge, a library, things like that. There's one main banquet room down here where we'll have our welcome reception tomorrow night. The guest rooms are on the top two floors. In between are the rooms we'll use for the actual event. With the exception of the larger lectures,

THE GIRL ON THE RETREAT

which will be held in the auditorium in the basement. They have movie nights there and sometimes live performances."

He sounds like a brochure.

"You seem to know this place pretty well," I remark.

Dan shrugs. "I've been here a few times. That's why I knew it would be perfect for this event. I thought it would be better than one of those miserable conference centers or a chain hotel with a bunch of people wandering around." He nods toward the far side of the lobby. "We can pick up the key to your room over there."

I'd rather him just set my bag down and let me go up to my room by myself, but I can't think of a polite way to say that. He's already making his way toward a large wooden desk that brings to mind luxury hotels from half a century ago. The man behind it fits seamlessly, his suit precisely tailored and pocket square folded sharply enough to cause puncture wounds. He lifts his head away from the large book he's scribbling notes into and offers a hint of a smile as Dan approaches.

"Mr. Vreeland," he says. His tone says this is not the first time he's spoken with Dan today. "I hope you're finding everything satisfactory."

"Everything is fantastic, Stanford. Thank you. I want to introduce you to one of our esteemed expert speakers. This is Agent Emma Griffin from the Federal Bureau of Investigations. She so graciously agreed to fill the space left vacant by Mr. Bremmer," Dan says.

"Lovely to meet you," the man says.

I nod. "You, too."

"She just needs to check in and get her room key."

Stanford opens a drawer at the top of the desk and sifts through reservation cards inside. He pulls one out and transfers information from it into the big book he was writing in. Turning to a large board on the wall behind him, he takes a key hanging from one of the hooks and sets in on the counter in front of me. He adds a brochure about the resort and slides them toward me with a smile.

"We have you in room 13. Enjoy your stay."

CHAPTER EIGHT

THERE'S ONLY ONE SMALL ELEVATOR TUCKED IN THE BACK OF THE lobby area, which doesn't seem very efficient for a venue that frequently hosts large events. I guess they want to maintain more of the vintage appeal by not having banks of brushed chrome taking up large swaths of space in the grand lobby. And I don't know much about the intricacies of architecture and construction, but I'm assuming adding an elevator shaft to an existing building likely isn't the easiest feat if the contractors don't want to completely rip apart a large part of the structure.

And so Dan and I pile into the elevator with my suitcases at my feet. He smiles to himself as the elevator rises, obviously excited about the event starting soon.

"You said something about a welcome reception," I say. "What's that?"

"Oh!" Dan says, seeming almost startled by the omission. "I'm sorry. Yes! It's going to be the kickoff to the whole event. Most of the

THE GIRL ON THE RETREAT

registered guests are arriving tomorrow afternoon and then in the evening we'll all gather together for a dinner and reception to welcome everybody and make introductions. Then everything officially starts the next morning. It should be a fun time."

"Sounds great," I say as the elevator doors open and we make our way down the hall toward my room. "Is there anything I need to do before then?"

"Just settle in and enjoy the resort. Get comfortable! Dinner will be served in the dining room downstairs, or you can call for room service. The lounge has coffee and snacks available throughout the day. If you need anything, you can talk to Stanford at the front desk or call housekeeping directly. The number is next to the phone in the room."

"Great. Thank you."

"You'll also find a schedule for the week, menus, descriptions of the workshops and seminars, some suggestions for activities during your downtime. All the information," he says.

"Perfect."

"I'll leave you to it. If you need to talk to me, just come find me. I'll be around. Thank you so much again for doing this. I'm hoping to have a chance to dip into some of your talks. I look forward to hearing your perspective," Dan says.

He waves and heads back down the hall toward the elevator. Like I do any time I go into a hotel, I look around to make sure I know exactly where the stairwell is and the easiest way to get to it from my room. In my line of work, it's never a good idea to depend entirely on an elevator. Having been trapped in one more than once, I am very familiar with their fallibility. Being forced to squeeze out from the hatch on the top of a broken-down elevator car that's stuck in between floors is not a fun afternoon activity I'd recommend to anyone.

Elevators also have the distinct disadvantage of being fully enclosed. When you step inside one, you are essentially in a box and can't see anything going on around you. Which means those doors could open up and you have no idea what's going to appear just inches away from you. Scrambling up and down stairs might require more cardio exertion, but if done correctly takes less time than an elevator, and you know if someone is coming behind you. I'd much rather take my chances against someone in a stairwell with all the space available than being trapped in a little cube with them.

I finally locate the stairs, which isn't actually a stairwell at all but a considerably residential-looking flight leading down from a landing opened off of a small hallway from the corridor of rooms. The way the floor is set up, with all the guest rooms in a horseshoe shape with a small gathering area in the center and then the landing leading down, has me wondering if there is actually another elevator on the far side of the lobby. Having two wings of guest rooms would make sense considering the atrium in the center of the lobby bisecting the upper floors. I can't imagine they only have these few rooms and the other half of the floor is just empty space.

The key to the room works smoothly, a nice contrast to some of the scuffles I've gotten into with hotel locks while in the field, and the door opens to a cool, airy room. It continues the balance of contemporary amenities with vintage elegance, relying heavily on white with hints of blush while also featuring a prominently placed television and phone. A set of glass French doors leads to a bedroom to the side and the bathroom attached is twice the size of mine at home.

This can't be how all the rooms in this place look. I go back into the main area of the room and approach a basket sitting on a table next to the window. Enrobed in a froth of white tulle and tied with a bow meticulously matched to the blush accents of the room, the basket nearly overflows with gourmet chocolates and fruit as well as a bottle of sparkling wine. It reminds me of the one that was brought to my house after the fundraising run. My immediate thought is this was intended for the original speaker, but when I check the card tucked into the tulle, I see my name. Dan really does pay attention to details. His thank you gifts might lack a bit of diversity and creativity, but I imagine streamlining that responsibility is a good time and money saver. Efficiency in high-powered business.

The same brochure Stanford gave me at the front desk sits on top of a stack of other papers and a quick glance inside confirms my suspicions about the rooms. Both their layout and their luxury. The top floor of the resort where I am is comprised of suites like mine, while the one below has more conventional rooms. They don't have the separate bedroom and expansive bathroom, but even those smaller rooms are beautifully appointed. I can see why this venue would draw companies for retreats and conventions, and even vacationers who long for relaxing, lush surroundings.

Skimming through the rest of the brochure tells me the resort offers a spa, several dining options including custom picnics to enjoy around the grounds, and outdoor recreation like walking trails, gardens, and a stable offering leisure riding. All of that would sound very tempting if I was on vacation, but I'm here to work, which means I need to focus.

THE GIRL ON THE RETREAT

Getting here a day before the guests gives me the chance to get oriented in the space and really prepare for the whole experience. Though Dan is the only person I saw when I arrived, it doesn't make sense that I'm the only one he would ask to come early. Stanford didn't seem surprised when Dan introduced me, so there have to be others around here. I skim through the descriptions of the sessions and the names of the various rooms and spaces where they'll be held before heading over to the phone to call Sam. I let him know I got here and tell him what's been happening so far.

"Are you going to leisure ride?" he asks.

"You know, I just might. But before I think about any of that, I really need to figure this place out and work on my presentations," I say.

"Of course, you do," he chuckles.

"What's that supposed to mean?" I ask.

"You can't bring yourself to relax, can you?"

"I relax plenty. We just went on a vacation," I say.

"We went on an extended weekend getaway," he corrects me.

"And it was wonderful. But that's not what this is. I'm not here to commune with nature."

"Is that what we were doing?" he asks. I can just imagine the sparkle in his eyes and the boyish smile.

"Yes," I say, brushing past the question as he laughs. "But I'm here for this event. I want to do the best I can with it."

"You always do," Sam says. "I just wish you'd let yourself take it easy. You've been handed a week at what sounds like a pretty amazing resort. I know you take this seriously, and I admire you for that, but you should enjoy it, too."

"I thought you were the one who said you weren't sure I should do it when I found out it was a week long," I point out.

"Well, I don't love the idea of you being away for that long. But since you're there, I think you should at least try to have some fun."

"I'll do my best," I tell him.

"Good."

"But right now I need to go find the room where my seminar is and finish my presentation."

My husband lets out a dramatic sigh. "Alright. You go do that. At least stop and eat something decent at some point. Don't just go to the vending machine."

"Oh, this is not the kind of place with vending machines," I tell him. "But there is a lounge with drinks and snacks at all times."

"All times?" Sam asks.

"That's what Dan told me. I think I'm going to be testing that declaration in the middle of the night."

"I'm sure you will. Call me tomorrow. I love you."

"Love you. Goodnight in advance. Don't work too hard this week," I say.

"Unless I am sitting in my squad car or behind my desk, or I am actively chasing someone, I'm going to be spending the week in my underwear in front of the TV," Sam tells me. "I already went to the video store and rented a stack of all the movies you won't watch with me."

"You do that. Bye."

He won't. Sam gets on me about putting too much energy and effort into my work, but he is deeply committed to his career as well, if maybe not quite as intense.

I take the schedule and descriptions with me, make sure I have the key to the room, and head out to explore the venue.

CHAPTER NINE

Him

THE WORDS ON THE PAPER POSTED ON THE WALL IN FRONT OF him were direct and clear. That was the way he preferred it. There was no room for ambiguity. He needed to know exactly what was wanted and expected so he could make sure to take every step in fulfilling it. Without that precision, it was a waste of time. Only perfection mattered.

Beside that paper was another. The questionnaire had taken him several revisions to be just the way he wanted it. The way he needed it. It wasn't the only way he got the information he needed from them. In order to even get as far as filling out the form and providing answers to the in-depth questions it asked, they had to go through several interviews and meetings. They had to be recommended or sponsored by someone he already knew.

This was not something he left up to chance. He had to ensure every one of them understood what they were doing and were the right type of people. Not everyone is. He knew that. He also found that not all of them did.

He'd noticed that about people from the time he was young. He spent his time observing, absorbing people and their behaviors, categorizing them. And one thing he learned above all else was that equality—innate, human equality—doesn't exist. It was a nice fiction, a fairy tale. But that's all it was. He knew that as a child and he knew that now as an adult.

People are not the same. Not among each other and not to themselves.

People are different inside their heads than they are outside of them.

So many believe there's so much more within them than there will ever be. They think they know what they want and can handle getting it, only to find that's not true. They believe themselves to be one kind of person, only to discover when they get down to it that they could *never* be that kind of person.

That was where things could get very complicated. If he were to simply accept anyone who came his way and halfway mentioned that they'd heard what he did, there was far too high a chance of a person discovering themselves far too late.

That could prove... inconvenient.

There were ways to amend that kind of issue. He'd had to do it before. But it wasn't something he relished. It took up his time and effort, things he would much rather be using elsewhere. Instead, he would rather sift out the merely curious first, then separate the grit, clarify and strain, and finally distill what was left down into the very fine select.

Only then, when they'd shown themselves and he felt confident that they were what and who they said they were, did he give them the questionnaire. It was both a moment of excitement and the biggest test they'd encountered. The stark black ink against cold white paper gave no hiding places. They were asked raw questions without any margin for sensitivity or subtlety. These questions demanded thorough, detailed, unwavering answers.

He read one of the answers again before going to the large cabinet against one wall. It looked to the world like a highly polished antique armoire. But inside, instead of clothing, there were hatchets and axes, along with an assortment of smaller edged weapons that didn't suit the

THE GIRL ON THE RETREAT

chest on the other side of the room containing daggers and knives, or the multi-locked room hung with swords and larger blades. He considered everything inside before selecting two of the objects, a large woodsman's axe and a compact camping hatchet.

He set them on a table spread with a white cloth and placed a card beside them, took a picture, then made a note in a small book on the table in front of the papers on the wall. Going back to the white-clothed table, he put on gloves and carefully cleaned the handles and heads, then went to work lightly sanding the handles so he could apply a new coat of finish and sealant.

He smiled as he worked, thinking of the yellowing map of the old campground in the book on the table and the postcard that was already in the mail. It was the moment tools turned into weapons.

He was always careful with this screening process, but he didn't take the rest of it too seriously. There was no reason to. It was all just a bit of frivolity.

CHAPTER TEN

There's a decidedly grand feeling to walking down the staircase through the next floor of rooms. It's not a huge, sweeping staircase, but the thick carpeting and ornate banisters give the feeling I should be wearing a large ballgown and gazing adoringly.

The details of the first floor of guest rooms are different than the hallway above. Different color themes and less opulent floral arrangements and art set the two areas apart. It's still beautiful and I detour away from the stairs to venture down the hallway and see more. In contrast to the upper floor bathed in shades of cream and gold, this floor is jewel tones of blue and purple. The two floors are tastefully reminiscent of peafowl, the bolder peacock on this floor and the elegant peahen on the top, a subtle but effective nod to the era evoked by the rest of the hotel.

The curiosity is getting to me as I walk along the corridor of rooms, looking at the doors and wondering exactly what's beyond them. The pictures in the brochure only show small bits of the rooms, such as the

THE GIRL ON THE RETREAT

French doors in the suite, and for some reason I really want to know what the rest of it looks like. Every door is closed and there's no indication any of them are actually occupied yet. There's a very light scent of bleach in the air. Not enough to be unpleasant. Just enough to smell clean.

Not getting anything else out of my exploration of this floor, I go back to the stairs and venture down one more floor to where the conference events themselves will be held. Just like the two floors of guest rooms, this floor is split into two horseshoe-shaped halves to accommodate the atrium in the lobby. I hope there's very clear guidance for guests as to how they are supposed to get to each of the classes or I have a feeling many will spend a good portion of at least the first day wandering around not knowing where they are supposed to go.

I expected to find someone on this floor, but it's just as quiet as the others. The only thing keeping it from being uncomfortably eerie is reminding myself that I got here early in the afternoon, likely before the other speakers. My career is not one that gives me the stability of a consistent schedule from day to day. There are days when I'm in the field and running nonstop 20 hours out of the day. Then there are stretches when I'm consulting on cases, working the logistic elements of an investigation, or sometimes even between cases, when I'm at home nearly all the time.

What it lacks in predictability it makes up for in flexibility, so at least there's that.

I'm assuming the rest of the speakers will start trickling in during the evening and everyone will be here by morning. It won't give latecomers much of a chance to get settled in and ready before the guests come, but since Dan mentioned they've been planning this for over a year, the others are probably fully prepared at this point.

The list Dan gave me still has the name of the speaker I'm replacing crossed out with mine written next to it in each of the time slots I'm expected to fill. It makes sense the materials would have already been ordered from the printer by the time the change was made, so this is one of the original sheets. I don't mind, but the slash of black ink and hastily scribbled name does take something away from the polish of the rest of the preparation.

The schedule is arranged by windows of time so guests can select what they want to do during each of the segments throughout the day. Almost all of the time slots feature at least three different options, broken up by lunch in the middle of the day and one seminar in the late afternoon that everyone attends. There's a different presenter for these seminars each day. Mine is in the middle of the week.

Now that I've caught on to the peacock theme of the resort, I'm noticing more subtle details that carry it through the space. Ornate metal legs on small tables incorporate feathers. Furniture, art, and the carpeting bring in pops of color without them being too much. In one open space near a window, nestled in a corner, sits a golden peacock statue. It's surprisingly subtle for a gold peacock and I'm decidedly impressed by the creative eye of whoever decorated the resort.

I finally find the first room that has my name listed next to it and peek in. I was expecting a basic conference type room but instead find something closer to a parlor. One wall is nearly taken up by a massive white fireplace, a few antique volumes positioned on the mantle and supported by gold peacock bookends. The rest of the relatively small space is filled with armchairs and settees as well as two chaise lounges and a handful of ottomans. All give the impression of vintage luxury in their shapes, colors, and patterns but are clearly modern pieces designed with far more comfort in mind than the elegance people prioritized a century ago. I can see myself draped across one of those lounges with good book and a crackling fire at the end of the day.

But that image of myself is wearing an era-appropriate gauzy peignor and slippers I should probably not wander around the convention in and that are certainly not packed in my suitcase, so the feasibility of that happening is low.

The next room I come to is larger, with an oblong polished table down the center and chairs surrounding it. A sideboard against one wall adds a touch of hospitality to the far more traditional convention space. There's a stack of papers sitting in the middle of the table and small notebooks with pens lying across them in front of each of the chairs. I step further into the room so I can get a better look. The notebooks are plain black, but the pens have been branded with the name of event.

I pick up one of the papers and read through a series of paragraphs describing different potentially dangerous scenarios. At the end of each are questions asking the participant to think about the danger present in that situation, what they think they would do if that happened to them, and any kind of emotions or feelings thinking about that particular situation brought to mind.

This is clearly one of the personal safety seminars and a quick glance at the schedule confirms Dan is the one hosting it. The details of the preparation, right down to the pens, told me as much. I set the paper back down on the stack, tapping it into place so the stack remains straight. It's hard to read the kinds of scenarios outlined there, but it also makes me feel good about my decision to be here. This is the reason I decided so many years ago to walk away from the life and career path I'd thought I was going to have and instead devote myself to the FBI.

Too often people think about personal safety or self-defense as a response mechanism. Martial arts classes or carrying around pepper spray and ear-splitting horns or whistles. Those are part of it, of course, but this shows another side of it. There's more to protecting yourself and avoiding, or at the very least managing, dangers than just knowing how to fight back.

I find another room I'll be using for one of the workshops, this one much like the first but with a heavier, darker feeling to the decor. I can imagine men gathering here to smoke cigars and make that simultaneously important and useless-sounding muttering that always seems to happen in movies about times more than a couple of decades ago.

As I get toward the end of the hallway, I find a room with the door closed. The others have been standing open, making it easy to glance inside and get a feel for the different spaces. This one being closed makes me pause. I check the schedule and confirm there is a workshop being held in this room. Something referred to as "See Through the Eyes of the Investigator." It sounds like a questionable foray into the computer-game experiences that have been getting popular.

I step up to the door. Ignoring my curiosity has never been my strong suit. It makes me a far better special agent. It also makes me terrible at not spoiling surprises, being precisely clear on boundaries, following protocols to the letter, and, in one particularly spectacular display, preserving the structure of my home. Using a sledgehammer to smash down the wall in the attic of my grandparents' house was perhaps not the most dignified I've ever been, but it did reveal critical information about my past that had been sealed up in a room in hopes no one would ever see it again.

There could be a serious reason this room is closed off rather than standing at least partially open the way the rest of them are. But if that was the case, the door would be locked rather than opening easily when I press the handle the way it just did. I open the door gradually and wait for a second for… something. I'm not entirely sure what, but that's why I wait.

Much like the stairwells, over my more than a decade in the Bureau, I've learned a thing or two about walking into closed rooms unexpectedly. If Xavier were here, he would admonish me for not knocking before trying the handle. Not for trying the handle or opening the door, just for not giving whoever, or whatever, may be inside proper polite notice of my intentions.

"Hello?" I call quietly into the space for good measure. The other rooms had at least some lights on, but this one is completely dark.

No one responds and I run my hand along the wall beside the door to find a light switch. I can't find one, so I push the door all the way open to let light from the hallway in. Stepping inside, I give my eyes a second to adjust. The positioning of this room means there isn't even a window to provide any illumination, so I have to rely on just the light that comes through the door to get me around.

I finally find a lamp a ridiculous distance from the door and flip it on. The glow of the bulb shows the large fixture sitting on a round marble table beside an impressive wingback chair. It casts a hazy light over the other side of the room where a semi-circle of more contemporary chairs has been set around an easel holding a large pad of blank paper and another supports a board covered in pictures and documents.

The pictures catch my eye. Even with the insufficient lighting I can tell those are crime scene images. And not recreations or the modified ones that replace obliterated body parts and pools of blood with strategically placed black boxes and bars. I cross the room and step between two chairs that look like they'd be better suited to a wedding reception than a true crime workshop to get to the displays.

Nothing is left to the imagination in the crime scene photos. I'm surprised to see them just put up like this. I'm used to seeing this kind of thing all the time, both in photos and in person, but most people aren't. Even if they are fascinated by criminology, coming face to face with a mutilated body that spent a good amount of time outside before it was found is startling at best.

Pictures like these are rarely shared with the public in their unaltered form. Sometimes they come up in the course of an interrogation, but even then they are kept in a folder or facedown on the table before being shown to the person being interviewed. And at that point the shock value is the point. Suddenly showing a person something so gruesome and hard-hitting should elicit a response and gauging that response can help to guide the investigation.

In this situation, the pictures are just out there in the open, ready to stun whoever walks into this room.

I look closer at the documents posted on the board with the pictures and see they are reports from the investigation. At least these are partially redacted, preserving the integrity of some of the information

THE GIRL ON THE RETREAT

they contain. This is especially pertinent to me when I read the name of the victim and realize I've heard of the case.

Vicki Freeman, thirty-six years old, found brutalized in a wooded area close to a busy roadway. A month ago.

The recentness of the crime is unsettling. This is still very much an active investigation. I'm not involved with it, but one of Sam's friends from his training academy years in Ashburn is one of the investigators. He called Sam when it was assigned to him, wondering if I'd heard anything about it. He described the cruel, gruesome nature of the killing and said it sounded like something I'd be a part of. He isn't wrong with the sentiment, but the Bureau hasn't gotten involved with the case.

The pictures and information put on display this way feels intrusive and potentially compromising. Having people who fancy themselves logical, super-intelligent citizen detectives fawn all over this kind of information could lead to a severe conflict of interest. Information could get leaked. Something said could detour the investigation and waste time and effort on the part of the actual investigators.

I shake my head as I look over the papers and see what is being displayed openly. The hair on the back of my neck stands up when I hear a voice behind me.

"Can't help but get yourself involved, can you, Agent Griffin?"

CHAPTER ELEVEN

MY PALM TINGLES WITH THE INSTINCT TO REACH FOR MY GUN, but I leave it where it is and turn around. The man behind me looks familiar. He's standing at the doorway, but when I meet his dark eyes, a slight smile crosses his face. It doesn't do much to soften the strong line of his jaw or intensity of his gaze.

"Kyle Harris," he says, coming toward me. "We met at the run."

He extends his hand and I take it, remembering the very brief encounter we'd had a couple weeks ago. I nod.

"Right. Hello, Mr. Harris."

"Kyle, please," he insists. "I'm sorry if I startled you. I didn't realize you had already arrived, and I came up here to check on the setup. You just can't resist a good crime, can you?"

"A good crime?" I ask.

He gestures toward the display. "Something this fascinating. A beautiful woman. A vicious crime. No leads. It's truly ideal, isn't it?"

"I don't know if that's the way I would describe a murder," I say.

"I'm sorry. I don't mean to sound disrespectful," he says. "I think it's coming out wrong. I just figured, since you're examining it so closely, you would understand what I'm saying."

I glance around and point to indicate the space around me. "I couldn't see it clearly. I couldn't find the light switch."

He walks across the room and uses a light panel to turn on the overhead lighting.

"Ah. Well, that's convenient."

Kyle laughs. "I think they hope people will only use the lamps because it fits with the decor better. It's a lot of commitment."

I nod. "I'm sorry for coming in, by the way. I know the door was closed. I was just having a look around and getting familiar with the layout of everything so I'm ready for the event to start."

"No worries. I probably shut the door without realizing it after getting everything in place. What do you think?" he asks, coming closer to the display and sweeping his eyes over it.

"You are leading this workshop?" I ask.

I don't remember seeing his name next to the title. Of course, I wasn't paying too much attention to the names of the speakers since I had no expectation of knowing any of them other than Dan. I'm still holding the papers, but it would probably look unduly suspicious for me to consult it while he's standing here.

"Yes," he confirms, glancing briefly at me. He pauses, then gives a slight shrug. "Well, kind of. I'm moderating the group. I have an interest in things like this, which I think I shared with you at the run, but I'm not a member of law enforcement. I don't really have the knowledge that's needed for this kind of workshop."

"What kind of workshop it is, exactly? Because I have to admit, it's kind of concerning to me," I say.

Kyle looks over at me. "Concerning to you? Why is that?"

"These pictures, for one. There's a reason modified versions are what are shown in newspapers and on the news. People not in law enforcement don't encounter things like this on a regular basis and it's too much to just force it on people without them realizing what they are going to encounter."

"They are adults, Agent Griffin. And they did sign up for this retreat. I think only showing sanitized versions of crime scene imagery is a disservice to the victims and to the investigation. Not to mention the idea of personal safety. Not confronting the gruesome realities of murders like this distances people from tragedy. It stops them from thinking about the full scope of these horrors. That means they are going to be less motivated to understand the crime and engage with solving it. And they will be less likely to think about them in terms of a cautionary tale, possibly putting themselves in the same situations or not taking the need to think carefully as seriously as they should," Kyle says. "I think we need to give them more credit than that."

"I can agree with you on some elements of that," I say. "I do think it's important to be upfront and honest about the extent and brutality of crime. Too often it's minimized, and that leaves people not putting enough thought and energy into reducing crime in all communities. But what you said about them engaging with solving the crimes. That's also what I'm talking about."

"What do you mean?" he asks.

"All this information that's being provided to them is very sensitive. Much of it is confidential and would never be publicized. Not in the newspapers, not on the news, not in a press conference. You said yourself that you are not a member of law enforcement, so you don't have the knowledge or experience. I, obviously, do. Some of these details are things that wouldn't be released because they are central to the investigation. That's especially true for a crime that's so recent.

"This murder occurred a month ago. That's extremely recent. It seems exploitive and intrusive. But more than that, allowing civilians to play detective and attempt to solve an active crime is a dangerous precedent. Too many lines of thought and irresponsible actions can lead to compromising the entire investigation. The killer could completely escape detection. And even if they are found, a good lawyer could invalidate all the evidence and find technical flaws in the case as it's presented because of this workshop's involvement."

"I understand your concerns. And, of course, I respect them because they're coming from you and your extensive expertise. I want to assure you I would never do anything to compromise a criminal investigation. I might find cases like this fascinating, but I don't root for the bad guy as it were. I wouldn't want someone responsible for something like this to get away. And I certainly wouldn't want the family of a victim like this to have to go through the suffering of a monster escaping consequence because of anything I might have done.

"But as I said, I'm only moderating the workshop. A detective actually involved in this case is the one leading it. He's going to be presenting all of the information and answering questions. I'm simply there to help moderate the conversation and keep people involved. Warren and I have had several conversations about how this is going to run, and he will be very careful to not reveal more than would be permitted by the investigation.

"I probably misspoke when I insinuated that this workshop is about the group participating in the investigation, or somehow launching their own investigation," he admits. "It really is what the title says. Looking through the eyes of the investigator. The goal is to give insight into how an investigation begins and what the earliest parts of that look like. He won't be entertaining theories or encouraging the participants to try to answer questions. Instead, they'll find out what an investigator thinks when they first arrive at a scene, the kinds of clues that they search for, how they look for suspects, things like that. The case itself is really just an example. They'll be talking about investigation of cases in general."

I nod. "That's better than I thought." I look at the pictures again, then tilt a look in his direction. "Actually, when I first read the title of the class I thought it had something to do with one of those computer simulations."

Kyle laughs again. "That's an idea for next year. Though I don't think that a virtual experience of being chased by a killer would be very popular."

I cringe and shake my head. "No. That's not going to be a hit."

"Alright, well the other speakers will be arriving later and there are still some details that need to be finished up before everything gets underway. Is there anything you need? Anything we can do for you?" he asks.

"No. I'm fine. Thank you."

"Okay. Well, dinner will be available in the dining room or through room service in a few hours. It might be your last chance to eat a meal in peace for the next week." Kyle leans down slightly like he doesn't want anyone to overhear what he's saying. "I'd take advantage of it."

I laugh. "I think I might. Actually, I'll walk out with you. Let me hit the lights now that I actually know where they are."

Kyle snickers as I cross to the light switch and flip it down. He steps out of the room and I turn off the lamp, plunging the room back into darkness and making spots dance in front of my eyes before following him out.

We walk down the short stretch of corridor together to get back to the main hallway, then go our separate ways. He's headed for the elevator and I go back to the steps. I'm curious about the other half of the resort and as far as I can tell, there's no way to pass through to the other half of the upper floors without going down to the lobby and climbing the stairs or using the elevator to go up. It occurs to me as I walk down the steps that I'm likely to run into Kyle again in the lobby when he comes out of the elevator and I get to the steps, but it is what it is.

The lobby has livened up slightly when I reach it. Two women sit in the chairs near the fireplace, each holding a cup of coffee as they lean toward each other and chat quietly. I stand corrected. Neither of them glances up as I pass, but Stanford at the desk gives me a cursory nod and tight smile before going back to his book.

It makes me think of Myrna from Feathered Nest. It's been a long time since I've seen or spoken to her, and I make a mental note to give her a call when this week is over.

I notice a few more peacock details as I make my way to the stairs. It's become a game now. When I reach the base of the steps, I see they look identical to the ones on the other side. For some reason I expected them to be different. Perhaps color-coded carpeting to visually set them apart. My heart tugs a little and I add another bullet point in my mental notes: call Xavier.

I haven't seen him since the day of the run, which is much longer than usual. Especially now that he and Dean live a good portion of the time in my grandparents' home just a couple blocks away, we often see each other every day. Dean might take a case that takes him out of town for a while, but even then I can't remember the last time I went a week without seeing him.

I push away the sad feeling by letting myself laugh at the thought of how much those two have changed my life. I didn't expect either one of them. I certainly didn't expect they would become vital aspects of my life and remain that way years after we met. I've become so used to them that I sometimes forget life even existed without them. Sam and I will reminisce about the earliest days we were in love, before I went into the FBI Academy and long before we got married, and I will find myself inserting Dean or Xavier into my visualizations. It just feels like they were there.

But they weren't, and it's not until a moment like this one, when something stands out to me this much, that their impact on me really sinks in. Before I met Xavier, I never would have thought about the color of carpeting on hotel steps. Not unless it was particularly offensive and I just couldn't wrap my head around the thought that someone had actually chosen that on purpose.

Now I think about the two sides of the lobby, their perfectly symmetrical staircases, and their matching carpeting, and all I think is how much easier it would be for Xavier if the two were different colors. Rather than having to think about something like which door he'd use to walk into the lobby and which direction he needed to turn, he would just have to find the right color. To someone who doesn't know him, that might sound like a deficit. That's far from the truth. Xavier is the most intelligent person I have ever known. He just processes things differently from others.

That makes me thankful for the large front desk. Since there's only that one on this side of the lobby, he would be able to tell if he was going the right direction when he noticed it.

As I climb the stairs to the first landing, I notice one other small difference. A plaque on the wall looks like it might be a historic marker or a label for a piece of art that's been removed. Instead, it's a directional sign indicating that the resort's indoor pool is down the hall to the left.

I want to see the pool, but first I need to assuage my curiosity. I climb to the top floor and see that it is identical to the one where I'm staying. The same goes for the next floor down. The mirror image is somehow both reassuring and disquieting.

On the event floor, I consult the schedule again and visit a few of the rooms. My workshops seem to be equally divided between the two sides of the resort, but fortunately the times are such that I'm not going to be scooping up my notes and running across the lobby after one class to try to get to the next on time.

There isn't anything particularly exciting on this side. Another of the rooms has been set up with a half-circle of chairs and a large pad of paper on an easel in the middle, but there's nothing written on it and no board full of case details. The schedule says this will host a workshop about home safety techniques. I have a brief, ridiculous moment of wondering if the woman leading it will just write "LOCKS" across the paper and then dismiss the workshop.

Finished with visiting the rooms, I decide to go down to the pool. I'm not in the habit of packing a bathing suit when I go somewhere for work, but if it's especially appealing and seems warm enough to make up for the mental reminder that it's still a very cold February outside, I might just dip out and buy one in the nearest town tomorrow morning before everything gets going.

I go back to the landing and follow the sign to the left. I'd already gone this way to see the meeting rooms but hadn't been looking for the pool access. I find it in a corner, a simple door marked with a plaque proclaiming "POOL." I can't imagine the pool is actually located on this floor of the resort and when I open the door I see it isn't.

The door leads to another set of stairs, this one a combination of the richly carpeted stairs leading down to the lobby and a traditional stairwell. I follow it down and realize it's bringing me past the lobby. Finally I reach another door much like the one at the top of the stairs and go through it into a hallway that stretches forward, then turns. I've taken several steps down the hall when the smell of chlorine tinges the air. Each breath gets a little thicker as I continue the rest of the way down the corridor and out into the cavernous pool room.

Having just walked down the steps and the hallway, I try to visualize where I am in the building. It seems this is beneath the floor of the lobby, the turns of the stairs and the hall reorienting me as I descended to lead me out onto this floor.

The lighting is soft, complementing the gold-embellished white and cream tiles and creating more of a relaxing, soothing environment than a boisterous family free-for-all that frequently breaks out at hotel pools. Particularly in cold weather when children have reached their limit.

I walk around the perimeter of the pool and tell myself I will definitely be venturing out to find a swimsuit somewhere tomorrow. Spring Break is not too far away. Surely someone will have started stocking their swimwear to prepare the young locals.

Before I head back down the hallway, I realize I didn't actually visit all of the rooms where I'll be speaking. Dan told me there was a seminar hall down in the refurbished basement area that would accommodate the larger audiences. A door across the pool between two others labeled as locker rooms says "BASEMENT."

I cross to it and open the door. I'm not surprised to find a set of steps without the lush carpeting. No one needs carpeting on basement steps leading from a pool. I follow the steps down and come to another room with deep square pools set into the floor. Steam rises up from the surface of the water. The lighting here is even dimmer, the colors richer and darker. Maybe this will be where my new swimsuit ends up.

I eventually find another door. It's not marked, but I go through it anyway. It brings me into yet another hallway. This is starting to feel like a hamster maze. It just further hints at the different lives this building has lived and all the ways people have molded and changed it to fit their whims.

This hallway is narrower than the others and carries the distinct feeling that I'm not supposed to be here. There are no directional signs, no decorative wall sconces. It feels like someone forgot to lock the door I went through. Rather than turning back, I decide to keep following the hall. Even if this area is intended for the staff of the resort, I figure it's going to lead to the public areas eventually. It wouldn't be very useful

THE GIRL ON THE RETREAT

to have staff move through hallways that don't give them access to the areas the guests use.

At least, that was my theory as I turned corners and kept walking, eventually coming to a locked door. Letting out an exasperated sigh, I turn back around and retrace my steps. I've been going for a few yards when I notice another door to my left I hadn't seen at first. The knob turns easily and I dip my head through to see what's beyond it. Only emergency lights up at the top of the walls are on, but they give enough of a glow for me to see this is a commercial kitchen. There's no action inside and no scent of food, so I'm guessing it's not the kitchen that's used daily, but one set aside for larger events.

I can see the doors leading out on the other side of the kitchen, light filtering in from under it, and head for it. I push through the doors and step out into a short corridor. I can see the end of it ahead along with brighter light and furniture that tells me I've at least managed to weave my way back to the guest areas of the resort.

I walk out of the corridor into what looks almost like the lobby of an old movie theater, complete with a gilded concessions stand boasting a large popcorn maker and elaborate display case I'm sure gets filled with all kinds of goodies during movie nights. The large, black double doors to the side of the stand must lead to the seminar hall. I step through them and walk up a ramp to look out over a sea of folded blue velvet chairs. It's no megaplex, but there are at least several dozen seats.

The stage at the front of the room has a velvet curtain hanging down over the movie screen, providing a backdrop for the speakers who will be hosting seminars here during the week. I'm getting hungry, so now that I've found the seminar room and gotten a look at it, I want to go by the lounge to get a snack before going back to my room to work on my talk.

I head back to the ramp but voices stop me. They're coming from the other side of the room, in the shadowy corner leading down what I'm assuming is another ramp to a second set of doors. They are muffled and hushed, so I can't understand all the words, but I can tell it's a man and a woman. Even without the words, I'm getting a clear impression of the tone. The conversation sounds sultry, almost seductive, and I feel even more out of place than I had in the staff hallway. I dart down the ramp and out through the double doors before whomever they are see me and things get far more awkward.

CHAPTER TWELVE

THE SNACKS IN THE LOUNGE ARE ENOUGH TO CARRY ME THROUGH until late evening and the extensive room service menu fuels me through several more hours of working on my presentations. I keep the TV on for noise to fill the quiet. Two more people took suites on this floor, but the rest are still empty. There aren't enough speakers to fill all of the suites, which means they split us across the two sides of the resort. I'm sure there's an official reason for it. Maybe it's supposed to give each of us the sense of greater privacy. Or perhaps it's because the guest rooms on the floors below will be full and the organizers want to encourage interaction between the speakers and the attendees.

Whatever the reason they've come up with, when evening goes to night and then tips over midnight, the partially filled floor reaches a kind of quiet that seems almost manufactured. I don't really know what show is playing or what's happening on it, but the voices are reassuring. Finally, I finish the work I wanted to get done and crawl into bed. Part of me worries tonight will be one of those nights when I can't sleep. Those happen to me far less frequently than they used to, but more often than I like.

Turns out, I shouldn't have been concerned. I'd drifted off easily and didn't wake until the phone buzzed loudly on the nightstand beside the bed. Groaning through the groggy confusion that comes along with waking up in a hotel on the first morning, I reach over for the phone. I'm expecting it to be Sam, calling me from his morning routine of coffee and orange juice, asking how to heat up the cinnamon rolls I left to thaw in the freezer. Like he does every time I'm away from home. I've debated leaving a note for him with the instructions, but I feel like that might ruin some of his plans for the days he's home alone.

He doesn't want me to feel like he's hovering around or infantilizing me with his worry, but if he's calling to ask for guidance toward achieving the world's most perfect cinnamon roll, it's not about him checking in. Even though he's definitely checking on me.

"Morning, babe," I say.

"Um, good morning to you, Agent Griffin. This is Stanford at the desk."

The man's uncomfortable voice has me scrambling to sit upright, pulling the comforter up around me like he can somehow see me.

"Oh. Stanford. I'm sorry. I thought you were my husband," I say. Somehow, I don't think I'm making this moment any better.

"No, ma'am. Mr. Vreeland took the liberty of scheduling a wakeup call for you. Breakfast will be available in half an hour."

"Thank you," I say.

"Have a nice day," Stanford says, hanging up so fast I wouldn't be surprised if he was already taking the handset away from his head as he was talking.

Now that my eyes are less bleary, I glance over at the clock and see that it's six. I'd really like to call Dan and ask what kind of fresh hell nonsense a wake-up call before the sun is awake is, but since I don't have his room number, I just flop back onto the bed. I change position a few times, but can't find that cozy, comfortable sleep the phone jostled me out of. After a few minutes, I let out a sigh.

I am officially awake.

It wouldn't be my first choice for a morning when I actually slept well, especially one that is right before what could be a very busy and stressful week. But at least I get to hit the ground running and can make the most of the day. I climb out of bed and head for the bathroom and the promise of a hot shower that gets the blood in my veins moving. It's not all that much earlier than I'd be waking up with Sam, but the late-night work had me really looking forward to that extra hour or so.

The shower does its job and by the time I get out, I'm seeing straight and wondering what's on offer for breakfast. I consider going down to the dining room, but it's easier to just call for room service and get ready for the day while I wait. By the time the cart appears outside my door, I'm dressed and just finishing my makeup. The food looks exceptional, and I bring it to the table next to the tall window at the far side of the room to eat while I gaze out over the beautiful landscape. The sun has just gotten up and there's still a faint haze over the rolling grass and manicured hedges.

A flicker of movement catches my eye and I lean closer to the window so I can get a better look. There's a figure moving across the grounds with a determined stride, head tucked down into the wind and one hand clutching the neck of a dark coat closed. I can't see any features, but by the size of the figure and the way it's moving, I would guess it's a man. The hand that isn't holding his coat is shoved deep in his pocket, his arm stiff like he's holding something.

I wonder if he's a member of the staff or if one of the speakers has a thing for early morning constitutionals. He seems to be moving at a fast, sure pace, like he has a specific destination and is familiar with how to get there rather than just wandering casually. He disappears behind a hedge and I go back to my breakfast. When I'm finished, it's time for my journey to the nearest shopping destination to try to find a swimsuit.

The swimsuit mission goes surprisingly smooth. Stanford, not making eye contact, gives me suggestions of where I might want to check and even makes a couple of calls for me to check for current stock. I get directions and head out. I find a simple black one piece at the first shop and am back at the resort in less than an hour. Remembering the locker rooms at the pool, I take my new suit and head to the other side of the lobby.

I am still not one to relish the idea of doing countless laps to greet the morning, but a few leisurely sweeps back and forth along the length of the water feels good. I even think I'll treat myself with a visit to the hot tubs. Getting out of the pool, I take one of the towels stacked in a warming case on one wall and wrap it around myself for the brief journey over to the other room. Whoever maintains these areas for the resort is obviously already anticipating the surge of guests coming later today because not only is the water in the tubs hotter than it was yesterday, but the surface of each pool rolls and rumbles with the effect of underwater jets.

I walk down the steps leading into the sunken pool and sink down to my shoulders. My eyes close as I settle onto a seat made into one of the corners and rest my head back against the side. Everything relaxes. This could be dangerous.

I try to remember if there is a doctor-recommended maximum time to spend in a hot tub, but let's be honest, I don't really care. I don't have high blood pressure or a heart condition. My skin is fairly resistant to the raisin effect. And I believe I have the faculties to know if I am being internally cooked and remove myself from the situation. I'm not going to worry about it.

I'm not sure how much time has passed when the sound of loud talking jolts me out of my peaceful state. These are definitely not the same voices I heard yesterday. Rather than a man and a woman having a silky, suggestive-sounding conversation, this is at least two women talking excitedly at what sounds like the top of their lungs. A high-pitched giggle punctures through the hazy warm air. It reverberates off the tile in the adjoining pool room and seems to be coming closer.

"Is this it?" one of the women asks.

"I don't know. It doesn't say on the door."

There's a knock. "Hello?"

The other women, I can tell now that it's three, laugh.

"Did you just knock and call out to a hot tub?"

"I don't think it's going to answer you, Chrissy."

They laugh again and I start reluctantly climbing out of the tub. I don't want to leave the hot water and relentless bubbles, but I also don't want to be in the room with the three of them for too long. I'm sure they are lovely people. They just have no volume moderation and I have a feeling they don't have a particularly calming presence.

I'm just wrapping up in my towel when they come into the room. They're still talking but stop when they notice me.

"Oh. Sorry! We didn't realize anyone was in here," one of them says.

I shake my head. "It's fine. I was just finishing up. Enjoy!"

I walk around them and dip out of the room. As the door is closing, I hear one of them lower her voice to a whisper.

"Did she look familiar to you? I feel like I've seen her before."

My second shower of the day washes away the chlorine and I'm on to my next set of clothes when I head downstairs. The guests have clearly started to arrive already, so I want to take my chance to explore the rest of the resort while I have it. The temperature has risen nicely since early this morning and I'm comfortable with just a sweater over my jeans and my boots as I walk through the sunroom and out the back door.

I walk along the edge of the paved drive and eventually find a path leading off into the grounds themselves. A small signpost provides directions to the hedge maze, stable, walking trails, and orchard. I head for the stables, wishing I'd brought a camera with me so I could take a picture for Sam. I don't think he actually believes I'd take a ride around the paddock during this conference.

The building that appears at the end of a long stretch of the paved walkway is far from what the word "stable" brings to mind. Towering and white, it fits seamlessly with the resort itself. The double doors are secured open, revealing a wide, clean concrete walkway through the center. I breathe in the smell of fresh straw and apples when I walk in. Large stalls line either side of the sun-filled building. A few have horses eating from baskets attached to the walls but most are empty.

I walk up to the first, a huge male with a shimmering mahogany coat. The golden plaque on the door to his stall reads "Sampson." I smile as he notices me and leans his head toward me. I touch the side of his face and run my hand down his soft, velvety nose. I walk through the stable, visiting each of the horses as I go. When I reach the final stall, a young man comes in through the second set of double doors. The jeans, plaid button-up shirt, and boots he's wearing, not to mention the bale of hay on his shoulder, are so on the nose it almost seems like a costume. Like maybe he's just a prop to give more legitimacy to the stable.

He smiles at me as he tosses the bale into one of the empty stalls. "Hi, there."

"Hello," I say.

"I'm Grant."

He extends his hand toward me, then realizes he is still wearing his thick work gloves and yanks one off before trying again.

"Emma," I say. "The horses are beautiful. I hope it's okay that I came in here."

"'Course, it is. That's why they're here. I like to think they consider me their best friend, but I know they're not going to turn down attention."

He gives a charming laugh. There's a bright sparkle in his eyes that shows how much he genuinely loves the work he does here. It's the kind of fulfilled joy that comes from doing something that's been in your blood from birth.

"I know a few people like that," I say.

"I'd say that's likely. I'd also say that's why I generally prefer horses to people," he says.

"Sounds about right to me."

"Would you like to see the rest of 'em? These guys are taking a bit of a rest, but the others are out in the field."

"Sure," I nod.

He gestures for me to follow him and we go out of the stable and onto a dirt path. We walk around a corral and down a slightly sloping hill to a paddock. I was expecting something smaller, but the white fence surrounds a field so large I can't see the far edge of it. Five horses are visible, looking majestic as they chew the grass and sun their faces. Grant makes a clicking sound with his tongue and the closest horse lifts his head to look over.

He seems to think for a second about whether he feels like coming over, then decides it's worth it when Grant produces a peppermint out of his pocket.

"This is Bentley. He's a sucker for peppermint."

"Me, too," I tell the beautiful brown and white Paint. I look at Grant, remembering the figure from this morning. "Do you bring them out for walks around the grounds early in the morning?"

He gives me the kind of confused, quizzical look only people that young can master.

"What do you mean?" he asks.

"When I was eating breakfast in my room this morning I saw someone walking across the grounds and it looked like they were kind of coming this direction. I thought it might be you."

He shakes his head. "I doubt it. I go straight to the stable from my cottage. It's in the opposite direction of the main resort."

"You live on property?"

He nods, feeding Bentley another peppermint.

"A few of us staff do. Especially the ones of us who take care of the grounds or the horses," he says.

"How about Stanford?" I ask.

A little smile curves his lips. "Definitely Stanford. This place is his life." He pats Bentley's side and grins a little wider. "You want a ride?"

Almost an hour later I'm climbing down out of the saddle and releasing the tight clip of the helmet locked under my chin. The ride was fun and invigorating, but I probably would have enjoyed it more if it was a little warmer. The day is mild but somehow felt much harsher up on Bentley's back. Grant and I walk back toward the stable where I'll return the boots and helmet I borrowed for the ride, when a blood-chilling scream sends the horses running across the field.

CHAPTER THIRTEEN

WITHOUT HESITATION, I TAKE OFF RUNNING IN THE DIRECTION of the scream. Grant comes behind me, gaining on me and quickly overcoming my pace. I fall into step behind him, knowing he is familiar with the grounds and will know how to navigate them more efficiently.

We go out of the stable and to the left, cutting across an open grassy area before getting back on the paved path and going further into the grounds in what I think is the direction of the orchard. There was only one scream. Nothing came after it but silence. That isn't reassuring. It makes the urgency surge inside me.

A scream might be frightening, but it's a sign of life. As long as I can hear the sound of someone's voice, it means they are still breathing. They are alive. When they go silent, I don't know anymore.

As we get close to the orchard, I see three people standing in the middle of the pathway. There's no obvious danger, no one visible on the ground. They turn to look when they hear our footsteps coming toward us.

"What's going on here?" I ask, slowing to a stop beside them.

The only man in the group steps aside and points down at the ground. I carefully move a sobbing woman to the side so I can look and see that a large area of the pale, sandy dirt has been stained dark red.

"It's blood," one of the women whispers. The voice sounds familiar and when I look at her face I realize it's one of the women from the hot tub room earlier. "You. We saw you earlier."

I nod. "Emma Griffin, FBI. Did any of you see anything?"

"Oh, my god. You're her. Agent Griffin," the second woman says.

"Yes. Tell me what happened."

The women look at each other and for a moment I think they are going to break out in schoolgirl squeals. Their eyes widen and one of them reaches out to take hold of the other's wrist.

"It's really her."

"Can you get over it for a second and tell her what happened?" Grant asks. "You screamed like you were hurt."

"Somebody is," the man says. "Look at all that blood."

"It is blood, isn't it?" one of the women asks, looking at me with wide, imploring eyes. "That's what that is."

It is. The color is familiar, and the smell, though faint and mixed with dirt, unmistakable. The size of the spot and the depth that it's saturated the ground indicates a fairly considerable quantity.

"Yes," I confirm. They gasp and I hold up a hand to stop them. "That doesn't mean anything. It's blood, yes, but we are right in front of woods. I would venture to say there are animals in those woods, don't you think?"

"It's an orchard," the man says. "Not exactly a wild forest."

"It's a heritage orchard. There is natural forestry growing around it and well beyond it," Grant adds.

"Which, again, means there are animals," I say.

"Tons. We've had wolves, coyotes, deer, all sorts of small things like rabbits, a couple of bears. A couple years back there was a mountain lion."

"See? The most likely explanation is a predator had a great meal here this morning," I say.

"Are you sure?" one of the women asks.

"You came here for the true crime and personal safety retreat, right?" I ask.

THE GIRL ON THE RETREAT

The group nods and for the first time I think about the fact that there were three women this morning and now there are only two. It doesn't really mean anything. They aren't physically attached to one another. But it catches my attention.

"Yes," says the smaller of the two women, a blonde with bright green eyes and a sprinkling of freckles across her nose and cheeks. "We're really interested in crime stories. That's how we know you. We couldn't believe it when we found out you're a speaker."

"Alright, so let's get a little head start. We will go ahead and treat this like a potential crime scene. I'll show you how I would go through the thought process of figuring out what happened if I just happened to come upon a pool of blood somewhere. Now, I'm going to go on the record right from the beginning as saying I believe this is evidence of perfectly normal animal behavior. Unpleasant, yes, but nothing to be worried about.

"However, I don't settle. I pay attention to every detail and I don't take things for granted. Something I've learned during my career is that things aren't always what they seem. It's a cliché, but it's true. You can't ever fully trust what something seems like on the surface. The only thing you can trust is what you find out when you look deeper. So I am going to show you how to look deeper."

Maybe I'm getting into the spirit of this whole thing. Maybe I just don't want these people going back and telling all the guests that there's been a murder and no one is doing anything about it. Whatever the reason, I have them all step back to stand alongside me and describe the scene as I see it through the lens of my training and experience.

"The first thing we want to do is eliminate all the traces of our interference with the scene. We don't want to confuse anything we might have left behind as being something that pertains to what happened here. Identify where you were standing and if you moved around so we can see the footprint patterns."

Once they all track out where they left prints in the dirt, I nod. "Alright, now we look around and see if there are any other footprints or tire impressions around here. That would tell us there was definitely a person here at some point, possibly more than one, and if they might have approached in a vehicle."

We look around but don't see any other impressions in the dirt. There are a couple of places where the grass beyond the curved end of the paved pathway transitions over into the dirt leading into the forest that look compressed or torn and we note them.

"But that could be from an animal as well," the man, who I learned is named Gordon, points out.

"That is very true. So now we have at least two different narratives forming and some support for both of them. As of right now, they are both possibilities, so they have to both be given equal credence and attention. If you start to lean too heavily into one of them without there being just cause to eliminate the other, it could distract the investigation and lead to missing vital clues that would steer the search in another direction.

"Now that we have checked for signs of who might have been here, we look for other tangible clues. Items that might point to where this blood came from and how it got here. This needs to be done carefully and strategically to avoid compromising the scene. We start right at the focus point of the scene, in this case, the blood, and methodically move outward."

We look around in the area for a few moments, gradually moving outward and closer to the trees since there was nothing that caught any of our attention closer to the path or the grassy area around the resort. We end up near the tree line and the women, Chrissy and Sabrina, hesitate. They exchange a look. Gordon presses right ahead, Grant close behind him as I linger back with the women. I don't want them to feel like they have been abandoned if either of them are still feeling uncomfortable or afraid.

Moments later, Gordon comes back out of the trees holding something in his hand.

"What's that?" Chrissy asks.

"A chunk of fur from some animal," he says, holding the gray swath out to us in his palm. He pokes it with his finger, flipping it over slightly. "There's some dry blood on it."

Sabrina looks like she feels a bit sick at the reveal, which is interesting considering her proclaimed fascination with crime. I wonder how she will react to the crime scene photos if she decides to attend Kyle Harris's workshop during the week.

"Alright, so here we go," I say. "We examined the area around the scene and didn't find any indication of any other people. No footprints, tire impressions, or anything else. There's no weapon or personal effects anywhere in the vicinity. And now there's what appears to be the remnants of an animal that got into quite the confrontation with something bigger and more ferocious. With all this evidence available to us, what is the narrative we believe?"

THE GIRL ON THE RETREAT

They all agree the most likely explanation is the grisly demise of an animal at the teeth of another. Coming to the conclusion seems to thrill them. Chrissy and Sabrina look flushed as they wave and then head back in the direction of the resort, arm in arm. Gordon waits behind and looks at me with a slightly scrutinizing eye. I stare back at him.

"This is all part of the retreat, isn't it?" he asks. "This isn't actually where an animal got attacked. You set it up as a special bonus activity if someone stumbled on it. Right?"

I shake my head. "No. At least, not that I know of. If someone did that, I didn't have anything to do with it."

"So, you just happened to be here to help us with our investigation?" he asks, a playful note in his voice like he thinks we are sharing some kind of secret.

"I was at the stable. My husband challenged me to ride a horse, so I did," I say.

I don't usually feel any need to justify things or explain myself, but I want to make the reality of the situation very clear to him. He seems convinced this was all a game hidden like a shimmery Easter egg for anyone who just happened by it. Just like I didn't want them spreading the possibility of a murder on the grounds, I really don't want him boasting about being involved in an unadvertised special session of retreat and getting private tutoring by one of the speakers.

"We heard the scream and thought something horrible happened," Grant says. "We came to see if we could help."

The camaraderie from the young man is sweet, even with the obvious note of frustration in his voice.

"Oh, really?" Gordon asks.

"It's kind of what I do," I say. "I hear screaming and think something is wrong, and I go to it."

"Chrissy was startled by the blood," he says.

"That scream sounded like a bit more than being startled," I note.

"That's Chrissy." Gordon says this like it's plenty of information for anyone to know her fully. "Well, the girls wanted to look at the fruit trees even though I told them there wouldn't be any fruit or even flowers at this time of year. I should probably go in and make sure they aren't looking for any other clues. Because," he continues, giving me another one of those looks that says there's something unspoken between us, "we already figured it out."

He heads into the orchard and I shake my head, letting out a breath. Grant is eyeing me and I lift my eyebrows at him in a silent question.

"You're somebody," he says.

"Mr. Rogers taught me that we're all somebody," I reply, starting back toward the resort not feeling quite as perky as I did when I first got off the horse.

"I mean, you're *somebody*," Grant says, changing his emphasis slightly. "They were completely freaking out about you."

He's smiling as he walks along beside me, nearly bouncing like a puppy as he goes.

"They weren't exactly freaking out," I say. "I'm sure you heard I'm an FBI agent. I've been involved in some high-profile cases."

"And so now you're doing this event," he says.

I nod. "Yes, I am."

His eyes slide over to me. "Was that whole thing a set up?"

"The blood? No, I didn't set that up. Don't you think if I knew something like that was going to happen, I wouldn't run the way I did? In riding boots?" I look down at my feet. "Which I need to bring back to the stable."

I turn and head toward the stable.

"Commitment to the buildup," he suggests.

"Sorry to disappoint you. Thanks for coming, though. If something had happened, I'd have appreciated your backup."

CHAPTER FOURTEEN

Him

NO ONE WENT INTO THE WELL-CONCEALED LOWER PORTION OF his house. He called it the Dark Wing. This wasn't a basement. Certainly not a dungeon. He'd never sink to that kind of overwrought cliché. There were no cells or dingy stone walls. No barred windows. The rooms were clean and meticulously organized. Designed specifically the way he wanted them.

After all, it was his space. Only for him. He would never allow anyone inside. He enjoyed the privacy, but there was also the element of preservation. He was like a magician who didn't want to reveal his tricks. That was one way he liked to look at what he did down in the Dark Wing. He made magic.

Like he always did, he brought his box of goodies upstairs and into a large sitting room where his special guests met with him. In the moments before the next was set to arrive, he laid each of the prepared weapons out on a cloth-covered table. Photographs were displayed on wooden easels set at either corner of the table, and in the center was a black binder filled with pages in plastic sleeves. These contained maps, sketches, lists, and other documents. A completed and screened questionnaire was at the very front.

On the mantle of the large stone fireplace behind him was a locked metal box. Inside was a stack of money. Bills sourced from several different banks across the span of three assigned days. Beneath the stacks was a white envelope containing a thick stack of papers.

The large wooden door at the far side of the room opened and a tiny old woman came in carrying a tray with a tea set and a plate stacked high with cookies. Shortbread. Her specialty. She had been making them for him since he was a little boy.

"Thank you, Ellen," he said.

She bowed. "Is there anything else you need before your friend gets here?"

A smile tilted his lips. Ellen was more a mother to him as he was growing up than his own mother had been. Not that it was his mother's fault. It was the way she was raised. She didn't know how to fully be a mother. But Ellen did. She never had children of her own, so all that nurturing went into the family she served. When he became an adult and took over everything his father left behind, it was implied that Ellen was merely a part of the estate. He'd never look at her that way.

He offered to set her up for a beautiful retirement years ago. But she refused. She was old and seemed to be a little more hunched over every day, but she didn't want to stop. She'd been with the family since she was a teenager and walked off a boat into a thrilling and terrifying new world. Even with his reassurances she wouldn't be alone, she didn't want to stop working. It was all she knew.

He was glad she was still there. He didn't want to look for someone else who would inevitably never live up to his standards. There was no intention for him to ever have children. There would be no one for him to leave his estate to. It would do him no good to hire someone young and train them to be the ideal housekeeper for the benefit of a future generation.

He was glad for the genuine kindness that didn't make her vulnerable but let her believe the people who arrived and were ushered into his room were his friends. That she could ignore the weapons on the table and the pictures on the stands. She cared for him without hesitation.

And he was glad for her shortbread.

"No. That's all."

Ellen tipped her head down in acknowledgement. "I'll go start supper. Will your friend be staying?"

"No. It's a short visit."

She bowed again and walked out of the room. It wasn't long before the deep, heavy sound of the doorbell rang through the house. He didn't move from where he stood next to the table. A few moments later, the door at the front of the room opened and his houseman ushered in a man wearing an expensive suit and an expression somewhere between neutrality and a smile.

"Thank you, Gerard. Kent, please come in."

The man in the suit came forward while the other nodded and left the room, closing the door behind him. There was a moment of silence. This was Kent's first time in this room. That wasn't unusual. Many only came once. Perhaps they were fulfilled by their one experience. Perhaps they discovered something inside themselves during the course of it that told them they were capable of this but it wasn't what they thought it would be. Perhaps it was the cost. This was not something that came cheaply. It was a luxury, an indulgence. The type of people who came to him could afford it.

Like Kent. He was prepared to make the installment payment that day. Before Kent said anything, just as he was instructed, he took off his suit jacket and draped it across a wingback chair. It looked like he was going to settle in for a cup of the tea Ellen brought in, but instead, Kent backed up away from the jacket until he was almost standing at the door again.

The man walked around the opposite side of the chair and opened the jacket, flipping it to reveal the glossy inner lining. He ran his hand along it, feeling for anything between the layers. He didn't like this part. He didn't like the suspicion or taking away from the enjoyment of the rest of it. But he had to be careful. Every step of the way, he couldn't let himself be lax.

When he didn't feel anything concealed within the lining of the jacket, he reached into the inside pocket and pull out a thick envelope. Taking out the cash inside, he brought it to the table where Ellen left the tea and cookies. Nodding at the other chair, he sat down and removed a thick, blue rubber band from around the stack of bills. Kent came over and sat across from him.

"This is everything?" he asked.

"Everything for this installment, yes," Kent replied.

"And you understand that this cannot be spoken of to anyone? There are no exceptions. The story we agreed on is your truth. There is no other story that exists for why you got this money out of the bank and what you did with it," he said.

"I understand," Kent said.

He nodded, dividing the bills into a few smaller piles to make them easier to handle. They sat in silence as he counted out individual stacks and lined them up neatly along the table.

"Help yourself to tea," he said while he worked. "The cookies are exceptional."

"Thank you."

He didn't rush with the count. He wanted to ensure absolute accuracy. He didn't say anything when he finished the count and confirmed he was holding the right amount. There was nothing to say. He didn't feel the need to provide validation for someone doing exactly what they were supposed to do. He tucked the money into the metal box on the mantle and locked it.

Kent's eyes flickered briefly to the box. He knew Kent was thinking about the papers sitting beneath the cash in that box. The contents of those papers were things Kent would never want to be seen outside of this room. If everything went the way it was meant to, they never would be. It was his protection—carefully screened, confirmed and affirmed—ensuring complete participation and discretion.

"As we agreed, another payment is due the day of your experience and the final amount must be remitted to me immediately upon completion. You still understand that?"

"Yes."

"And you are in agreement?"

"Yes. You'll have it."

He watched him carefully. He'd been listening to the tone in each of the few words Kent had said. He was sifting through the sound, trying to find notes that might indicate his unspoken thoughts and feelings. There was no hesitation in Kent's voice. Nothing that indicated he was feeling nervous or having any second thoughts. This also wasn't unusual. Though there were many who only came to this room once, there were many others who couldn't seem to stop.

The cost didn't deter them. The money meant nothing compared to the fulfillment they got from it. The rush. These people also learned something about themselves during their first experience. They learned the kill was something more than just something they fantasized about, something they wanted. They enjoyed it. They came back for more. They became addicted.

"Then let's have some fun. Come see what I have for you."

Kent took one more sip of his tea before setting down the cup and eagerly approaching the table where the man was standing. He offered Kent the black binder.

"This contains all the details for how your experience will play out. There are several sketches of the location and recommendations for how to position yourself and how to manage different scenarios that may arise with her. Don't worry. I'll be nearby if anything should not go according to how you envision it. But you can rest assured, I've taken every precaution to make sure it goes smoothly and is exactly what you want.

"After we've gone over everything else, you're welcome to relax here and go through the details. I'll answer any questions you have and we can address anything that isn't to your liking. Remember, this is about what you want. If I can make it happen for you, that's what I'm going to do. I'm going to ask that the contents of the binder be destroyed before you leave today, but there are some pictures in the back you are welcome to keep for your own collection."

"Sounds good," Kent replied.

He smiled. "Perfect. Now to these. You requested compact ax-type weapons. These are what I selected for you."

Kent looked over the weapons laid out in front of him and ran his fingers along the edge of one of the blades. He smiled.

"This will work nicely."

CHAPTER FIFTEEN

I STOP BY THE LOUNGE WHEN I GET BACK TO THE MAIN BUILDING. It's been a long time since I've ridden a horse, and I forgot how much of an appetite it could build up. The welcome reception isn't for another few hours, so I grab a plate of the snacks provided in the sun-filled room and start back toward my room. I want to visit the library I didn't get a chance to look at last night, but I'm not going to bring food around the books, so that will have to stay on my list of things I hope to get to during this week.

I step out into the lobby and almost immediately hear a gasp and realize someone is rushing toward me. It's Chrissy and Sabrina.

Sabrina reaches out toward me like she wants to grab onto me, but I put my plate of food and the drink in my hand between me and her so she can't.

"It's you," she says. "It seems like everywhere we turn, there you are."

"We are at a fairly small resort for a specific event," I reply. "It kind of is that I'm everywhere."

THE GIRL ON THE RETREAT

They laugh like I'm hilarious and look at each other like they're communicating something without speaking. These are women who have known each other a long time.

"We wanted to say thank you. For out there," Sabrina says, twisting slightly at her waist and gesturing behind her like she's indicating the orchard.

I shake my head dismissively. "No need to thank me. I'm just glad no one was hurt and there wasn't anything serious happening."

"But if there was, you could handle it. You always do," Chrissy says.

"It's my job," I say with a little smile.

"You're so modest," Sabrina says. "It's obvious this is so much more than just your job. We've followed your cases and seen you speak. You care so much."

This is one of those moments when the inspirational thing to say would be that I think law enforcement agents care about what they are doing and put the same kind of thought, energy, and emotion into their work that I do. That would just be a sound clip for an after-school special movie, though. I'm far enough into my career, and into my life in general, to know that's not always the case.

Not everyone enters this line of work because of their desire to keep people safe. There are some with selfish motivations and others who are fed into the career because it's what's expected of them. Others who may start with good intentions and take too many compromises. And then those who simply don't care and never did. It's a job, a set of procedures to complete, no different than going to an office and filling out paperwork, just with different circumstances.

Sabrina reaches into the large bag she's now holding over her shoulder. I didn't notice her having it while we were at the orchard, which means she got it in the brief time between them getting back from their walk and me coming out of the lounge. Out of the bag she produces a small black camera. She gives me a sheepish look.

"I don't know if it's okay, but can we take our picture with you?" she asks.

"We mean, not if it's going to compromise anything. If you need to keep your identity concealed or something…" Chrissy quickly adds.

"She doesn't do undercover work anymore. She's too recognizable. And she's here doing this event. People know who she is." She looks at me. "Right?"

I give a tight-lipped nod. "Right. I haven't done undercover work in a long time because of the high-profile cases I've worked over the last few years. My face ended up on TV and in too many media publications for me to be able to successfully go undercover. And besides, my name is all over the brochures for this place. It would be pretty silly for me to try to stay incognito."

It might not be exactly an enthusiastic response but it's the truth. The women are treating me like the celebrity Dan has called me and it's awkward. I appreciate how excited they are, I'm just not sure how I'm supposed to act. I am still an active agent and intend to be for quite a long time. I don't want to seem like I'm trying to be a media personality. But I suppose this isn't too much different than lending the appeal of my name to the fundraising run or the event itself. If I'm going to appeal to people, I have to expect some level of attention.

It's only after we have taken a few pictures that the women seem to notice I'm holding my plate and cup. Sabrina's eyes widen a little bit.

"Oh. You were trying to eat. I'm sorry. We won't take up any more of your time. We're really looking forward to your workshops."

"I am, too. It should be interesting."

"Will you be at the welcome reception tonight?" Chrissy asks.

"I think everybody's supposed to be there."

"Then, maybe we'll see you there."

The women wave and I turn to head to my room. The lobby is starting to fill up and I realize one of the shuttles from the off-site parking lot must have just arrived. People are milling about with keys and paperwork while others line up at the desk waiting for their turn to be checked in. I can see Stanford working double time to try to work through the line smoothly.

Heading up the stairs, I hear someone coming down in front of me and step to the side to get out of their path. As I'm turning the corner, another man I recognize from the run appears. He's looking down as he adjusts his tie and only looks up when he realizes he's not alone in the corridor. Recognition flashes across his eyes. He points at me.

"You're the FBI agent, right? Emma?" he asks.

I nod. "Agent Emma Griffin. And you're...Tom Murphy."

He smiles and nods back, obviously appreciating the recognition. That appreciation has nothing to do with the fact that it's me doing the recognition. He just likes people knowing his name.

"That's right. Looks like you and I had the same thought. I was just heading down to see what was set up in the lounge," he says.

I lift my plate and cup up slightly to acknowledge the mirrored plans.

"Looks pretty good," I say.

He smirks and we continue in our own directions for a few steps before I hear his voice behind me.

THE GIRL ON THE RETREAT

"Were you able to find all of the rooms alright?" he asks.

I give him a quizzical look. "All of the rooms?"

"I heard you were looking around the other night, trying to find the rooms where you'll do your workshops and seminar," he says.

"Oh. Right. Yeah. I found them."

"Good. It's easy to get turned around in this place."

He smiles and heads down the stairs. Something about the words doesn't sit well with me. They were easily explainable. It's not all that out of the ordinary to think Kyle Harris mentioned to him that he'd run into me in the workshop room. But it still feels odd as I continue to my room and settle on the bed to watch the news as I eat.

The day feels long and erratic already and I don't realize I've drifted to sleep until my eyes snap open. The clock on the table beside the bed tells me I've napped away a good portion of the afternoon and don't have a lot of time before I'm supposed to meet with the organizers to prepare for the reception. In consideration of riding the horse and tromping around investigating the blood by the orchard, I get into my third shower of the day.

The pool of blood is still in the corner of my mind as I wash my hair and let the hot water burn away the fog in my brain. I know the explanation we came up with is the most logical one, especially with the piece of bloodied fur and the lack of footprints or tire impressions in the area, but there was something strange about it. The location of it was unusual. Grant said there were wild animals in the area, including large predators that occasionally came onto the property. I don't doubt that. This resort is not near any densely populated areas and the surrounding land is thick forest and mountain.

But animals don't generally kill out in the open when they have the option of being shielded, especially in areas with frequent human activity. The blood was so close to the trees it just seems whatever predator was out there would have dragged the prey into the woods for the kill and to consume it. The piece of fur was also the only sign of the animal left, but the blood was still wet. Unless it was a very small prey animal and large predator animal, it would take more than a few moments to fully ingest the animal, and the amount of blood seemed to indicate something larger than that.

I would think there would have been more of the animal left, or the predator would have still been nearby when Chrissy, Sabrina, and Gordon came on the scene.

I push the thoughts out of my mind. There's something about this place. It's seamless on the surface and eerily beautiful, giving the impression of existing within two time periods simultaneously. Like at any moment I could step through a door or over a threshold and find myself in a different time, unable to get back to my own. It's at once dreamy and mesmerizing, making me want to just sink in and never leave, and quietly unnerving. It's cotton candy spun from sugar misted with poison.

It's obviously getting to me and the event hasn't even fully started.

CHAPTER SIXTEEN

In the papers Dan left for me in my room there was a note describing that evening's welcome reception and asking all the speakers to arrive early. This is our formal chance for those of us who don't know each other to meet before the guests start arriving. He also wants to go over the agenda for the evening so any of us who might have last-minute additions to the descriptions of our workshops or anything we might want him to say during his introductions, we can let him know.

He hadn't told me about the welcome reception when he first described the event on the phone, so I didn't know to bring any evening clothes. I've been to enough similar events to know to pack at least business attire, so I walk into the reception hall wearing the suit I usually wear when I go to headquarters. It's black and well fitted, perfectly appropriate, but certainly more business and less evening than the dresses two of the other three women in the room are wearing.

From the dynamic seeming to play out with body language between two of the women and two of the men, I'm guessing those two are the wives of two of the speakers, rather than speakers themselves. I recognize one of the men as Tom Murphy, who I'd encountered on the steps, and the other is Dan. Tom's wife is the other woman in the room not wearing a dress. She's opted for wide-legged, sequined evening pants and a vibrant blue blouse that seems almost like she chose it to fit with the decor of the resort.

Dan notices me and gestures with a bright smile for me to come over. His wife is exactly what I would have envisioned. A warm, genuine smile on her round face, a cloud of blonde curls ending up above the shoulders, a soft body that looks like Dan just loves to snuggle. I have no personal experience, obviously, but he strikes me as a snuggler. The way he gazes at his wife is pure and sincere, eyes filled with love and adoration even after the many years they've spent together. When I saw her at a distance, I thought her dress was black, but as they get closer, I realize it's actually a shade of dark purple. I'm starting to feel like I missed a couple of pieces of information about this event.

"Emma, I want you to meet my wife. Honey, this is Agent Emma Griffin. Emma, my beautiful wife Chelsea."

"It's nice to meet you," I say.

"You, too," Chelsea replies, shaking my hand. "Dan has told me so much about you. Everything you've done truly sounds amazing." She looks around as if she's taking in the surroundings of the entire resort, not just the room where we're standing. "All of this isn't really my thing." She turns to her husband and places a hand in the center of his chest like she's comforting him. "I know, sweetheart. I know you love it, but I just can't get myself to enjoy it. It just gives me the heebie-jeebies."

She shudders to show the effect and I smile.

"Don't worry. You're not the only one. My best friend is a consultant for the Bureau but absolutely *will not* go in the field for the same reason. Her mother still refuses to consider her in the FBI and won't let either of us talk about any of our cases when we are at her house. Now she's engaged, to my other best friend, actually, and he is an agent. She's not happy about it. Not because of who he is. She loves Eric. Just because she doesn't want to hear any of it or have to worry about any of us. I'm fairly sure she's come up with fake careers for all three of us for when she talks about us to her friends."

Chelsea giggles. It's an effervescent sound that makes Dan smile even more.

"I just came for tonight to celebrate the start of the event, then I'll spend the rest of the week in our cottage."

"You have a cottage around here?" I ask.

THE GIRL ON THE RETREAT

"The resort has a few little ones. They don't generally rent them out to guests. They were built here for staff a few decades ago when this was more of a summer retreat for the wealthy families from the cities. But I come here so frequently they made an exception so Chelsea can enjoy herself around the resort without being stuck in the middle of the conference," Dan explains.

"That's right. Grant down at the stable said he lives on property. I'm guessing he has one of those cottages."

"The one who takes care of the horses? Yep, he lives down there, too. I've actually known him since he was just a little slip of a thing. His father used to watch over the horses here," Dan tells me.

"I had a feeling that wasn't something he'd just picked up recently," I confirm.

Dan's eyes flicker over my shoulder. "Looks like our final two just got here. We can get started."

I twist to watch him as he heads for the door to greet Kyle Harris and another man I met at the run: Cory Mellon. The name pops into my head. He's the one who didn't hesitate to tell me he had no idea who I was. It was a refreshing comment and at the same time one of those situations when I'm not sure why he felt the need to say it. I wasn't giving him a spontaneous oral exam on the greatest highlights of my career. I was just being introduced. Yet, he seemed compelled to make note of not being familiar with who I was or why I was there.

Maybe it was just because he'd been listening to the other men gush and felt like I needed some humbling. Maybe he just didn't want to go along with the crowd and wanted to feel cool and aloof. Whatever the reason, this time he sees me, Cory Mellon locks eyes with me and strides purposefully in my direction.

"Emma Griffin," he says, extending his hand with far more enthusiasm than he did when we met. "We met at the run."

"I remember. Hello, Mr. Mellon."

"Please. Mr. Mellon is my father." I hope the cringe I feel doesn't appear on my face. I didn't know people actually said that in real life. "I'm Mr. Mellon the Second." He laughs at the unexpected redemption of his cliché. "No. It's just Cory."

I smile. "Hello, Cory."

"You know, I felt really bad after we met at the run. Dan was… I'll put it as less than pleased at me after I said what I did and I figured I must have really missed something. I did some looking into you."

"Oh, you did?" I ask.

"Oh, yes. I have to say, you've had quite the career."

It isn't exactly a compliment, but I'm going to put more meaning into the fact that he actually came to me to apologize for being rude. At least, I think that's what he's attempting to do. He seems to have his own way about him. Arrogant and conceited, to be sure, but there was at least a hint of that in all of the men leading up this foundation. Even Dan showed off about the cottage. But there's something just under his surface that's almost approachable in its awkwardness. Like he was the nerdy college roommate of a frat boy jock and it rubbed off on him.

"That is certainly one way to put it," I say.

"I actually followed one of your cases really closely," he says, his eyes sinking down and to the side as he tries to find the right words for what he's trying to tell me. "Something with your boyfriend? He disappeared and then showed back up and then was murdered?"

I nod, my lips pressing hard together as I try to keep looking calm.

"Yes. My ex-boyfriend but also my friend. That was a very challenging case," I say.

"Are you going to talk about it during one of your workshops?" he asks.

"I wasn't planning on it," I tell him.

I try not to think too much about the years marred by the gloom of the entire horrific saga surrounding Greg. It's with me every day through scars on my body and my mind, as well as the shocking wealth no one knew he had but he left completely to me. I won't forget the things I went through in those years, the things I saw and was forced to do. I won't forget him. But my life is so much more now. That didn't stop me, even though that was the hope in the twisted, deranged mind of the man who left him for dead once and then ensured it was finished a second time. I kept going. I kept living. And I've devoted a huge amount of money to various projects and causes I hope would honor Greg and the life he gave up thinking he was doing it for love.

"No. I'm not planning on talking about that in any of my workshops," I say.

"Too bad," Cory says with a visible downward tug of the corners of his mouth. "I would have liked to dip in and watch some of that." Dan clears his throat somewhere across the room and Cory points toward him. "Looks like we're getting started."

He walks away and I turn to watch the group of speakers move toward Dan, where he's standing on a low stage on the other side of a dance floor surrounded by dining tables. It looks like a generic wedding reception but without the massive cake and with centerpieces designed with dark-colored flowers and detailing such as a rope draped in one of the vases and a pipe propped against another.

"Hello, everyone! I'm so excited to see all of you now that everyone has arrived. Welcome! I'm thrilled you were all able to join us and I am looking forward to an incredible week. This is a first-of-its-kind venture, as far as any of us in the Omnia Foundation know. There have been events focused on true crime and events focused on personal safety and awareness, but blending them together was completely new.

"I don't even remember which of us came up with the idea originally, but there was a conversation about teaching people what serial killers do in one room while showing people how to stop them from doing it in another. It sounds like a joke. Right? Like somewhere in there should be a parody of the DMV or a factory where one floor painstakingly hand-blows glass pieces, sends them on a conveyor belt to a grinder to be made into sand, then to be made into soda bottles."

The crowd politely titters at the story, more to acknowledge they heard it instead of thinking it was actually funny.

"Anyway, we had a little laugh about it at first, but then within a few days one of us brought it up again and was like… you know, this might not actually be such a bad idea. Think about it. And we did. We considered the draw of true crime and the desire to understand the people who commit crimes, the ones who fall victim to them, and the ones who fight them. Then we recentered on the primary goal and focus of Omnia, which is to raise awareness of crime—particularly violent crime—and educate vulnerable populations on how to properly prepare, protect, and preserve themselves.

"It occurred to us that learning about crimes and giving into that fascination can be a form of entertainment for sure. But it can also be an effective funnel toward better self-awareness and defense. If people can look deeply into these sensational crimes and take them apart to better understand each element, each step, they can see the failings of common sense, awareness, and reaction that created serious danger for the victims. But they can also see the motivations and tactics of the perpetrator. Getting into this mindset helps to provide a jumping-off place, a reference point for the self-defense and personal safety lessons. These two work closely together to create a retreat atmosphere meant to be fun, thrilling, and exciting but also highly informative and empowering.

"Our hope is that everyone who comes here will spend each day going through a full range of emotions. We want them to laugh at the games and activities and some of your stories. We want to bring them humor and relaxation, and hopefully help them meet some new friends.

We want them to cry when they think of the victims of the cases and what they went through, but also for the life and journeys of the perpetrators and the things they encountered. We want them to gasp in fear thinking of the dangers that could be lurking around every corner. We want them to feel sick, considering what one human being is capable of doing to another. We want them to feel anger at the same thing.

"Most of all, we want them to feel like they leave this place more educated, more confident, more powerful than they were before. Even if just because they learned something new about a case they followed and it gave them a different perspective. Or because they picked up one tip for how to handle a tense situation. Whatever it is, we want them to feel like their time here was a changing experience. I, for one, can't wait to sit in on as many workshops and seminars as I possibly can and learn some new things myself. I look forward to getting to know each of you better and thank you so much for helping me bring this vision to life.

"Please come get a program for this evening and head on over to the bar to enjoy a drink and an hors d'oeuvres before the guests arrive. Dinner will be served in about half an hour. Then we'll have dancing and socializing. There are a couple of extra little activities and events going on after the reception tonight throughout the resort, so feel free to enjoy any of those."

He steps down off the stage and there is the brief tense moment where people wonder if they are supposed to applaud or not. Dan was clearly channeling an inspirational speaker, but this doesn't seem like a clapping kind of situation. Instead, the group of presenters and their dates dissipate, some heading for the bar while others start searching the tables for their name cards.

I walk over to the nearest table and take a closer look at the centerpiece. This one has a large knife embedded down in the gel surrounding the flowers. I check each of the names and don't find mine, so I move on to the next table. The next has a wrench sitting beneath the vase. I'm starting to catch on.

"Funny, aren't they?" a voice behind me asks.

I straighten and turn around. A tall, beautiful woman with long mahogany hair and vibrant green eyes is right behind me. Her black satin high heels lift her up to a few inches taller than me and she, too, seems to have gotten the memo with a subtle gold feather detail at the waist of her black dress.

"Funny?" I ask.

THE GIRL ON THE RETREAT

She nods and gestures toward the centerpiece. "Those. They're funny, right? They're like *Clue*. You know. 'In the ballroom with the lead pipe.' Have you played it?"

Oh, I most certainly have. Just the thought of the game brings out the crankiness in me. Game nights with Janet and Paul across the street are always a bit rowdy and competitive in the most fun way, but they're brought to another level when we walk in the house and Paul has set his first-run *Clue* game out on the table. I've tried to convince him before that it's technically a collectible so we really shouldn't be playing it because we could damage the board or lose one of the itty-bitty metal weapons, but it doesn't ever do any good. When we see that box, we know what's coming: the FBI agent is not going to be able to figure out Mr. Boddy's damn murder.

CHAPTER SEVENTEEN

"I'VE PLAYED IT A FEW TIMES," I TELL THE WOMAN. "IT IS A pretty cute theme. I'm not so sure it is appropriate for the self-defense portion of the retreat. But I guess Dan did say he wanted to bring some humor and make sure everyone enjoys themselves."

"Exactly. I'm sure this is going to be a really useful week and the people who signed up are going to learn a ton. But really they just want to come and have a fun time. I think that's important. Being able to add humor to things. Don't you agree?"

I start to agree, but the woman doesn't wait for my answer.

"Life is already hard enough. It does it all by itself. That's what my grandmother always used to teach me. I would come to her and tell her about a problem I was having, or be upset because I wanted to play a game a certain way and none of the other kids was taking it seriously enough, or whatever. You know how kids are. Anyway, I would be so worked up and Granny would tell me to calm down and find a reason to laugh about it: 'Life is hard enough, Daisy. It does it all by itself. You don't need to help it along. Find a way to laugh at it and then you really have control. You can't be scared of what you laugh at.' I just keep that going through my head whenever something isn't going my way."

"Sounds like your grandmother is a pretty special woman," I say.

"She was. Unfortunately, she's not with us anymore. It's been about three years now."

"Oh. I'm so sorry for your loss," I tell her.

A soft moment of nostalgia brushes a hint of a smile across her lips.

"Thank you. She was really sick for a long time, and she kept saying she was at peace and ready to just get on with it. Sometimes she would have arguments with the cancer, like she thought if she made it angry enough it would just get more aggressive and she would finally be done with it. She never was a particularly patient woman. One time when she was about eighty-five she called my daddy to tell him she'd fallen and thought she might be hurt. He asked when it happened and she said two days before but she had too much to do so she didn't call anybody."

I laugh out loud at that. "Sounds like my own grandmother."

Daisy grins. "Mind you, this woman never learned how to drive a car. She had quite the social life when her siblings were alive and she was close with her neighbors at her apartment complex. At this point her siblings and her friends were all gone. We never could figure out what it was she was doing that kept her so busy. Granny then told my father he needed to help her because it was really starting to hurt and she wanted the doctor to take a look.

"This is the point when my father reminded her that she lived in an assisted living facility where there was literally a medical office downstairs and a nurse's station on every other floor. He asked why she didn't call one of them for help and Granny said she didn't have it in her to sit around and wait for them, she needed *him* to take her to the hospital and get something for the pain so she could continue on with her day. Perhaps I should have mentioned he lived three states away."

I chuckle. "Well, of course he was a better candidate to get her to the hospital without trying her patience than any of the medical staff at the facility."

Daisy titters. "There you go. You're understanding my Granny now. He eventually got her to call, and good thing. Turns out she'd had three broken ribs and a fractured hip. And she spent two days in her favorite chair, watching Wheel of Fortune, and making a million of those little things. You know those things…" Daisy makes a gesture with her fingers like she's squeezing something small repeatedly. "They're made out of plastic with bits of yarn woven into them. You see them on Christmas trees and have Hershey's Kisses inside."

"Oh," I say, "the cheek squeezers. I know exactly what you're talking about." The visual of the little cheek squeezers immediately comes to mind. "When I was very small my grandmother used to make those for me, too. They looked like little green frogs and she nestled them into the branches of the Christmas tree. I didn't understand why she made frogs for the tree and not something else, like a Santa or even just a solid color made to look like a wrapped present. Once I was an adult she told me it was just because that was the way she liked them and she wasn't going to change for anybody or anything. But that was her."

It's Daisy's turn to laugh. "I think they would have gotten along famously."

"There you are."

A man's voice comes from behind me. I turn around and am briefly confused to see Gordon walking up to the table. I can't imagine why he would have been looking for me, then I realize he's looking over my shoulder at Daisy. I look back at her and see a bright smile on her face, her sparkling eyes a little wider.

"Hey, sweetie," she says, reaching out an arm to pull him toward her for a quick hug.

They exchange kisses on the cheek and he looks down into her face. It's the same kind of gesture as Dan Vreeland, but the feeling is different. This is still new. Their body language says they are familiar enough with each other to have likely been together a year or so, but the relationship is still fairly surface-level. They aren't moving with the depth and intensity of Dan and his wife, that kind of anchored connection that unifies them into one unit. Instead, the connection is still forming, still based largely on attraction and spark. It's very much there but green.

"I see you got caught up talking again," Gordon says with a smile, giving Daisy a playful jostle that reminds me of Sam.

"Caught me," Daisy says, putting her hands up with a little shrug like she's surrendering. "You'd gone off to talk to Bingham and I saw Agent Griffin over here. I was so jealous I didn't get to meet her with the rest of you, so I came over to talk to her."

That's when it occurs to me I have seen her before. This is the third woman from the spa room. The one missing from Chrissy and Sabrina at the orchard and in the lobby.

"Which we actually haven't done," I say, extending a hand toward her. "Emma."

THE GIRL ON THE RETREAT

A flush goes across her cheeks and she shakes her head like she's jostling herself out of something.

"Right. Sorry. I'm Daisy, Gordon's fiancée."

"It's nice to meet you. And congratulations," I say.

"Thank you," she says. "I still can't believe it myself sometimes. It's been a whirlwind." She looks over at Gordon. "Right? I wasn't even thinking about meeting someone a year and a half ago, and now here I am planning a wedding in six months."

Gordon leans over to kiss her on the cheek. "We've got to find our table, babe. Dinner is going to start soon."

"Oh. Right." She looks at me with an almost apologetic smile. "It was so nice to finally meet you. I hope to see more of you this week."

I nod. "I'm sure you will."

She waves and Gordon takes her by the arm to escort her across the dance floor to more of the tables.

CHAPTER EIGHTEEN

The tables are starting to fill up and finally I catch sight of Dan, who gestures at me to come over to the table where he's standing. It's positioned closest to the stage, set back slightly from the dance floor. As I approach, I notice one empty seat.

"Here," Dan says, gesturing at that seat. "I have you up here with me."

Chelsea leans forward in her seat to wave her fingers at me as I take my seat. I smile and wave back at her. I'm glad to be at the same table as her. I hadn't gotten a program the way he'd instructed during his speech because I'd gotten distracted by the centerpieces and then wrapped up in conversation with Daisy. There's one sitting at my spot, however, and I pick it up to glance over it.

"You don't have a drink," Dan notes.

I realize everyone else at the table has something other than their customary glass of water and shake my head.

"No. I didn't get a chance to go over to the bar," I say.

"Let me get you something," he offers. "What do you like?"

I hold up a hand to stop him. "No, it's fine. You don't have to do that. Water is plenty and I can go over there and get something if I change my mind."

"Nonsense. I'm already standing and you need a cocktail. What can I get for you?"

I have to smile at his justification that he's standing when I just barely sat down, but I know there's no point in arguing with him.

"I don't really know," I admit.

The truth is, I'm not that big of a drinker. I'll have the occasional glass of wine with dinner or some whiskey in my tea when I'm sick, but it's just not a big part of my daily life so I'm not particularly up on the cocktail game. I'm about to tell him to just bring me whatever white wine they have available, but he's already starting to walk away.

"I'll surprise you."

As soon as he is away from the table, Chelsea picks up the pink drink in front of her and moves over into the seat beside me.

"I'm going to steal Dan's seat so I can talk to you," she says. She lowers her voice to a playful conspiratorial whisper. "Do you think he'll notice?"

I lean toward her. "Maybe you should switch the name cards. Then it will be undetectable."

She laughs but does switch the cards just as Dan appears back at the side of the table. He's holding a drink in either hand, a glass of iced tea and something extremely blue. My heart sinks a little when he hands the intensely blue one to me and keeps the iced tea for himself.

"Well," I remark, eyeing the drink, "this is vibrant."

"It's a Blue Lagoon," he says.

"Like the movie?" I ask with a slight cringe. Nearly five years on since seeing it with Sam at the theater and I'm not fully over the slight chill aspects of that film send down my spine. But I know there are a lot of very dedicated devotees of the movie, so it's not out of the realm of possibility that they created a cocktail as an homage.

"No. Might be trendy now because of it, I suppose, but it predates the movie by a couple of decades. I'm actually familiar with it because it's always what my Pops drinks at cocktail parties during the holidays. It always stood out to me. Everyone else has their mulled wine and eggnog or cranberry spritzers and then here's my father with his tropical blue drink. One year Mom had used all the oranges for the mulled wine bowl and candied slices on top of the fruit cake so there wasn't a fresh slice available when Pops wanted his cocktail."

Chelsea has started giggling at this point, her hand over her mouth like she's trying to hold it together. Dan looks at her in delight, the shared memory passing between the two of them.

"That's right," she says through her laughter. "She didn't want him to be disappointed by not having his orange slice in his cocktail, so she fished one out of the mulled wine and used that as garnish. It was dripping down into the drink when she handed it to him, so from then on, he called it a Purple Swamp."

I chuckle at the story and remove the very fresh, decidedly un-mulled orange slice off the edge of my glass to set aside so it doesn't fall when I take my obligatory sip. The flavor is intense right from the second it hits my tongue. Extremely sweet and far stronger on the alcohol than I was anticipating considering its neon color, but the orange-tinged lemonade flavor surprises me. I'm not really sure what kind of flavor I was expecting, but that wasn't it.

It's not unpleasant and I can see myself working my way through one of these while lounging on the beach or sitting by the pool during vacation, especially if I could find a couple of tiny drink umbrellas, but I won't be finishing this one tonight. I take one more sip and set the drink down, picking up the program again. I open it and a piece of white paper flutters out, landing on the floor beside Chelsea's chair. She picks it up and hands it to me.

"Oh," I say. "It's about me."

I show her the paper that notes Lucas Bremmer won't be in attendance at the retreat and introduces me as the replacement.

"I'm sorry there wasn't time to actually fix the programs," Dan says. "I wanted to do something a little grander to introduce you to the attendees who didn't know about the change, but this is all we could do with the time squeeze."

"No need to apologize. A fancy introduction is not necessary," I tell him. "I just hope the change itself doesn't disappoint people."

"Everyone I've talked to is thrilled you're here," Dan says.

"It's true," Chelsea assures me, resting her fingertips on my arm. "I've heard a lot of the guests talking about it. Daisy Gallagher in particular talked about you nonstop before the weekend even started."

"To be fair, that's not really off course for Daisy. The nonstop talking part," Dan says with a heavy touch of mirth. "But she is genuinely excited to meet you."

"You know Daisy?" I ask.

"Of course," Dan says. "She's one of the leaders of the retreat. She's doing part of the personal safety track."

THE GIRL ON THE RETREAT

He gestures toward the program and I scan through the list of presenters before finding her name alongside a portrait of her beaming toward the camera.

"I actually saw her this morning and then just formally met her before I came over here to sit," I say. "She was with a couple of friends when I first saw her, so I thought she was just a guest and showed up at the reception early."

Reading through the brief biography beside Daisy's picture tells me she is a fitness and aerobics instructor, as well as a counselor at a shelter. Her body more than testifies to her dedication to physical health, and her friendly, funny personality would make it easy for even traumatized people to trust her and be willing to talk. Maybe that's what's behind the openness with me. She certainly felt warm and welcoming despite talking my ear off.

The program doesn't have a full schedule, I'm assuming that was distributed to guests when they checked in, but it does spotlight a couple of program offerings. Daisy's name on one of them catches my eye. The description offers guests the opportunity to get a fresh, fun start on the day with a Jazzercise session meant to encourage physical strength, flexibility, and wellbeing and get everyone focused for the work ahead.

It's a lot of words that might not really mean much of anything, but at the same time, could be truly impactful. I've never done Jazzercise before, but I hear it's pretty trendy lately. I make a plan to go to the first session in the morning. Maybe that will become the way I start each day during the week.

Before dinner starts, I need to visit the restroom, so I excuse myself and leave the banquet hall. I don't see any, but there's a hallway ahead and that seems like a logical place to keep a restroom out of the way but still accessible.

I turn the corner and see a tiny sign near the top of a door indicating I've found what I was looking for. Just as I'm getting to it, the door opens and a young woman bursts out. She nearly runs into me, mumbles an apology, and runs down the hall in the opposite direction from where I came. I watch her and see her take another corner. Almost immediately, there are tense, raised voices. Hearing that kind of aggression always creates an instinctive spike of protectiveness in me. That girl could not have been older than her early twenties, if that, and the harshness in the voice of the man yelling at her could quickly turn into something worse.

"Where the hell have you been?" he demands.

"I'm sorry," she says and starts to continue, but his voice bites hers off.

"Sorry doesn't mean shit. You were supposed to be here over an hour ago. I sent half the dishwashing staff out searching for you. What is going on?"

"Something came up that was unavoidable," she says.

"Something came up?" he asks in disbelief. "Did you seriously just tell me *something came up* and that's why you are more than an hour late to work for the first night of an event hosted by some of the wealthiest, most powerful men in this state?"

"I can't tell you anything else. It's very personal," the girl says.

Her voice is starting to shake. She obviously feels intimidated by this man, and I can't blame her. It's clear he is her boss, and he's furious. Because of his position, however, I'm less concerned about her safety than I would be if I thought this man might be her husband or boyfriend, or even her father.

"I don't care about your damn personal life. When you're working for me, you don't have a personal life. Your life is this resort and the people spending out of their asses to stay here, you got it?" he sneers. "We've been prepping for this event for six months. You not being here when you were supposed to be meant I had to double up work on other people and not get things done when they were scheduled to be done. You better get in that kitchen and work harder and faster than you ever have in your life to make up for this. You're going to be lucky if any of them want anything to do with you and you best be prepared to do the cleanup yourself tonight."

"By myself?" she asks in disbelief.

"Are you arguing with me?" he growls, his voice rising enough that I'm wondering if everybody inside the reception can hear him.

The music playing in the background isn't very loud. Maybe all the conversations going on will drown him out. If not, it will be uncomfortable at best for Dan and the rest of the host group.

"No. I'm not arguing. I'll do whatever I need to do," she relents.

The longer I listen to her, the more familiar her voice sounds. I can't place it and it might just be that she sounds like most girls her age, but it sticks with me. The man has already launched into her again and a second later, Dan appears beside me.

"Emma?" he asks. "What's going on?"

"I'm not sure. I was coming to the restroom. But I saw a girl run out and when she got down the hall, I could hear this starting."

I point toward the hallway to indicate the ongoing heated conversation. Dan nods.

THE GIRL ON THE RETREAT

"I just heard what I thought was shouting. I'm sure everything's fine. I'm just going to go check."

He heads for the corridor and I dip into the restroom. When I come out, I can hear him talking.

"This kind of behavior is really unacceptable. There are several hundred people right on the other side of that wall who have paid a considerable amount of money to attend this event. They're expecting the highest quality, and that's what I expect to give them. I chose this venue because of its luxury and the service I've come to know."

"Is everything alright? What's going on here?"

I turn to look over my shoulder and see that Stanford is the latest person to join me in the hallway. His eyebrows furrow together as he stares down the hallway toward the voices. The loud, gruff man is now trying to calm and cajole Dan, but it doesn't seem to be doing much good.

"There's a bit of a conflict going on," I tell Stanford. "Nothing too severe. From what I've gathered, one of the kitchen staff was late arriving and her boss is angry with her. Dan Vreeland came out of the reception to confront them after hearing them shouting."

Stanford looks at me with a cocked eyebrow that screams judgment and condemnation.

"And you just happen to be hearing all of this?" he asks.

I realize it does sound like I've just planted myself in the hallway and am eavesdropping on the drama going on down the hall like it's an afternoon soap opera.

"Observation is part of my job. I pay attention to what's happening around me," I reply.

He looks like he's going to argue with me, then seems to remember who I am and why I'd need to be vigilant, and stops himself.

"You can go back to the reception," he says.

"I don't need your permission to go or not," I say.

There's a brief moment of standoff before he turns on his heel and rushes down the hallway toward the ongoing conversation.

"How can I help?" I hear him ask.

Both Dan and the gruff-sounding man start talking at the same time, trying to one-up each other in volume until Stanford stops them.

"Mr. Vreeland, I'm very sorry about this situation. I understand it is frustrating to you and you are concerned about the experience for your guests. Please allow the resort staff to handle this for you while you enjoy yourself," Stanford says. "I know you have worked extremely hard to put this event together and we are honored you chose our resort as your venue. It's very important to me that you are happy with all aspects. I apologize deeply for the disruption to your event, but I don't want you to give up any more of your time. Please, allow me to take care of this and find a way to make it up to you."

"It isn't your fault," Dan says. "You've gone above and beyond for Omnia."

"And I would like to continue to do that. Please go back to your guests and let me settle this," Stanford insists.

Dan finally relents and comes around the corner, noticing I'm still standing where he left me.

"Emma, I didn't realize you were still here," he says.

"Things seemed to be getting fairly heated and I wasn't comfortable just walking away from it," I tell him.

He slouches a bit, letting out a breath. "That makes sense. But I'm sorry you had to see it."

"Don't be. It's what I do. That's why you have me here, right?" I ask, giving him a little smile to reassure him. "And it's really no big deal. It's not like we're here for a stuffy wedding or a weeklong church service. Most of the people in that room can't wait to start talking crime. If they noticed the yelling at all, they didn't care and probably won't even remember. Or they'll think it's part of some roleplay event."

"You think so?" he asks.

"Absolutely. Let's get back in there. I'm starving."

Dan grins. "Me, too."

CHAPTER NINETEEN

WE GET BACK INTO THE RECEPTION HALL JUST IN TIME TO SEE the waitstaff stream through a door to the side of the room. By the orientation of it in comparison to the hallway I was just in, I can guess the offshoot hallway where the conflict boiled over leads to the kitchen and then this door comes off of it further down. If I have to make another guess, I would say there is likely a door to the outside at the far end of that hallway and likely a parking lot and delivery dock right just beyond to allow supplies and staff to enter seamlessly and without any guests witnessing it.

Everyone in the room seems to be talking and the music is a little louder, creating a bubbling, energetic atmosphere. I lift my hands to indicate the sound, showing Dan that the screaming was likely inaudible to the majority of the people in the room, and even those who did hear it were obviously not that seriously affected by it. Looking to either side as we hurry back to our table, I don't see anyone who looks upset or agitated. Instead, everyone is smiling, laughing, and talking. I wonder how many of them know each other and how many are forming new friendships.

My eyes catch Daisy sitting beside Gordon. Chrissy and Sabrina are at the same table, but neither appears to have a date. They don't look bothered by that. Both hold drinks as they laugh and lean across closer to Daisy to chat. She notices me out of the corner of her eye and turns toward me, waving her fingers happily. The other women follow her gaze and I see their faces brighten. They join her waving and I wave back. Chrissy pushes her chair back from the table like she's going to get up and come toward me, but two waiters and a waitress approach their table to set plates in front of each person.

Their movements are carefully choreographed so that they are reaching down from the same side of the person and the plates touch the table at the exact same moment, ladies getting theirs first, followed by the men. I follow Dan back to our table and we sit down at places already set with fresh, incredible-looking salads.

I glance over to the next table being served on our side of the room and see the young woman who ran from the bathroom and right into the clutches of her angry boss. She's wearing the same crisp black and white uniform as the other members of the waitstaff, but her expression is strained. Her eyes are slightly swollen and her makeup doesn't look exactly right, like she'd started crying and washed away some of her eye makeup, and so she had to replace it hastily, resulting in clumps and shadowy smudging under her eyes.

I'm sure that whole experience wasn't fun for her, but she's keeping it together. She moves right along with the others and doesn't miss a beat as they serve the table and head back toward the door to the kitchen to gather more plates.

"This looks delicious," I marvel, looking down at my plate.

"Doesn't it?" Chelsea asks beside me.

I notice the pink drink she'd been sipping before I headed for the bathroom has now been replaced with something garishly green. Just the color harkens to mind a sour apple flavor. I don't particularly enjoy the idea of drinking something sour, except for lemonade, of course. She already has her fork in her hand and is carefully sifting through the contents of the plate.

By the time the next course comes out, Chelsea has replaced her finished green drink for a Blue Lagoon. My matching cocktail is languishing at the corner of my setting, but I accept her cheers when she offers her glass out to me and take a sip.

THE GIRL ON THE RETREAT

The waitstaff comes and takes the plates away from in front of us, replacing them with a small plate featuring several cheeses and accompaniments. It looks delicious, but I'm already feeling full, so I'm glad for the small size of the serving.

"Just wait until you see dessert," Dan says as he leans toward the middle of the table so it's clear he's speaking to all of us. "I special-ordered it."

"What is it?" Chelsea asks.

"You'll find out. I don't want to ruin the surprise," he tells his wife with a wink and a playful tap on her nose. "Enjoy your cheese course, I'll be right back."

He gets up and heads back for the stage. The DJ lowers the music. He's tucked off into a corner so he's barely visible. I'm assuming because he doesn't fit into the aesthetic of the rest of the environment. Dan smiles at him, then turns to the group.

"Hello, again! I hope everyone enjoyed dinner and conversations with some new friends. Dessert will be served in a little while, but for now, we're going to get the music going and welcome everybody out onto the dance floor! Come on out here and show us your best moves!"

As he steps down off the stage, the music shifts from soft dinner music to a loud, energetic song that fills the entire space and immediately draws people out of their seats into the middle of the floor. Not everyone heads out into the flashing, colored lights suddenly pulsing in the darkened center of the space, but nearly everybody who hasn't joined in is tapping their feet or watching with that expression on their face that says it is way outside of their character to jump in but they are strongly considering it.

I stay where I am, content to just watch. As soon as Dan gets back to the table, he takes Chelsea's hand and they head out into the chaos. After a couple of songs, they disappear and the next time I see them, Chelsea is holding yet another drink. This one's a pale yellow color. She comes over to me and takes my hand, trying to pull me up off my chair. I shake my head, but she keeps tugging, making me laugh with her overdone wiggling until I finally give in and let her bring me out to the dance floor.

My mother was a ballerina in Russia when she was young, but my dancing is far less refined than hers. Both of my parents encouraged me to practice martial arts just about from the time I was able to stand and it kept me active, and once I joined the Academy, working out became a part of my usual routine. Somewhere along the line these disciplines blended and when I get out on a dance floor there's somewhat of a disconnect between what my brain thinks my body is doing and what it is actually doing.

But I am also not one to back down in the face of looking ridiculous, so with Chelsea's cheerful face and everyone else's enthusiasm pushing me along, I join in. I get through a few songs, but I'm relieved when the doors open and several waitstaff roll a large table into the room. A massive, elaborately decorated cake sits in the center surrounded by several other platters of delectable looking treats. One appears to be a cheesecake with red mirror glaze and a sugar knife sticking out of it.

I understand Dan's intention to create an event that is fun and memorable, but I'm having trouble balancing all the different energies that seem to be coming together. The playful touches are fun, but they stand in stark contrast to the intense seriousness of the topics covered in the workshops and the self-defense lessons. I hope it all comes together.

Some people continue dancing while others drift over to the dessert table to choose sweets. That's the group I join. I'm already missing Sam from watching the couples around me laughing and gazing at each other, but seeing the tiered displays and platters of gorgeous desserts makes me miss him even more. Sam has a notorious sweet tooth and I know he would consider this elaborate table a personal challenge. The plates sitting on the side waiting for guests to serve themselves are small, which means my husband would be strategically trying to decide how many of the desserts he'd be able to fit within the available surface space and return as many times as necessary to try everything.

This would likely all be accompanied by some grumbling about how he should have been properly forewarned about dessert so he could prepare himself properly during the other courses of the meal.

The dancing worked up a bit of an appetite, but space is still at a premium, so I select my post-dinner treats carefully. I return to the table and a few moments later, Dan and Chelsea come from the direction of the bar.

"They're serving dessert cocktails," Chelsea announces.

Her voice has taken on a bit of a slur. I've tried not to pay too close attention to the number of drinks she's downed since the beginning of the evening. It's not my job to regulate her intake of alcohol. But I can't help but notice the effect those drinks seem to be having on her.

"Do they have coffee?" I ask.

She nods over the rim of a glass filled with something that looks like a milkshake but that I'm sure would not be a good choice for children.

"Absolutely," she says.

"Perfect. I'm going to get a cup. Anybody want some?"

THE GIRL ON THE RETREAT

Everybody shakes their head and I keep my eyes on Chelsea for an extra second to make sure she doesn't change her mind. When she doesn't, I go to the bar and peruse the impressive selection of flavored brews, syrups, creamers, and even toppings. I was up for just a hot cup of black dark roast, but the availability of all the fun extras is too tempting to pass up. Still determined to eat the desserts I chose, I restrain myself and only drizzle some coconut syrup and creamy caramel into my coffee, then top it with a swirl of whipped cream.

Back at the table, most of Chelsea's creamy, chocolate-drizzled drink is gone along with a good portion of her desserts. She and Dan go for refills and by the time I've finished my plate, she's gotten through another dessert-like cocktail and is sipping a cup of coffee heavily augmented with Irish cream. I'm not watching her carefully, knowing she has to be feeling the effect at this point.

The night is wearing on, but there doesn't seem to be any indication of things winding down. Everybody is having fun dancing and eating, some are caught up in intense conversations, others are just lingering near the dessert table. Dan is clearly far more invested in this than the other men. I haven't seen any of the others flitting around anywhere near as much as he has been, trying to interact with as many people as he possibly can and keeping everything going.

That's what he's doing when Cyndi Lauper bursts through the speakers. Chelsea gasps and bounds to her feet.

"I love this song!" she declares loudly.

Her feet stumble a little bit beneath her as she turns and heads for the dance floor.

"Chelsea," I call after her. "Are you okay?"

She doesn't respond but looks around. "Where's Dan? Dan!"

Dan is across the room talking to Kyle Harris and the people at his table, too far away to hear his wife calling for him over the sound of the music throbbing. He walks over to the next table and greets the eager-looking guests, catching Chelsea's attention.

"There he is!" she exclaims. "Dan! Come on and dance with me. Do you remember this song?"

She throws her arms up in the air and lets out a cheer, spinning around with her eyes closed. This is not a good combination for someone who has consumed as many drinks as Chelsea. I get to my feet, heading toward her. I'm almost to her when her feet tangle and she tips over, but I manage to catch her.

"I've got you," I say, helping her back to her feet.

"Emma!" she says. "I love this song."

"I know," I say gently. "I heard you. But maybe you should kind of take it easy."

"No. I want to dance." She tries to take a step out of my arms but isn't steady enough to stay upright. She nearly tumbles again and I put an arm around her to hold her upright. "Wow."

"Yeah. You've had fun tonight."

She groans as I hear Dan calling her name. He must have seen what was happening and has come over to check on his wife.

"She's alright," I tell him before he gets all the way across the dance floor. His expression is filled with worry. "She's just feeling all the celebration a bit."

"Oh, honey," he says. He looks around at the reception, clearly torn. "I'm supposed to be here until everyone is gone. But she really needs to lie down."

"I'll take her. I'm feeling tired myself. If you can give me a key, I'll bring her to her cottage and make sure she gets settled in. That way you can stay here and do what you need to do, and she can sleep it off."

"Are you sure?" he asks. "I don't want you to have to do that."

"I'm sure. It's perfectly fine. Like I said, I'm feeling tired, too. I was going to slip out and head up to my room to get some rest before tomorrow, anyway. I can just get her to the cottage before that. You should be here handling this. Don't worry about it."

Dan looks hesitant, but finally acquiesces. "The key should be in her handbag. It's Cabin Four." He takes Chelsea by the shoulders and looks into her face. "Honey, Emma is going to take you back to the cabin so you can get some sleep. I'll be there before you know it, alright?"

The way they described it earlier almost sounded as though Chelsea was staying at the cabin alone while Dan stayed in the main building with all the others. It makes me feel better to know the couple is staying together and he'll be there with her tonight.

"She's going to be fine," I tell him again. "Just enjoy yourself and maybe bring some food with you back to the cabin. Something as fatty as possible. She's going to have a hell of a hangover in the morning and that will help. She'll also need a big breakfast."

I don't know why I feel the need to instruct him on how to take care of his wife. She's an adult. Probably a few years older than me. I'm sure she knows how to handle herself when she's drinking. He may have even seen her this way before and knows exactly what to do when she goes over the edge a touch. But I feel protective over her, and something tells me even if she is fond of a tipple every now and again, this level of indulgence is reserved just for special occasions such as this one.

THE GIRL ON THE RETREAT

Guiding Chelsea back to the table, I find her handbag and open it to make sure the key is there. I find it and close the bag back up. Chelsea leans against her chair, downing a glass of water. When she's finished, I take her arm and steer her toward the lobby. Several people have spilled out of the reception into the lobby where it's cooler, brighter, and quieter. I walk right past them without looking directly at any of them. I want as little attention as possible brought to Chelsea in this condition.

We get through the lobby and into the sunroom without any complication, then out into the sharply cold night air. Neither of us have a jacket or wrap to protect us, but there's no point in turning around now. The cold will help to break through her fog a bit and will keep our pace up so we get to the cottage as fast as possible. I didn't see any of them from the stable or even while I was near the orchard, so I'm not sure how far away they are. Grant and Dan both mentioned they are generally occupied by staff, so I can't imagine they are going to be readily visible to guests just walking around the grounds. It's the accommodation equivalent of the back staircases.

There's a little twinge when thinking about it that way, the elitist discrimination feeling awkward and uncomfortable when put into that context. At the same time, I can see why it would be a good thing for those who work at the resort. They get their own space away from where they spend their days working and don't have to worry about still feeling on duty because they are seen by the guests. It's far too frequent that entitled people believe if they see someone who looks like they work in a location, even if they are clearly not active at that moment, the staff member should immediately jump to doing whatever the customer wants. That has to be stressful and frustrating, and keeping their quarters away from the rest of the resort gives the much-needed distance to stop that from happening. The staff can get away for the night and just relax.

I hurry down the paved path as fast as I can bring Chelsea without worrying she's going to fall over, paying attention to the small signs next to it. Small lights embedded down in the dirt shine up on them, illuminating the instructions on them. None of them indicate cottages, so I go to the drive that leads to the parking area and continue along it.

Finally there's a small stone gate with a plaque stating "No Guests." This has to be it. A path forms up into the grass at the side of the drive and leads along the incline of the hill and over the side of the gate, then into a stand of trees. It's darker here than is really comfortable, and I hope there is more moonlight when I'm on my way back to the main building.

"How are you doing, Chelsea?" I ask.

She glances over at me. "Feeling okay."

"Good." Ahead of us I see a cluster of white cabins. "It looks like we're almost there."

We get to the little structures and I find the one Dan and Chelsea are staying in. We climb the somewhat rickety wooden front steps carefully and I use the key from her bag to unlock the door. I lean my head inside and listen for a second, then open the door the rest of the way and bring her inside. That gesture is compulsion when I'm entering a dark, unfamiliar building. It's just a little resort cottage, but I never really know what might be waiting for me.

Feeling along the wall, I find a light switch and fill the space with warm light from an overhead fixture. It shows a cozy living area with a fireplace, furniture, and a dining table off to the side. There's no kitchen since presumably the staff would eat up at the main building or get food there and bring it back here, but there is a short hallway leading away from the living room. That must be where the bedroom is, so I bring Chelsea toward it.

She's shaking slightly in my grasp and her head is moving in small circles like she can't keep it upright. I bring her into the bedroom and see the bathroom just beyond the bed.

"Why don't I get a shower running for you?" I offer.

Chelsea nods and I guide her to the edge of the bed so she can sit down before going into the bathroom to get the water running. The tub is an old-fashioned ball foot model that makes me smile. It sits on a floor of tiny tiles with a small embedded design in the center that matches the motifs in the lobby of the main building. This was definitely not a cottage built just for the staff. Details like that are meant to be noticed and appreciated by guests.

The water gets warm and I switch it over to come from the shower head. Gathering towels from a shelf, I turn to call for Chelsea, and find her standing right behind me.

CHAPTER TWENTY

CHELSEA'S SUDDEN APPEARANCE ONLY INCHES FROM MY FACE startles a gasp from me and I take a step back. She stares at me for a second, then turns her head to look in the mirror. Her reflection stares back at her with suddenly tired eyes, her makeup worn away from the sweat of dancing for hours. There's a flushed redness in her cheeks from the cold and the alcohol.

"Oh, wow," she says, walking up to the sink and leaning to look more closely in the mirror. "Look at me. I look awful."

I recover from the momentary shock and shake my head.

"No, you don't. Come on. The water is going. You'll feel so much better once you've gotten clean. Here are some towels." I set them on the counter, not sure why I moved them in the first place considering I just set them down inches from where they were on the shelf. "I'm going to wait out in the living room until you get out. Call for me if you need anything."

I'm sure she's going to be absolutely fine, but I don't want to leave until I know for sure she is safely out of the shower and tucked into bed. It's all too easy for anyone to slip and fall, especially when they're as drunk as she is.

I settle onto the couch in the living room and reach for a magazine sitting on the coffee table. The daily lives of celebrities has never been something that's really demanded my attention and I find myself bored flipping through page after page of what people are wearing, who is supposedly sleeping with who, and where someone was seen walking their dog. Setting the magazine back down, I glance around the room. I notice a book sitting on the armrest of one of the rocking chairs set on either side of the fireplace and stand up to get it.

Bound in blue fabric, the volume looks old and worn, like it has been read many times. It doesn't have as much age on it as the books in the room where I'm having my first workshop tomorrow, but enough that I can imagine it being read by either Chelsea or Dan when they were younger. Since I'm going to make the leap into assuming the magazine on the coffee table belongs to Chelsea, the book is probably Dan's. Though, I may be wrong. There have been plenty of times I've seen Dean get swept up in one of these magazines while sitting in a waiting room, drawn into the stories like he's watching a soap opera. Which far more men do than will admit. They like the drama just as much as the women.

I sit down in the rocking chair and turn on the floor lamp behind me. The book turns out to be a sweeping fantasy epic. Within the first couple of pages, I'm lost in the rhythm of the storytelling and very concerned about whether the princess is going to escape her evil captor trying to force her into a loveless marriage and vanquish the dragon set to guard her before her planned wedding to the man she loves. I appreciate the sword smuggled in the layers of her dress and her unwavering resolve to do some serious damage on her way out of this situation. I also wish the valiant knight would move his ass a little faster to provide some backup.

And I'm also glad Xavier isn't here to explain to me all the historical inaccuracies regarding the clothing choices, the concept of a marriage for love, particularly between a knight and a princess, and the weaponry being used, while also scolding Sam for his lack of whimsy when he can't embrace that said incorrect sword blade is being used to kill a dragon.

There is a tense soundtrack playing in my head and reaching a dramatic crescendo as the princess runs down a tightly spiraling stone staircase at the back of the tower where she's kept when I notice the

THE GIRL ON THE RETREAT

sound of the shower has stopped. Setting the book down, I go to the closed bedroom door and put my head close to it.

"Chelsea? Are you okay in there?" I ask.

"You can come in," she says.

I open the door and find her in pajamas, pulling back the comforter. I help her and take her arm to provide support while she gets in. She flops down onto the mattress and rests her head on the pillow. As I cover her with the blanket, she meets my eyes.

"I'm so sorry," she whispers. "I can't believe I did this."

Chelsea closes her eyes and covers them with one hand, her lips pressed together like she's fighting tears.

"It's alright. Really. You don't need to be upset about it. You had fun and now you're back here safe. That's all that matters," I say.

"Did I embarrass Dan?" she asks.

I shake my head. "No. He was worried about you and wanted to make sure you were going to be okay, but no one was watching. Everybody was having their own good time and didn't even notice us leave. Tomorrow, no one is even going to remember if they did see us talking about leaving."

She looks at me again. "Thank you for helping me."

"Of course. Now, you close your eyes and get some sleep. Do you know if there's any Tylenol in the bathroom?" I ask.

Chelsea's eyes are already drifting down and she mumbles something but I don't understand it. I take it upon myself to go into the bathroom and look through the few items on the counter. I find a bottle of pain reliever and bring it along with a cup of water back into the bedroom and set it on the table beside her. I turn off the lamp on that nightstand while leaving the other on so she isn't too disoriented if she wakes up, then head for the door.

"Emma?" she asks in a sleepy, blurry voice.

"Hmm?" I ask.

"Can you stay for a little while? Just until I'm really asleep. I don't like falling asleep in an empty house."

I smile softly, knowing so much of that comes from her deep connection to her husband. "Sure. I'll just be sitting out in the living room. Okay?"

"Can you sit in here?" she asks.

There's a small chair against the wall next to the window, a tiny round table tucked up beside it.

"Absolutely. Just give me a second. I'll be right back."

I go back to the living room and return with the book, settling in for at least a few more minutes of finding out what's going to happen. The lamp I left on is the one closest to me, creating some strange shadows on the other side of the room. I've sunken into the story and am not sure how long I've been sitting here when one of those shadows moves.

I notice it just out of the top of my vision, over the edge of the book. It looks like the dim pool in the opposite corner of the room melted down and a piece of it split off, then moved across the bed. Something has just crossed by the window. Setting the book down, I get up and look out the window. I don't see anything, but the hairs on the back of my neck are tingling. There's a sound at the front of the cottage like something hitting the front porch.

Chelsea is sleeping peacefully, and I move quietly as I cross the room so I don't disturb her. I go into the living room and look through the window there. More moonlight spills down across the grass but I don't see any movement. The peephole shows an empty porch, but I open the door and step out onto it to make sure. I don't see anything until I take another couple of steps forward and look down. Something is sitting on the middle step, up against the corner rather than in the middle as if it was dropped or tossed there rather than being placed.

Looking around, I still don't see anyone, so I crouch down to get a better look. I can't identify the blue object, so I pick it up and turn it around in my hands to look at it from all angles. It looks like a mass of melted plastic, but I don't know what it could have been or why it ended up on this cottage porch. This, along with the shadow moving past Chelsea's window, makes me uncomfortable leaving her. It could be nothing. It's likely nothing. I don't take those kinds of risks.

Going back into the cottage, I lock the door and throw the chain lock. I go to each of the windows and release the drapes so they fall down over gauzy curtains meant to allow sunlight to stream in during the day. With those gauzy curtains as the only thing hanging over the windows, anyone who might be outside could easily see right in. That done, I go back into the bedroom and make sure that window is covered as well. Taking up the book again, I sit down beside Chelsea's sleeping form to wait.

The door opens an hour later and I stand up to walk out into the hallway so Dan isn't startled by me still being here. I hold up a hand to him.

"She's sleeping," I say softly.

"Thank you. I appreciate you bringing her back here." His eyes flitter around for a second like he's not positive what he's supposed to say next. "I thought you were just going to drop her off and head back to your room."

"I was," I tell him. "But I didn't want to leave her while she was in the shower. Then she asked me to stay while she fell asleep."

"Oh. Yeah, she doesn't like to sleep in an empty house."

"She mentioned that," I say.

"Thank you again. Really. I know this wasn't exactly what you had in mind when you were thinking about this evening," Dan says.

"Really, it's fine. I was glad to do it. She's sleeping peacefully. I put some water and Tylenol next to the bed for her so she can take it when she wakes up. It should help with the hangover. Does she usually get them when she's been drinking?" I ask.

I realize as it comes out of my mouth that it's an incredibly personal question I probably shouldn't have asked in this particular context. He's not being interrogated. I can only hope it's the genuine concern I feel for Chelsea that comes across and not me being nosy and invasive. Dan looks at me for a brief second, then shakes his head.

"No. Honestly, I've never seen her like this. She doesn't drink very often and when she does, she might get a little tipsy, but not like this. I'm actually really shocked to see her get this way. I know she was really nervous about the retreat, and I guess that might have made her act out a bit more than usual. I just don't understand how it got this bad," he admits.

I look at him with confusion. "Dan, she was drinking the whole night. Just about every time I looked at her, she had a new drink in her hand. Even with dessert."

"Emma, I ordered her drinks myself. The Blue Lagoon had alcohol and she had one spiked milkshake, but the rest were virgin. Just juice and soda," he says.

"What about her coffee? The Irish Cream smell was strong."

"Creamer," he tells me. "It's non-alcoholic."

"Did Chelsea know her drinks weren't all hard?" I ask.

"Of course. She comes from a family with a high degree of alcoholism. She lost an uncle, her grandfather, and a couple of cousins to it. She was nearly killed in a drunk driving accident involving her sister, who didn't make it. There were two other people in the car who were killed as well."

"That's horrible," I say. "I'm surprised she drinks at all."

"She didn't for a very long time. She completely avoided any alcohol and even stayed away from events that were going to have it. She'd even leave weddings before the reception because she didn't want to be around alcohol. After a while, she was able to work through by realizing it had gone from just an avoidance to an aversion and that wasn't healthy. Eventually, she figured out ways to just drink small amounts and develop a healthy relationship with it, instead of having to be all or nothing."

"That makes sense. I imagine the virgin cocktails help her feel like she's still able to take part in things. But a cocktail with dinner and then a spiked milkshake a couple of hours later isn't anywhere near enough alcohol to get someone drunk like that," I say. "How could she have been that affected if that was all she had?"

He shakes his head, glancing over my shoulder like he's trying to get a glimpse of his wife in the bedroom. "I don't know. That's why I came back here as soon as I could. I asked the DJ to kind of wrap things up to encourage people to leave and as soon as I could, I got out of there and came here. I wanted to make sure she's alright, that there wasn't something else that was going on."

He looks stressed and exhausted. I start toward the door. "You need to get some rest. Big day tomorrow. Call me if you need anything, okay?"

"Thanks, Emma. Goodnight."

"Goodnight." I take another step, then remember the strange plastic object on the steps and turn back to him. "I heard a sound on the front porch and when I went out there, I found this on the step. Do you have any idea what it is?"

Dan takes it from my hand and turns it around the same way I did, then frowns. "Melted plastic?" He hands it back to me. "No. I have no idea. I guess it's possible it was in the trash in here when they were cleaning and it was just dropped when the cleaning staff left."

"Maybe. Okay, I'm going to head back to the main building. I'll see you tomorrow."

"See you tomorrow."

I wish even more that I'd brought a coat when I step out and find the wind harsher and the temperature even lower. But I didn't think I was going to braving the elements tonight. Maybe I should have taken the couple of minutes to go upstairs and grab a coat. I could have even used the elevator. But Chelsea was obviously in a bad way, and I didn't want to make her wait any longer to get a good shower and into a comfortable bed than she absolutely had to. And I certainly didn't want to jostle her with any kind of unnecessary motion.

It's fine. I got across the grounds once, I can do it again.

THE GIRL ON THE RETREAT

At least wearing my suit to the reception has a distinct benefit over all the gowns and high heels in this way. It might not be flashy and fancy, but it allows for much faster movement.

The grounds are intensely quiet as I head for the main building ahead. The moonlight is bright enough, and there are lights embedded in the ground along the path, which is nice. When I can avoid crossing unfamiliar terrain in the dark, I tend to.

The hill is picking up and I can see the main building ahead when a feeling brushes across the back of my neck. It's nothing tangible, not like a bug fluttering past or someone actually touching me. Instead, it's the sensation of eyes focused on my skin. My steps slow as I tune into my surroundings. I wait for a sound, a flicker of movement. Everything is still and silent, but the feeling is still there. Rather than looking further into the darkness, I focus my eyes on the halos of illumination around the lights in the ground. They bleed between the blades of grass and spill onto the pathways, in small sections between them blending until there is a faint river of light along each side.

I wait for it to be broken by a shadow or a footstep. My breath comes out in puffs of white. It reverberates in my ears. I'm very aware of everything around me, the blood coursing through me, the tingle in my fingertips. My gun is at my hip. My knife in the band of my bra. After a few more beats of nothingness, I tell myself I don't need either and continue on.

I've gone only a few more steps when I hear a sharp intake of breath somewhere to my right. Stopping, I turn toward it, my hand going to my hip by instinct. There was a time when I didn't put my holster on all the time, when I would run into the darkness without it, when I'd pretend I could separate myself from being an agent when I wasn't active. Those days are gone. I learned.

Nothing has changed. The still darkness is unbroken. The flow of light shows no shadows.

I move in the direction of the breath, but even in the moonlight, I don't see anyone—until in the distance, at the edge of the hedge maze, I see a figure moving quickly away from the woods. They aren't looking my direction, but toward the main building. From the distance I can't tell who they are. They rush toward the end of the maze and then suddenly take a sharp turn and disappear around the corner.

I wait for a few seconds, then decide to continue to my room. If someone is out gallivanting through the grounds in the rush after the reception, good for them. I hope they're wearing a coat, but that's really all I can offer them.

Going back down onto the drive, I walk along the edge toward the grounds. I feel the sensation of the eyes on me again and moments later hear the unmistakable sound of footsteps. I go a little faster. The footsteps are erratic, coming in a burst and then disappearing for a few seconds only to return. In one of the quiet stretches, I look behind me and see nothing. I can still feel the pursuit as I jog the last few dozen yards to the back door of the resort. I grab for the handle.

It doesn't move. The door is locked. I hear the footsteps falling steadily behind me now and I spin around with my gun in my hand.

The figure coming toward me is dressed in all black and stays far enough away from the light at the edges of the drive that I can't see any of their features.

"Stop!" I shout, taking a step toward them just as I feel hands clamp down around my upper arm.

The figure skids to a partial stop and pivots to run in the opposite direction and I turn to the person gripping me.

"Daisy?"

CHAPTER TWENTY-ONE

WILD EYES LOOK BACK AT ME THROUGH SMUDGED MAKEUP. Her lipstick is worn and her cheeks are red, and her hair that had fallen so thick and perfect at the reception is now messy and tousled. She's no longer wearing the dress she'd been wearing, but a pair of lounge pants and a sweatshirt.

"Who was that?" she asks.

"I don't know. Daisy, what are you doing out here?"

"I was taking a walk. I couldn't sleep."

"Taking a walk?" I ask.

"Right. After all the excitement at the reception, I thought I would be exhausted and just fall right to sleep, but I couldn't get myself to settle in. When Gordon got back to the room, he was just about dead on his feet and I didn't want to keep him up by being awake, so I thought a walk would do me good," she says. "I was coming back and realized that person was chasing me." She lets out a shuddering sigh and pulls her arms tight around her. "So much for no more excitement for the night, right?"

I keep looking at her makeup and her hair. "You couldn't sleep so you came out here to wander around the grounds?"

"Right," she confirms.

"No coat or flashlight?" I ask.

"Where are yours?" she asks. "Come on, I want to go inside. Whoever that person was might come back."

She reaches around me to open the door but has the same trouble with the latch.

"It's locked," I tell her. "They must have locked it after the reception cleared out."

"What are we going to do?" she asks, sounding right on the edge of panic. "We're stuck out here in this cold. It's probably below freezing out here. How long are we going to last? What if this is what that guy wanted? He wanted us to get locked out here so he could come back for us."

She was heading in the direction of another of her long tirades, so I take her by the shoulders to stop her. "Daisy, calm down. They're gone. Honestly, it was probably someone staying here or a member of the staff and they were just trying to get back inside. They probably didn't even realize you thought they were following you."

"They were running right behind me," she insists.

"You came up from my left side and that person came up behind and slightly to the side."

"Right."

"So, if they were chasing you, wouldn't they have been to my left as well? Why would they chase you and then detour themselves away from you but keep coming?" I ask.

"If they were just trying to get inside, why did they turn and run away like that?" she asks.

"Because I had a gun pointed at them," I say. "The impulse of an FBI agent who hears someone running up behind them in the dark."

"Oh. Right." She cups her hands and presses them to the glass so she can try to look through into the sunroom. There are a few lights on inside, but most of the areas are darkened. "I don't see anyone in there. I'm freezing. What are we going to do?"

"This isn't the only entrance. Let's check the front door," I suggest.

We walk around the side of the resort, my legs starting to feel heavy and my hands stinging with the cold. I try some of the visualization exercises that are so popular now, imagining myself stretched out on my favorite blue beach blanket and moving my feet off the edge so I can bury my toes in the hot sand as the sun bakes me. According to the class Xavier made all of us go to at the Sherwood community center, this is supposed to somehow circumvent the actual input my brain is currently processing and convince it I'm actually experiencing those things so I don't feel the cold.

It is not working.

We get around to the front of the resort and find the lights to either side of the front door are on, casting a welcoming glow across the porch and down the steps. We rush up the steps toward the door. I'm hoping that the door will be unlocked, even though the resort is closed to any other guests, and I highly doubt this is the type of place where people just show up in the middle of the night for a last-minute reservation.

But one tug at the door confirms that it's definitely locked.

Daisy sags beside me, letting out a sound that's somewhere between exasperation and despair as her head falls back. I notice a small box with a button beside the door.

"Look. It's an intercom," I say. I press the button and wait for a response. "I hope it doesn't just connect to the front desk. Though, let's be real, Stanford is probably standing behind it right now."

"Hello?" a voice comes through the speaker.

I open my mouth, then close it, bringing myself a little closer to the intercom. "Stanford?"

Oh, I sincerely hope he is not actually at the desk in the dark.

"Yes, ma'am."

He sounds slightly groggy and I wonder if the intercom connects to the desk and to his apartment as well. Grant mentioned he lived on the property but not in one of the cottages like the other staff. It doesn't surprise me that he'd have an apartment in the main building, allowing him to stay close to everything and respond to anything he might need to. I can't imagine he is actually the only person who oversees the resort, but as of now, the only other staff I've encountered are the kitchen workers.

"We're locked out," I say. "Could you please come let us in?"

"I'm sorry, we aren't accepting further reservations. There is a private event being hosted at the resort this week."

I glance over at Daisy and see her peering around, her arms wrapped tight around herself as if she's looking for someone. I know she's thinking about the person who ran toward us. I'm trying not to think about the shadow in the cottage. There's nothing to prove whoever it was meant any kind of harm, and they might have been so startled by me that they ran away rather than letting me know who they were. Even if that isn't the case, they know now that I have a gun readily accessible. It wouldn't be well advised to try to come for us again.

"I know," I say into the speaker. "This is Emma Griffin. I'm here with Daisy Gallagher." There's no response. "We're speakers for the event?"

"Yes, Agent Griffin, I understand. You say you are locked out?" he asks.

"Yes. We tried to get through the back door into the sunroom and it wouldn't open, so we came to the front and it won't open, either."

"The sunroom door should not be locked," he says. "That door is always kept unlocked."

"Well, it must have been locked accidentally. Neither of us were able to open it and now we're at the front. It's extremely cold out here. Could you please let us in?" I ask.

I'm losing my patience but fighting to keep my voice steady. It's the wee hours of the morning at this point, and even though I'm sure he was at the reception until the bitter end to supervise the entire thing all the way through cleanup, Stanford also strikes me as someone who doesn't take much time falling asleep at night. He's so in control he wouldn't tolerate his brain being so insubordinate as to require winding down before falling directly to sleep. He probably doesn't even need an alarm clock to get up in the morning. But likely has two.

"Give me a few moments. I'll be right with you," he says.

The intercom goes quiet and I step away from it, turning back to Daisy. She has her head back again, but I realize she's staring at the ceiling.

"What are you looking at?" I ask.

"The ceiling," she says. "Why is it blue? The rest of this place is white."

I glance up and see the particular shade of blue coating the ceiling of the porch overhang.

"It's called haint blue. It's an old Southern tradition," I tell her. It's supposed to protect the home from spirits because it looks like water and folklore says spirits can't cross water, so they'd avoid anything that looks like it."

"Oh." Daisy looks over at me. "That seems like something I should know. Right? Doesn't that seem like I should know it?"

I laugh. "It's very valuable information."

She bounces a little. "Where is he?"

"I'm pretty sure he was in bed," I say. "He probably needed to get up and get dressed before coming down here."

"Oh. Right. That makes sense. I don't see that man being okay with showing up at the door in his bathrobe," she says.

I chuckle. "No, I very much doubt he would be. And I have a feeling there's going to be an unpleasant talking to in store for whoever locked that back door tonight."

I join in with Daisy's bouncing. I'm getting very aware of the time and how little of the night is left before we have to be up for the morning. It was not great forethought for the party to get so rowdy and last well into the night while also scheduling the first workshops for far too early the next day. I am anticipating a challenging morning ahead.

Daisy presses herself close to one of the decorative glass panels to either side of the door. Gorgeous stained-glass pieces masterfully inset in clear glass are a visitor's first glimpse of the opulent peacock theming they'll encounter inside. These windows look original to the Victorian-era version of the structure. They would have been a display of tremendous wealth and class, an energy that still exudes from the surroundings, even with the updated, modern touches.

"It looks so different in there all dark and empty," she says.

"Do you think Gordon is going to wake up and be worried about you?" I ask.

"Hmmmm?" she asks, turning to look at me.

"Gordon," I say. "Do you think he's going to wonder where you are? I know my husband would roll over and wake up realizing I wasn't there. He'd be really worried about me." I let out a slight sigh. "He's actually probably really worried about me anyway. I didn't call him tonight and he will have been expecting to hear from me."

"Oh," Daisy says. She shakes her head. "No. I doubt he'll even notice I'm not there. He's a really heavy sleeper."

"But I thought you said you left to take a walk because you couldn't fall asleep and didn't want to keep him up," I say.

"Right. Well, he's a deep sleeper once he's asleep. I didn't want to stop him from falling asleep," she says. "You know, he was just really tired and wanted to get right to sleep because the workshops start in the morning and he didn't want to be totally exhausted. He thought I should get some sleep, too, because I'm going to be leading classes and need to have energy. But maybe that's part of not being able to go to sleep. Nerves, right? This is the biggest event I've ever done.

"I'm used to teaching much smaller classes, so all this is kind of a lot. It must have started getting to me when I saw them all at the reception and realized it was going to be that many people coming to my classes. I mean, not at the same time, obviously. And I guess not everybody who is signed up for the retreat is actually going to come to my classes, but it's going to be a lot of them. Right? You think people are going to want to come?"

"I'm sure they will," I try, but I already know the conversation train is rolling down that hill.

"But that was keeping me from sleeping and I didn't want it to keep him from falling asleep, so I went out for a walk. Moving my body is just part of my life. It always has been for as long as I can remember. I've just always been happiest and felt the best when I was moving. Not always Jazzercise, obviously. That really wasn't a thing when I was younger. I grew up on a farm, so I was really active doing those kinds of things and just running around with the other farm kids. That's why I should have known about the blue. The…"

"Haint," I say, filling in the silence that comes like a gasp for air after her long stretch of speech.

"Haint, right. That's why I feel like I should have known about that. How about you?" she asks.

"What about me?" I ask.

"Do you get nervous speaking in front of groups like this?" she asks.

"Oh. Um," I think for a second about how I'm going to answer. "Not really. I wouldn't say nervous. I'm used to talking to people. But this is the first time I'll be speaking to this large of a group at the same time, so I'm just wondering what it's going to be like and hoping I pull it off."

"You will," she says with a smile. "You're going to do an amazing job. You are just an incredible woman. I admire you so much. I'm sorry. I already said all this, right? And you probably hear it all the time."

I notice movement out of the corner of my eye and look through the glass expecting to see Stanford. Instead, someone is coming across the lobby from the direction of the sunroom. Daisy sees him, too, and knocks on the glass. The person pauses, hesitating as he stares at the front door. She waves enthusiastically and I decide looking friendly and unthreatening is going to be the best way to get me out of this cold, so I join her. He comes toward us and when he's close, I realize it's one of the waitstaff from earlier. He must recognize us because he turns the locks on the inside of the door and opens it.

"Thank you so much," I say, eagerly stepping into the warmth of the lobby. "We've been waiting out there."

"Why didn't you go to the back door?" he asks.

Daisy and I look at each other. "It was locked."

"Jared? What are you doing?"

Stanford is coming toward us, his eyebrows knitted together and a displeased expression on his face. Like I expected, he is fully dressed and ready to present himself just like he would if he was standing behind the desk. I can understand his desire to be professional and not seem too comfortable and familiar with the guests, but seeing him in a bathrobe and slippers would have been barely a price to pay to not stand in the cold for the last several minutes.

"I forgot something in the kitchen," Jared says. "I needed to come back for it and when I was crossing the lobby, I saw these guests outside and let them in. They're speakers for the event. I didn't think they should be out in the cold."

"Of course not," Stanford says, sounding almost flustered by being called out for even giving the appearance of not being a fully welcoming and hospitable host. "I only mean how did you get in?"

"The back door," Jared says.

Stanford looks over at Daisy and me. "I thought you said the back door was locked."

"It was," I say.

"We both tried it," Daisy adds.

"It was unlocked when I got to it," Jared says. "Just like always."

"Thank you, Jared," Stanford says. "You can go on to the kitchen now."

"Excuse me," I say, stopping the younger man as he starts away from us. He turns to me with raised eyebrows. "Were you here about ten minutes ago? At the back of the building? Did you come up and see us there?"

I omit the detail of the gun. There's no need to fray Stanford's nerves at this time of night. Jared shakes his head.

"No. I just got here a couple of minutes ago," he says.

"Alright. Thank you," I say.

Stanford gives a dismissing nod and Jared scurries away toward the kitchen. Stanford looks back at us.

"Perhaps the door was stuck because of the temperature," he suggests.

He doesn't actually believe it. There was no precipitation to freeze the door and it's generally warm, damp temperatures that make doors difficult to open. But it's easier for him to say that than to suggest we aren't capable of operating a standard door handle.

"It was locked," I insist. "Could he have unlocked it?"

"Impossible. Kitchen staff does not have keys to the main entrances of the resort. The head of the kitchen has a key to the delivery door, but that's it."

"Who does have a key to the front and back doors?" I ask.

"Me," he says. "Now, if there's nothing else I can do for either of you, I'll go back to bed."

We shake our heads and he nods in return, a silent exchange weighed down by the odd situation.

"We should get to bed, too," Daisy says when he's across the lobby.

All the strange explanations she gave are still running through my head as we head up the steps to the top floor. It could make sense. It's logical enough that though her fiancé is a heavy sleeper she wanted to get out of his way as he tried to fall asleep. But something about it felt odd.

We part ways at the top of the steps and I wave goodnight to her before walking down the hall to the tall window that takes up a large portion of the wall. I look out over the grounds. Some clouds have stretched across the moon, stifling some of the light. But even in the diminished glow I can see something moving. Something large that appears to be walking on four feet. It goes for the woods, pauses, then jumps and heads for the trees.

Baffled, I make my way to my room and debate calling Sam at this hour.

CHAPTER TWENTY-TWO

Him

H E WATCHED THE NEWS EVERY NIGHT.
Many people did, trying to find out what was happening in the world, staying informed, feeling like part of everything around them even if they are disconnected the rest of the time.

That wasn't why he did it. When he turned the TV on at night, he wasn't waiting to see what they had to tell him. He was looking for specific details.

He waited to hear mention of certain places, names, descriptions. He kept track. He liked the chase.

It was very rarely a matter of *if* they would find out. It was *when* and *how*.

It was part of the service he offered. His clients didn't have to think about anything beyond the fulfillment of their experience. He would ensure the rest of it was managed effectively and securely. They could walk away as soon as they had gotten what they wanted and he would step in to handle the aftermath. He crafted coverup stories and evidence trails. He dealt with cleaning up and destroying what was necessary.

That wasn't always the case. Sometimes it was part of the experience, chosen by the customer who came to him with their fantasies. They didn't just dream of the kill. They wanted to orchestrate every detail of it. From how their prey arrived, to the hunting grounds, to what will happen to what's left of them when the hunt is finished.

Either way, he tracked every detail in the weeks and months that followed, paying close attention to how every element of it was unfolding.

The announcement a person had gone missing.

The details they knew.

The discovery of a body.

The chase.

He took tremendous care to make sure it all worked the way it was meant to. Meticulous management protected his client and himself. The authorities had never caught up with him. He'd never lost a single client.

Tonight he watched to see if Melanie Bridges would be reported missing. She should have been at work early yesterday morning after taking her usual jog along the trail that skirted the edge of her neighborhood. Then she was supposed to be seen at a lunch date in the middle of the day. By the time neither one of those happened and she also didn't arrive for a meeting with the PTA in the evening, somebody should have noticed. By now, the alert should have gone up that a popular teacher who always arranged the school's fall festival and was known for her love of jogging and swimming had disappeared without a trace.

While he waited for the anchors to start in on the local news, he sifted through the newly developed photographs on the table in front of him. Having his own dark room certainly had its benefits. Turning over rolls of film filled with the kind of imagery he sold wouldn't work in any conventional development shop. He had no interest in coming up with explanations or dealing with the added scrutiny that could come from a curious clerk catching a glimpse of these little souvenirs.

As much as he loved crafting customized experiences for his clients and watching as they fulfilled their deepest desires, this was the primary portion of his business. These pictures were a safer, less extreme form of indulgence. Clients with these cravings but without the stomach or the drive, or perhaps the budget, to go full-in on completing their fantasies could hold these pictures and imagine themselves there. They could collect them like fine art. Hide away with them in the dark.

These were a small taste of what the hungry people who called him on heavily guarded numbers really wanted. Their desire to see a beautiful body meant something different than for the men who crept into the dark corners of peep shows and sex shops.

These men, and sometimes women, wanted true bodies. Corpses. Empty shells now devoid of any soul. The only time a picture of a person still full of life meant anything was when he was offering up a new choice of prey for those who didn't come to him with a specific kill in mind. The others wanted cold skin and hot blood. Some found their pleasure in bodies carefully posed while others just wanted them as they fell.

He'd found a bit of perverse enjoyment out of building his photography skills through the classes he took. Around him eager adult learning students clamored to perfectly frame flowers and capture just the right shimmer of light across open water at golden hour. They had optimism-filled conversations about finding a new hobby or wanting to start a business capturing couples on their wedding days. Some spoke of the need to express themselves artistically.

Maybe that was what he was doing. Maybe this was his art.

The thought made his lips tingle.

"Local fifth-grade teacher Melanie Bridges was last seen at a dinner with friends two days ago."

The mention of the name caught his attention and he set down the new stack of images to pay attention to what the anchor had to say.

"Those friends report Melanie told them she was going home to finalize a presentation she'd be making to the PTA. She seemed in good spirits and they had no concerns when she headed home. The school administration, however, noticed she did not arrive to teach her classes yesterday and when they called her home, she did not answer.

"Police conducted a welfare check at her home and did not see her vehicle or any other sign of her. At this time a canvas of her neighborhood is being organized in the hopes of finding her. Anyone with any information is asked to please contact the Springfield Police Department."

He smiled as he turned the TV off and went back to the pictures. He touched Melanie's face.

"Don't worry. If they don't find you within the next few weeks, we'll move it along for them. Kent specifically asked that you don't stay missing forever. He doesn't want you to stay in the creek all alone. Isn't that kind of him? Hopefully the log will dislodge and you'll float downstream with the snowmelt. By then, of course, there won't be any evidence for them to find. And they won't have any way of finding the campground fifty miles away. But at least they'll have your body back, won't they?"

He set the pictures aside to finish distributing between Kent's final portfolio and to the waiting collectors. Another was sitting at the corner of his desk. He picked it up and leaned back in his chair, gazing at the woman in it. Older than Melanie and with thick blonde hair rather than Melanie's dark brown. This woman hadn't left his mind since the first time he saw her. This picture wasn't taken for any of his clients. She was very much alive, her hair lifted up from her neck with her movement. Shorts showed off toned legs and the expression on her face displayed pure determination.

On the long table set up on the other side of the room were the detailed plans he'd been working on for the last several months. This would be the most intricate experience he'd ever orchestrated. Rather than just one client, he'd invited a few of his most loyal repeat customers and close friends. This exclusive hunt was unlike anything he'd ever offered. It promised to be a lavish and thrilling experience only he could pull off.

But it wasn't enough. He wasn't satisfied with what he'd already put in place. He wanted something special, a truly unique VIP offering befitting the caliber of guests partaking in this event. He'd been trying to come up with the perfect premium addition, something he could surprise them with to further elevate their experience. He'd been testing his idea, dipping just the tips of his fingers into the pool to see what he could stir up.

He stood up and carried the picture in his hand over to the table and set it down among images of thick trees, open grass, and custom-crafted weapons.

She was perfect.

CHAPTER TWENTY-THREE

WHEN I FINALLY GET BACK TO MY SUITE, I SEE IT WAS CLEANED while I was at the reception. It seems strange that the housekeeping staff would be working that late in the evening, but at the same time, I was taking a nap during the time when they would probably usually be cleaning rooms. It's a nice touch that they would have them come back through to take care of my room while I was out.

The room smells fresh and clean, and perfect, evenly spaced tracks from a vacuum cleaner mark the carpet. In the center of the table near the window is a small silver tray with several chocolates along with a single fresh flower. Beside it sits what looks like a jewelry box atop a cream-colored envelope. I move the box and pick up the envelope first. It has my name across it in sweeping penmanship. Inside is a notecard. I read over the brief message, then set the card down and pick up the jewelry box.

Opening it, I find the enamel pin described in the note. The event is divided into different tracks, each assigned a color used on the schedule, directional signage, and other materials for the event. Speakers and leaders for each of these tracks will wear pins in the color that corresponds to the track they belong to, making it easy for guests to quickly identify whether they are in the right place during any given event.

My pin is a rich emerald green and in the shape of a shield, golden lines through it creating the look of a coat of arms but without the individual detailing. It's large enough to be clearly obvious if worn on a lapel, and I go ahead and carry it into the bedroom to add it to the outfit I plan to wear for my first workshop in a few hours. That way I can't possibly forget it when I leave the room.

I look across the bedroom at the phone and am again tempted to call Sam. I miss the sound of his voice and I know he's worried about me. I'm surprised Stanford didn't tell me he'd called the front desk demanding to know where I was. My husband would never admit it, but he's a worrier. He likes to say he has an appropriate level of concern for his wife, just as any husband would. But the truth is, he is constantly worried something has happened or will happen to me at any given moment.

Not that I can really blame him. Over the decades I've known him, he's borne witness to plenty of incidents and events that probably justify his feeling that way. I only wish it didn't bother him so much.

Almost as though thinking about him brought more clarity to my mind, I realize there's a red light blinking on the phone. I go over to it and see it's an indicator for a voice message. Unsurprisingly, the message is from Sam. It brings a smile to my lips as I listen to him tell me about his day and send his hopes I'm having a good time and me not being in my room at that hour meant I was enjoying myself and not that I'd taken up with one of the other speakers and run away forever. It's the joke he always uses so he doesn't have to say he hopes nothing bad has happened to me. He ends the message telling me to call him no matter what time I get back in, so I take him at his word.

"Hello?" he asks, sounding groggy and a little confused.

"Hey, babe. I'm sorry to wake you up. You said call no matter what time it was," I say.

"No, no. I'm glad you called. Hi. I miss you."

There's still some sleepiness in his voice, but he's coming out of it.

"I miss you, too. I'm sorry I wasn't here earlier when you called," I say.

"It's okay. Did you have fun tonight?" he asks.

"Well..."

THE GIRL ON THE RETREAT

I tell him about the reception and having to bring Chelsea back to her cottage, the strange shadow and Dan's reaction to the way his wife was acting, then the doors being locked and being surprised by Daisy. It sounds like so much now that I say it out loud and suddenly I'm even more exhausted. I know I need to wash off my makeup and change my clothes, but I wish I didn't have to.

"What do you think was going on with Chelsea?" he asks.

"I really don't know. It's very strange. I guess there's a chance he could be lying about how much she usually drinks," I say.

"Or she could. Maybe he genuinely thinks she doesn't drink very much, but she overindulged tonight and he thought she was drinking her usual virgin drinks."

"I guess that's possible, but why would she do that? If she was going to drink alcohol, why wouldn't she tell him if he's right there? And he was almost always with her when she ordered the drinks. He actually brought a couple of them to her," I say.

"I don't know."

"There's something about this place, Sam. I wish I could describe it to you. It's gorgeous. The whole place is. But it's also eerie. Like I'm just waiting around for a ghost to walk down the hallway," I say.

"Don't say that to Xavier," Sam chortles. "He'll be on his way to you with one of his contraptions."

"I'll tell you again, the ghost hunting rods were not his idea. That's actually something people think work," I say.

"They also think those will show you where water is," Sam points out.

"I know. Anyway, that's not the point. There's just something about this whole resort that's… I don't even know the right words for it. I want to bring you here for a long vacation and I also want to get in my car and leave. My brain just won't stop. I keep thinking about the shadow at the cottage and the person who ran up on me while I was at the back door. I wonder if it was the same person, or if that shadow was Daisy. Why was that person coming toward me? They didn't seem to have any kind of weapon and weren't saying anything. It was probably just a member of the staff or even a guest that I scared the living hell out of and so they ran away and were too embarrassed to come back. And speaking of the door. I *know* it was locked. I tried it. Daisy tried it. That door was locked. But then the guy from the kitchen just walked right in like it was nothing."

"You said the manager guy is really stuffy," Sam says.

"Stanford? Yeah, he is."

"Could he have unlocked that door just to make a point?"

"I don't think he would go out of his way to do something like that. Besides, Jared would have seen him come to the door and unlock it. He would have had to go to the door without any of us seeing him, unlock it, then go away and wait for someone to walk through it. Which seems like kind of a gamble when there are two of your event speakers freezing to death on your front porch," I say.

"Go big or go home," he says.

"I don't really think that's applicable here," I say. He lets out a huge yawn. "You go on back to sleep. I'll talk to you tomorrow. I love you."

"Love you. Goodnight."

He already sounds partially asleep as I hang up. I drag myself to the bathroom for what is, by my calculations, the three hundredth shower I've taken since arriving here and finally crawl into bed. I don't even want to look at the clock. I have a distinct suspicion I don't need to and that another wakeup call is going to blast me out of my sleep way before I want it to anyway, so I curl up with my back to the clock and go to sleep.

Just as I suspected, I feel like I've been asleep ten minutes when the call comes to roust me from bed. As much as I crave the high school trick of asking for a few more minutes, I know that's not going to happen, so I get up and put on the clothes I'm glad I picked out for myself last night. It eliminates the need for me to think for the next fifteen minutes or so before I can get my blood actually flowing through my body.

The coffeemaker is a high-end model that I need to concentrate on just to figure out how to work it, but the coffee bubbling out of it within a few minutes smells glorious. I finish getting dressed and take a sip. This far exceeds anything I've had in a hotel before. Leaning against the counter, I take a few more sips before putting on my makeup and fixing my hair. I figure I'll have time after breakfast to come back here for my notes, so I leave my satchel and notepads and head out.

When I open the door, I nearly kick over a small vase of flowers. Purple carnations. I pick them up and see a card sticking out of the top of the vase. Expecting it to be from Dan as a kickoff of the morning, I read it. But it's not my name on the card. Instead, it says "Lucas."

I flip the card over and see another message.

"Ace of spades."

I flip the card back to the front again, just to make sure I didn't miss anything, but there's nothing else on either side. Just his name and "Ace of spades."

Scooping the vase off the carpet, I bring it with me downstairs into the lobby. The resort is gradually coming to life as people drift down the stairs and make their way into the lounge and down toward the dining room. An A-frame board displayed in front of the lounge lists the quick options for breakfast available there for those not interested in a full meal. I glance at it as I head for the front desk. A more elegant, framed board beside the door to the dining room holds a printed menu of the table service meal being served inside.

Stanford is standing in his usual place behind the desk and even though I'm sure he's tired, he looks just as polished as yesterday. He looks up as I approach. I'm expecting some sort of displeased scowl like he's really not happy to see me again so soon, but he offers me the same kind of slight smile he has given everyone else who comes to talk to him. Apparently we're going to go the route of pretending last night never happened. I'm alright with that.

"Good morning, Agent Griffin," he says. "What can I do for you?"

"Good morning, Stanford. I found this outside my door this morning," I put the vase on the counter in front of him. "The card has the name 'Lucas' on it. I'm assuming that's Lucas Bremmer."

"Oh, the speaker you replaced," he says.

"Yes," I say. "Do you know who brought them up?"

He shakes his head. "No. I would generally receive deliveries like these and have the housekeeping staff bring them to the room, but I didn't see these this morning. They must have come while I was overseeing setup for breakfast. I apologize."

"No need to apologize. It's fine. I was wondering, though, if you could tell me anything about Mr. Bremmer."

"What do you mean?" he frowns.

"Do you know why he wasn't able to be here?" I ask. "I know his cancellation was fairly sudden."

"Mr. Vreeland informed me of the change when he arrived Tuesday. He just said that there was a change in the schedule and a note needed to be printed to add to the program for the evening reception. The schedules themselves, other than the ones included in the speaker packets, hadn't been printed, so those were able to be modified before the printer sent them over. He told me Mr. Bremmer was unavoidably needed somewhere else, but he was very fortunate to have gotten an exceptional replacement. Which would be you," he says.

It's what I'm assuming is Stanford's version of flattery.

"And I feel very fortunate to have been able to step in," I say. "Well, I should go have breakfast before everything gets started. Thank you for your help."

"Oh, the flowers, Agent Griffin," he says as I walk away.

"They aren't for me," I say.

"But they are for someone who isn't going to be here. You might as well keep them in your room. They are lovely," he says.

"Alright," I agree, going back to the desk for the vase. "If someone mentions them, please let me know."

He gives me a somewhat quizzical face but agrees, and I head back for my room to put the vase on the table. Before leaving, I take the card and slip it into the nightstand drawer.

Time has ticked away since I got up, but I'm too hungry for one of the danishes or bagels being offered in the lounge to fill me up. It's cutting it close, but I head for the dining room. I slip in and see Dan, Chelsea, Tom Murphy, Kyle Harris, and the woman he was with at the reception sitting together at a round table to one side. Dan sees me as soon as I walk in and waves me over.

I notice they all have coffee in front of them, but there are no plates.

"Good morning, Emma," Dan says. "Coming for breakfast?"

I'm not sure what else it is that I would be doing in the dining room first thing in the morning, but I nod and smile anyway.

"Yes. I'm starving this morning," I say.

"I guess you danced it all off last night," he says with a laugh. "Please, join us."

"You are already all settled. I don't want to intrude."

"Nonsense. All we've gotten is our coffee. They haven't even brought the pastries yet. Please. There's a seat right there," Dan says, gesturing to the empty seat next to Chelsea.

There really is no polite way to get out of this particular invitation, so I walk around to the seat.

"Alright. Thank you." I sit down and Chelsea looks over at me with a shy smile.

I want to ask her how she is, but everyone at the table is watching me and I don't want to embarrass her. Instead, I smile at each of them.

"How did you sleep?" Dan asks.

"Really well," I say.

"I hope you weren't too chilly," Kyle says.

I look at him through narrowed eyes. That was a strange thing for him to say. He didn't know I went to Chelsea's cottage or that I was locked outside, though it seems that is exactly what he's referencing.

"No," I say. "I was fine."

"I was freezing!" the woman next to him says. "I piled on the blankets but just couldn't seem to get warm. It was like there was air leaking into the room or something."

THE GIRL ON THE RETREAT

"I don't think we got a chance to meet last night," I say to her. "I'm Emma Griffin."

"She's with the FBI," Dan adds.

"Yes," Kyle tells her. "She's here to talk about some of her cases and how crimes are investigated."

"I'm Ainsley. That's fascinating. I'll have to make sure to slip into one of your sessions. You're the green track, I see."

I glance down at my chest. I'd forgotten about the pin I'd put there last night. I'm glad I thought to attach it when I first got it.

"I am," I say. I look around the table at the others. "Red and blue. Are there others?"

Tom looks at his own scarlet pin, then at Dan's sapphire-hued one. "There's one more, isn't there?"

"Yellow," Dan says. "Did you pick up one of the schedules? Hopefully the colors will help keep things organized."

"I didn't, but I'll grab one after breakfast. Speaking of the schedule being updated, what can you tell me about Lucas Bremmer?" I ask.

"What do you mean?" Dan asks. "I told you about him when you first got here."

"I know you told me he's a writer and that he had to call out, but do you have any idea why? When you talked to him, did he sound distressed or anything?"

Everybody at the table is looking at me strangely and I don't particularly blame them. Two waitstaff come up at that moment to place trays of pastries in front of us. It breaks the stares and we all mumble our thanks to them until they walk away. I glance around at the rest of the room and notice one of the tables only has one server carrying two trays.

"I didn't get a chance to talk to him directly," Dan says. "He left a message with my receptionist. But I don't have any reason to believe there was anything seriously wrong. She didn't say he sounded upset or anything. Why?"

"Oh, no reason. I'm just curious. It's what I do. Some flowers showed up at my suite this morning with a card made out to him, which just got me thinking about why he would drop the event so unexpectedly," I say.

"There were flowers delivered to your room?" Dan frowns. "With a card to Lucas?"

He sounds genuinely confused and the mystery of how those flowers got to my door gets sharper in my mind.

"I brought it down to Stanford, but he said he didn't see who delivered it and didn't know who brought it up to my room," I say.

I don't mention the odd message written on the back of the card. I don't know what it means and I'm not sure if it's something to be shared with other people. The appearance of a woman at the side of the table makes us all turn. She looks nervous, her eyes locked on me.

"Agent Griffin?" she asks. "You are her, right? Agent Emma Griffin with the FBI?"

"Yes."

A shaky smile curves her lips. "I thought it was you, then I saw your name in the schedule and… I just can't believe you're here."

"Do you and Agent Griffin here know each other?" Tom Murphy asks with a slight edge of protectiveness in his voice.

I have a feeling he's more protective of his own space than he is me, but he's still acting as a valuable conductor in the conversation.

"Oh, no," she says, shaking her head. "Well, kind of. I know her. I'm Penny White. You worked on my cousin Sydney's case. It was a little while ago, I don't know if you would remember."

"Of course, I do," I say. I stand up and walk around the table to her. "I could never forget that case. How is your family doing?"

"Better. Sydney is doing really well. She finished her degree. She's been working with other people going through things similar to what she did. She's even talking about writing a book."

"Wow," I say. "That's amazing. I'm so glad to hear things are working out for her. Please say hello to her for me and to the rest of your family."

Penny smiles. "I will. Thank you." She hesitates, then opens her arms. I accept her hug. "Thank you for saving her."

She waves at the rest of the table and heads back to her own. I sit down, feeling tightness in my chest I try to swallow away with a gulp of water from the goblet in front of me. I look around for one of the waitstaff.

"Do you need something?" Dan asks.

"I was just hoping for a cup of coffee," I say.

"I'll get you one," he says.

"No, it's fine, I don't need you to…"

He's already up and gone. I can feel everyone looking at me, waiting for me to give them details about the interaction they just witnessed. When I don't offer them, Kyle leans toward me.

"What was that all about?" he asks. "What was her cousin's case?"

"It was a killer referred to as the Shepherd. She was a therapist at a university who used messages and personal connections to lure several young people to suicide."

THE GIRL ON THE RETREAT

I don't get into details. I don't want to delve into that again. I've thought of Sydney and the horror she went through many times since the case closed. What she experienced is a kind of torment and torture no one should ever be put through. I'm so glad to know she was able to get through to the other side and is reclaiming her life. It will never be the same or even what it could have been. But it will be something far more than the ruthless manipulator who had her under their control had wanted for her.

"The internet can be a really dark place," I say.

"The what?" Tom asks, but I roll my eyes. He must be joking. "I know there's a lot of good to be had with that kind of capability, but it's growing so fast and it seems like every time something good comes from it, there's something horrific like that, too," I continue. "It makes me miss when I was young and none of it existed."

Nostalgic silence settles over the table as we all think about our childhoods when the concept of the internet or even so much as a computer that could fit into a home was so far beyond our comprehension it was laughable.

"And on that note, I think I'd like to get back to the fun," Tom says. "I'm going to go find Dan and get some coffee for myself."

"Coffee actually sounds really good," Ainsley adds, looking at Kyle with big eyes.

"I guess I'm going to find some coffee, too," he says with a laugh.

The men get up and leave. As soon as they leave, Ainsley's face loses its sweet smile. She glances around with something much closer to disdain in her expression.

"They shouldn't be having to go find someone to help them. Isn't that the whole point of having a waitstaff?" she asks.

"There are a lot of people here," I point out.

She looks at me with icy eyes. "And it's their job." She lets out a sigh. "I'm going to powder my nose."

CHAPTER TWENTY-FOUR

A INSLEY SWEEPS OFF AND CHELSEA WATCHES HER GO. "I really dislike her."

"That wasn't the most pleasant I've ever heard someone be," I admit diplomatically. "You sound like you're pretty familiar with her."

"Dan, Tom, and Kyle get together a lot. Especially since Omnia formed. There are others in the group. Cory Mellon, Brad Carver, Gary Nielson. But Dan, Tom, and Kyle are the core of the group. Kyle started bringing Ainsley around with him just about as soon as they met. She puts on a good smile and can be sweet as pie when she's talking to Kyle, but as soon as he's not paying attention, that's the woman who comes out. I'm telling you, she's after a big ol' diamond and that's all that matters to her," Chelsea says.

"How long have they been together?" I ask.

"A few months," she says.

"And she's already angling to marry him?" I ask.

THE GIRL ON THE RETREAT

"When a man has as much money as Kyle Harris does, women don't care if they've ever met him at all. They want to marry him. She's just the one he got attached to."

"What about Lucas Bremmer? Or the guy with Daisy. Are they part of the group?" I ask.

"No. Lucas and Dan have gotten to know each other fairly well since he started planning this retreat. He was a fan of his writing before. But Lucas isn't a part of Omnia. And the guy with Daisy, Gordon, is a photographer. He worked with Dan's company some and that's how they met Daisy and figured she would be a good match for this event. Tom suggested he take some shots of the events for publicity and for future fundraising opportunities. Gordon's photography company is still fairly new, so any work he can get is going to help him. Not that he really needs it. He comes from some sort of money. I'm not sure what. I don't know him all that well," she says.

"How about you?" I ask. "How are you doing?"

She looks like she wishes I hadn't mentioned it, that she thought maybe there was a chance I would have just forgotten last night happened. If she was lucky, I was also drunk enough to not be in my right mind and maybe it just obliterated my memory.

"I'm alright. A bit of a headache. I appreciate the headache pills. Dan said you left them by the bed for me," she says.

"Listen, Chelsea, Dan told me you don't drink much. That those drinks you had were mostly non-alcoholic. Is that true?"

She nods. "I just had the one cocktail and the spiked milkshake. And honestly that had probably less than a shot worth of liquor in it, and by that time I'd eaten so much I wouldn't think it would affect me at all."

"So what happened?" I ask. "Because you seemed really drunk."

"I don't know. Maybe… maybe my nerves got to me? And that made the alcohol hit me harder?" she offers.

It's a weak suggestion that doesn't really add up to anything, but I don't have time to question it. Ainsley stalks back up to the table and drops down in her chair right as the guys show back up. They aren't carrying any coffee.

"The server will be back with some coffee in just a second," Dan says.

"And breakfast, I hope," Ainsley says.

Even as the words are coming out of her mouth I listen to the tone of her voice slip from the almost aggressive, disinterested tone to her sweet act. I wish I could say I wonder how effective that really is in getting the attention she wants from Kyle, but I know the answer. I've encountered plenty of couples who have gone through years of marriage and still barely know each other as they really are. Some people would just rather marry an idea than deal with being alone or doing the work of building a relationship with a real person who doesn't perfectly coordinate with them.

"Yes," Kyle says with a smile, leaning over to kiss her cheek. "And breakfast. The kitchen apologizes profusely."

"Apparently they are having some staff issues," Dan says.

"Again?" I ask.

He looks frustrated and embarrassed. "The same server. She never showed up for her shift this morning."

"I'm surprised I haven't heard the kitchen manager screaming the way he was the other night," I remark.

"Well, he's probably so overwhelmed he hasn't been able to come up for air long enough to start screaming," Dan tells me. "Apparently one of the line cooks didn't show up, either."

"Has anybody checked on them?" I ask.

"Stanford has been calling them and went to the line cook's cottage to see if he was there, but there wasn't any sign of him," Tom says. "I'm guessing that was actually what he was doing when those carnations were delivered."

"The server doesn't live in the cottages?" I ask.

"Most of the serving staff is local and commutes in. But Stanford called her home and there was no answer, either. So right now the kitchen is operating at a deficit," Dan says.

"They probably just had a little too much fun last night after the reception and are sleeping it off somewhere. They'll wake up, be embarrassed as hell, and come slinking back hoping they aren't going to get fired," Tom chuckles. "Which they probably won't be during this week, but the second the retreat is over, they'll be out. Kitchen staff is a dime a dozen around here. Kids from the local colleges flock to work at the tourist spots, especially here. They know this is where the high-end work is."

I don't like the lascivious note in Tom's voice, even though what he's saying isn't outlandish. The girl I saw at the reception looked right about that age. It wouldn't be too outlandish to imagine her blowing off steam and getting in over her head. Especially after the argument with her supervisor.

"No," Dan says. "I don't think so. That doesn't sound like Jared. He's not that kind of person."

THE GIRL ON THE RETREAT

"Jared?" I ask.

"Yes. He's been working in the kitchen for a few years. I've gotten to know him over the times I've been here for business and on vacation. He's a good guy. Responsible. Extremely strong work ethic. He has dreams of becoming a chef and has been working here to gain the skills and experience to get him there. He's not the kind of person to go out partying and miss work. It's just not him."

Our breakfast arrives and we tuck into the meal, aware of the shortened time before the workshops are set to begin. As we finish eating and start to leave, I hesitate, touching Dan's arm to signal for him to stop and talk to me.

"I saw Jared last night," I tell him.

"What do you mean?" he asks.

I take a breath. I didn't want to get into all the details about what happened after I left the cottage with him. He's going through enough right now and I don't want to add to any of his stress. But things are getting strange, and I want to know why.

I tell him about meeting up with Daisy and the locked back door, then having to call Stanford on the intercom to let us into the also-locked front door.

"We saw someone walk through the lobby from the sunroom area and he came to open the door for us. Stanford got there just a second later and called him Jared. He said he had forgotten something in the kitchen and that the back door was unlocked when he went to it," I say.

"And you're sure he said Jared?" Dan asks.

"Yes. Dan, there was someone else out there."

Tom Murphy comes back into dining room and I stop.

"Everything okay?" he asks.

"Of course," I say.

"Well, there's not much time before the first workshops. We need to get ready," he says. "Dan, Cory has a question for you about one of the seminars. I tried to answer it for him, but I think you probably know more than I do."

Dan nods and meets my eyes, but I don't let on that we were talking about anything important. I have no choice but to keep going as planned. Odd things are happening, but for now, I really have nothing but a collection of disconnected moments and strange incidents. They don't really point to anything specific. I'm here for a reason and I can't let myself be distracted by the feeling of being watched continuously rolling down my spine and the tingling of my instincts at the back of my skull.

I leave the dining room and head back to my room to brush my teeth and gather up my notes for the workshops. Before I leave, I look in the nightstand drawer to make sure the card is still there. It is and I slip it further beneath the leather-bound room service menu kept there. I don't know what it means, but something tells me I want to keep it out of sight.

CHAPTER TWENTY-FIVE

THE FIRST COUPLE OF WORKSHOPS OF THE DAY ARE FOCUSED ON specific topics, making the conversation easy to narrow down. We talk about what got me interested in being an agent, my earliest days in the FBI, and my first cases. Some of the questions they ask venture into deeply personal aspects of my life, including my mother's murder, my father's disappearance, and the horrors my uncle committed, and I shave away some of the details so I give them honest, accurate answers, but keep some close to my chest.

As the middle of the day approaches, I head to the other side of the lobby for a larger seminar-style class. My spot in the actual seminar room isn't until later in the week, so I have time to let my experiences with each of these earlier classes prepare me for that. This class is split into two parts with a break for lunch in the middle. It gives me a chance to make it more interactive and I look forward to engaging with the guests that way.

A few people are already scattered through the seats in the room when I arrive. I smile at them and set my satchel down on the table positioned at the front of the room. There's a large dry erase whiteboard set up behind it and I pick up one of the markers to write my name across it. I'm not sure why I have the compulsion to do that. Anyone who is here purposely signed up for this class and knows I'm leading it, but I don't like the empty white stretch of board and that's what I have to fill it with at the moment.

There're a few minutes left before the class starts and I busy myself going through my notes and pulling out the supplies I requested from Dan that he has waiting for me in a box set beside the table.

"How's your first day going, Emma?"

I look up to see Cory Mellon beside the table.

"Going well," I reply. "How about you?"

"Can't complain. I'm looking forward to this," he says, gesturing at my notes like he's expecting a burlesque show and the notepad is my prop.

"You're going to sit in?" I ask.

"Absolutely. Kyle and Tom, too."

He gestures out at the seats and I see the guys sitting in the center of the room, waving at me. I wave back.

"I hope you guys enjoy it," I say.

"I think we will."

The room has filled up as Cory makes his way over to the rest of the guys and I give it a few more seconds for everybody to settle. When they're in place, I smile.

"Hello, everybody, as you probably know my name is Emma Griffin and I am a Special Agent with the Federal Bureau of Investigations—or as you've probably heard it most often, the FBI. I entered the Academy the very second that I could and I became an agent at 23, the youngest age you can be to work in the Bureau. Over my career, I have seen and experienced everything you can probably imagine. Every type of criminal, every type of crime, and every type of coverup.

"It's been my job to find the people who do these things and stop them. I make sure they are brought to justice. But I also feel like I have another job in my life. A calling. The most important reason I entered the FBI was to protect people. I hate crime. I know that sounds like a tremendous cliché, and like it doesn't mean anything, but I assure you, I mean it in the simplest and most straightforward meaning of the words.

"I hate crime. I hate what it does to the individual victims. I hate what it does to our community. I hate what it does to society as a whole.

Crime doesn't just affect the people who are specifically targeted. There are countless others who are damaged when one person decides to take what they want, do what they want, and live how they want and to hell with everyone else.

"My personal experiences starting when I was very young drove me to take up this career. I committed myself to stop criminals and bring them to justice. But I am also committed to helping the members of my community protect themselves. I want everyone to be as safe and prepared as they possibly can, because danger is *everywhere*. I don't say that to scare anybody or to be dramatic. I say it as a simple fact. We don't know when the next crime is going to happen. Or the next catastrophe. The next tragedy. If we knew that, they wouldn't exist. Everyone would know what to expect, where not to go, what not to do, who not to associate with.

"But it isn't that simple. Which means everyone needs to be as prepared as possible to protect themselves at any point in their lives. No matter where they are or what they're doing, they need to be ready to react effectively to a potential threat. But it isn't just about being able to fight back or defend yourself physically."

"Or to run away," a voice calls from the audience.

I look out and see Kyle chuckling. I let out a short laugh and nod.

"Or run away," I echo him. "Underrated tool. Like I said, though, it's more than that. There are ways you can help yourself avoid these dangers to begin with and keep yourself safer in your daily life. That's what we're going to talk about today."

"Are you suggesting the victims are at fault for what happened to them?" someone asks from the audience.

I look out over them but don't see anyone who seems to want to take credit for the question. The men in the center of the room are looking around just like I am, trying to find who asked it. I decide it doesn't really matter who asked it, it's important to answer.

"Absolutely not," I say. "A victim is never to blame for being the target of a crime. That is extremely important for everyone to understand. It is not the fault of the victim that someone else decided to take it upon themselves to break the law and damage them in the process. No matter what the crime, no matter the circumstances. Theft, murder, rape. It doesn't matter. The only person who is to blame when it comes to a crime is the criminal. Period.

"But the truth and the very raw reality is that there are some victims who have put themselves into positions that make them more vulnerable. They've made decisions that put them in the line of the criminal and open themselves up to what happens. It's not their fault. They weren't asking for it. They didn't deserve it. But in some circumstances, they may have enabled it. That's uncomfortable for some people to hear. And it's uncomfortable because it makes things real. It takes away the abstract.

"We're not talking about blame here. We're talking about responsibility. Everyone has a responsibility to themselves and the people around them. I can't tell you how many times I've heard people argue about that. It's often said that we need to put more energy and effort into teaching people not to commit crimes. That we need to really focus on getting it through people's heads that it's wrong to hurt other people. It's wrong to steal, to kill, to rape. That if we can simply teach our young people not to think of these things as acceptable, then the world will be completely devoid of crime.

"But we all know that's not how it works. Of course, it's important for us to teach our children right from wrong. Of course, we should be instilling morals and values in them that we hope will shape them into good people, productive members of society, and people who won't victimize. But let me tell you something: I have encountered a lot of criminals in my day. More than I can count, and I promise you, they know what they are doing is wrong. They were taught that as children. They do it anyway.

"Which is why we can't just think about preventing crime in terms of teaching people not to victimize. We also have to teach people not to become victims. To take the responsibility of their safety and protection into their own hands. And as controversial as that may sound, I guarantee every single one of you already does it without even putting a moment of thought into it. I can prove it with one simple question. Do you lock your doors?"

A mutter rolls through the room. I know I'm making some of the people here very uncomfortable and others angry. Many people simply hope that they'll never be victims of a crime. They hope they'd never be in a situation like that in the first place. I believe in hope, but I believe in reality just as much. Maybe more. I won't apologize for what I'm saying. It's the truth. I've seen it time and time again, and I want to see it less.

"That's not the same thing," someone says from the audience.

"Why not?" I ask.

"Because locking your doors is just something you *do*. Most people, anyway. My mom still doesn't. It drives me crazy."

I find the man who's talking now. He doesn't sound like the person who spoke the first time, but I can see him watching me intently now.

THE GIRL ON THE RETREAT

"Why?" I ask, taking a few steps closer to him. "Why does it drive you crazy that your mother doesn't lock her doors?"

"Because..." he starts, but then his voice trails off and his cheeks go slightly pink as if he can hear the words he's about to say going through his head and realizes what's happening. He finally sighs, knowing he's already gotten himself this far and can't just pretend he didn't start it now. "Because somebody could just walk into her house and rob her or hurt her."

"Exactly," I say. "Every day every one of us does things to prevent crime and we might not even think about it. Locking our home, closing the windows, not leaving our keys in the car, parking under streetlights. Simple things that are so ingrained in our daily routines it's easy just to go through the motions without putting thought into why we're doing it. What I'm asking you to do is put thought into it. Every day, put thought into avoiding danger, paying attention to what's going on around you, protecting yourself, and protecting others. It's not foolproof. It's not guaranteed. Danger still exists. Criminals still exist. But it can help.

"So, let's get started. I'm going to tell you about some of the cases I've seen in my career with the Bureau, as well as some situations I've encountered through my husband's position as Sheriff in our hometown and my cousin Dean's career as a private investigator. I'll detail what happened and we'll talk about what could have gone differently."

CHAPTER TWENTY-SIX

T**HE TIME GOES BY QUICKLY AND SOON I REALIZE IT'S JUST A FEW** minutes before the lunch break.

"In just a couple of minutes we're going to take a break and get some lunch, but when we come back here, I'm going to change things up a little bit. I've been doing most of the talking and I want to know what's on your mind. I'm going to be handing out some paper and pens. During the break, think about what you want to contribute to this conversation or anything you might want to know about my career, or things I have encountered. Anything like that. When we get back, I'll choose some questions to answer and we'll see what kind of discussions we can get into. Just leave them on the desk whenever you're ready and I'll see you back here in an hour."

I hand out the slips of paper and pens Dan left in the box for me, take my satchel, and head out. I'm interested to see the kinds of questions that are going to appear on the table after lunch, but for right now, I'm hungry. Breakfast and dinner are the big stars of the food offerings during the week. To keep the schedule working smoothly, lunch breaks are staggered according to what sessions the guests choose and feature boxed meals alongside a buffet of sides, salads, and fruit in individual serving containers. The lounge has its customary snacks but also an array of desserts to complement the meals. This way everybody can grab what they want, find a place to settle in for their break, and then get back to their next workshop or seminar.

That's exactly what I do, snagging a box marked as containing an egg salad sandwich, adding a container of pasta salad and another of fruit, and quickly heading for the sunroom. I want a few minutes of quiet and the bright sunlight filtering through the windows lures me toward it.

No one else has ventured out of the warmth of the lobby into the comparative chill of the sunroom. It's cold out here but not so terrible that I can't tolerate it. It isn't the kind of soaking cold of winter. Spring is on the edges of the chill, promising something softer coming soon. I settle onto a white wicker couch and unpack my lunch on the table in front of me. From the bottom of my satchel I draw a paperback I've already read a dozen times but never tire of reading again.

There's a certain luxury in eating and reading all alone. I've only gotten a few minutes to savor it when Chrissy and Sabrina step out into the sunroom. They're carrying their own lunches and both are grinning broadly.

"Hi, Agent Griffin!" Chrissy says. "I can't believe we're running into you again!"

I can. They took my first three workshops this morning.

"Hi," I reply.

"Can we join you?" Sabrina asks, already sitting down and setting up her own box lunch.

"Sure."

"This has been such an amazing day," Chrissy says. "It's better than I even thought it would be. I'm having such a good time."

"That's good to hear," I say.

"That story you told about helping your old flame find his girlfriend's daughter was really inspiring," she says. "It really shows the kind of person you are."

"Well, that old flame is my husband now and it was his ex-girlfriend," I chuckle. "They hadn't dated in years."

"Still," Chrissy says. "That was really brave of you."

I take a bite of my sandwich to stem the stream of words that is trying to come out of my mouth.

"If I'm going to be described as 'brave' for anything I've done in my career, I don't think looking for the child of a woman I never heard of who dated a man I hadn't seen in seven years really qualifies," I say when I swallow.

The women start laughing as if I made some sort of joke. As their hysterics quiet, Sabrina cranes her neck to look back into the lobby.

"Where is she?" she mutters more to herself than to either of us.

"Daisy?" I ask.

She sits back and nods. "Yes. She was supposed to meet us for lunch. The only reason we're not in your seminar during this block is because she's teaching the class she's the most nervous about and we wanted to support her."

"As you should," I say. "How is she doing today?"

I hope the events of last night didn't affect her too much. I still don't believe what she told me about going for a walk because she couldn't sleep. The makeup and hairspray still in her hair were clear giveaways that she hadn't tried to settle into bed like she told me she did. But that doesn't minimize the fear she felt when the person came up on us. She obviously didn't know who it was and was frightened by their sudden appearance. I expected to see her at breakfast this morning, but I haven't seen her all day.

"She's fine," Chrissy says. "Maybe a little worked up."

"Worked up?" I ask.

"It's a big event for her. She's hoping she'll impress the Omnia guys like Gordon did and become a more regular part of their events. Her career really means a lot to her."

"Which I think surprises some people," Sabrina says.

There's a note in her voice that's not exactly pleasant, like she's making a snide remark without specifically directing it. Though I have a feeling I know who she's talking about.

"What do you mean?" I ask.

Chrissy sighs. "Gordon."

"Her fiancé," I say. "The man who was with the two of you at the orchard."

"That's him," Sabrina confirms. "Don't get me wrong, he can be a really nice guy and all, he's just…"

She's struggling to come up with the right words and Chrissy steps in to help her.

"He's just not right for Daisy. Not in all ways, anyhow. There are things about him she adores and that are really great for her. He takes good care of her, makes her feel beautiful, kind of whisked her away. But

THE GIRL ON THE RETREAT

then he also seems to have these... expectations of her. He wants her to be a wife."

I wait for there to be more to that, but there doesn't seem to be. "Is there a problem with that?"

"*Just* a wife," Sabrina clarifies. "As in, he doesn't want her doing things like this anymore once they get married. He thinks it's adorable that she teaches exercise."

"Adorable," Chrissy says again for emphasis. "He actually said that."

"Probably not the word Daisy would want to hear used to describe her work," I acknowledge.

"No. And he told her it would be fine with him if she had a small group just for ladies at a local community center or in the park or something, but that he thinks she should be spending her time at home and with him. He can support them and she should just enjoy the fact that she doesn't have to work," Sabrina says.

"The thing is, he does his photography. He could work for his family's business if he wanted to. He could even just live off his trust fund. It's not a huge amount, not like the Omnia guys, but it's enough that they'd be perfectly comfortable. Yet, he chooses to do the photography because he wants to be separate from his family and not defined by them."

"But you don't see him returning his trust fund or the company stocks," Sabrina adds.

"So, he doesn't think Daisy should try to build the career she wants, but he can pursue whatever hobbies he wants while thinking of them as some sort of calling," I say.

Chrissy gives me a wink and finger-gun. "She really doesn't like the double standard."

"I wouldn't think so. Has she talked to him about it?" I ask. "Really explained how she feels about it? I know she's excited to get married and all, but if she's feeling this way, maybe they need to slow down a bit."

"She's tried talking to him. She thought he'd heard her and was really understanding her when she booked this retreat. She was so excited that he was being supportive, but then she realized he was only saying he was okay with it because it was for Omnia, and he's been trying to get in even better with them for a long time. He's hoping this could launch him further in his own businesses so he can stand apart from his family once and for all. Or at least continue to pretend that's what he's doing. I don't have a doubt in my mind he's going to keep holding onto his association with his family and their business until the bitter end because it gives him leverage in certain circles. It's something to fall back on if he needs to."

"The point is, Daisy just wants to be Daisy. That's what she's always been. Unapologetically Daisy," Sabrina adds. "She's kind and sweet and a little over the top but an amazing heart. She wants to love and be loved, but she also wants to be herself. The only problem is, sometimes I don't know if she even knows who that is anymore."

"We want to like him. Really, we do. And most of the time, we do. I just don't want to see her give up who she was and is, or could be," Chrissy adds.

"I understand. I…" Out of the corner of my eye, I see movement on the other side of the sunroom wall. I look and see Grant storming down the walkway, his head in his hands. "Excuse me. I need to go talk with someone. Thanks for joining me. I'm sure I'll see you around."

I don't wait for their response but grab my satchel and rush out toward Grant. He's heading in the opposite direction now like he's pacing.

"Grant," I call out to him. "Hey. Wait." He turns around and I see his eyes are rimmed with red and his jaw is twitching with tension. "What's going on?"

"Bentley is missing," he says.

"Your horse? He's missing?" I ask.

He lets out a quick, short sob. "He was in his stall last night when I put all the horses up for the night. I had to go into town for an appointment this morning so I had another hand taking care of 'em until I got back. I just went to the field to check on them and Bentley isn't there. Stan said when he got to the stable this morning some of the stalls were open and a couple of the horses were already in the corral. He thought maybe I'd done that before I went into town and just didn't bother to tell him. Bentley wasn't in his stall and wasn't in the field when I checked."

"He didn't notice Bentley wasn't there?" I ask.

Grant shakes his head. "He doesn't work directly with the horses as much as I do," he says. "He mostly handles handyman work around the grounds. He didn't have any reason to think any of them were missing."

"I'd think he would have said something when he saw they were already out this morning," I say.

Grant scoffs. "Say something to who? Stanford in there? He's never gotten anywhere near any of those animals. He might have a heart attack if he got dirt anywhere near his suit. Like I said, Stan just figured I'd already turned some of them out for the morning. He didn't know Bentley wasn't there." Grant looks like he's going to cry again. "I have to find him. I don't understand how he could have gone anywhere unless someone purposely let him loose."

My mind goes back to last night and what I saw through the window at the end of the hall. The four-legged creature that ran into the trees in the moonlight. I tell Grant what I saw and his eyes widen.

"I'm going to go get Sampson. He'll bring me into the woods and we'll look for him. Thank you, Emma."

I watch him run back toward the stable, my heart churning. Glancing at my watch, I see I don't have a lot of time before I need to be back in the seminar, but there's enough for a fast call to Sam.

CHAPTER TWENTY-SEVEN

"**I**T'S STRANGE. I'LL GIVE IT TO YOU," Sam says. "But there could also be a really simple explanation. Someone thought they knew what they were doing with the horses and wanted to play with them after the stable was already closed for the night. They let some of them out into the corral and that one got away. They weren't able to catch it and were too scared to tell anyone, so they just left the rest of them where they were and went to bed. They probably figured a domesticated horse would end up coming back to its barn when it was ready to."

"That could be," I admit. "But what about the missing server and line cook? Or the card in the flowers? Or the person running up on Daisy and me last night and then running away?"

"They aren't officially missing yet. People just aren't sure where they are. I know you said Dan defended the guy and said he was really responsible, wouldn't just run off partying, all that, and I'm sure that's true to a degree. But how well does he actually know him? He's an employee he's run into a few times when he was there on trips? They might have exchanged a few words?"

"I think it was more than a few words," I say. "He knew Jared's biggest aspirations in life and was trying to find ways to support him in reaching those goals. That's not something you do just for someone you barely know."

"That's true. But people can do things that are out of character. That does happen. Maybe he was under so much pressure to do well that he ended up needing to break out of his shell just a little. Or he could have a crush on that girl and he wanted to do something to impress her. She wanted to go drinking or maybe they found a party with some drugs. He went with her, they did something stupid, they slept it off somewhere, and now are probably doing everything they can to come up with an explanation that's going to save their skin. It happens. People do ridiculous, out of character, out of the middle of nowhere things sometimes," Sam says.

"Like you marrying the heartless FBI agent who left you with barely a word for seven years?" I ask.

"Yep, like that."

He laughs, but I'm still feeling on edge.

"There was definitely someone out there last night. They went by the cottage while I was taking care of Chelsea, close enough that their shadow crossed her bed. Chelsea, by the way, who told me herself that she wasn't drinking enough to have gotten that messed up. And whoever it was followed me to the main building and came at me. They either went away because they saw Daisy there or because they saw my gun, but there was someone there," I say. "And then the flowers. Flowers no one saw delivered and no one can tell me how they got to my room, and that have a card made out to someone everyone knew wasn't going to be at the retreat."

"What do you think that means?" Sam asks.

My head feels oddly fuzzy all of a sudden, like all my thoughts have turned to cotton. I can hear Sam's voice, but I can't exactly make out what he's saying. Behind it, there's a sharp sound, a high-pitched beep I can't place. Stretching the phone cord as far as I can, I make it into the bathroom and turn on the water. Filling my palm, I press my cool hand to the back of my neck to shake myself out of the fog.

"Hmmm?" I ask Sam.

"I was asking what you think the words on the card meant. If anything else has stood out to you that might have anything to do with what it says," he says.

"No," I say. "It doesn't mean anything to me. I can't tell if it's a message as in something that Lucas would have been waiting for, like a signal or a coded answer to something, or if it's a threat of some kind. Whatever it is, nobody can tell me who stuffed it down in those carnations and put them in front of my door."

I stop. My own words prick the back of my mind but I can't figure out why.

"For right this second, Emma, there's no reason to be concerned. Just try to focus on why you're there. If anything else happens, you can deal with it then. But for now, don't get wrapped up in just the possibility of something going on," Sam says, again bringing me back into the conversation. "I know when you notice things that don't seem right, they bother you until you can figure out what they mean. It's why you're so good at what you do. But don't let it get to you so much that it takes over everything else. Okay?"

I don't really want to admit it but my husband makes sense. Observing everything around me closely and noticing details other people miss are some of my strongest skills. They've made me the agent I am, but they can also get in the way. At this second, I don't actually know that anything bad is happening. I've already told myself that, but hearing it from Sam is different. He's at a distance. He can look at the entire picture and get the full scope of it rather than being immersed in just the moment-to-moment unfolding of everything. That perspective is valuable and it helps me feel more grounded.

"Okay. Thank you for talking me down. I've got to get back to my seminar. I'll give you a call a bit later," I say.

"Alright. I love you."

"Love you."

The slightly unnerving feeling that has been trailing me since I got here is still tingling on the very surface of my skin as I hurry back toward the seminar room. There's such a strange sense here of being perfectly relaxed and at peace, and at the same time like I'm surrounded by a delicate glass capsule ready to shatter.

I hear my name as I climb the steps to the other side of the second floor and turn to see Dan jogging to catch up with me. I step off to the side to wait for him so I'm not in the way of the others trying to get to their next spot.

"Hey," he says when he gets to me.

"Hi," I say. "Everything alright?"

"I wanted to ask you about what you were trying to tell me earlier. I've been trying to get your attention all day, but it's like you haven't heard me."

I shake my head, surprised to hear him say that. I definitely didn't hear him at any point. I can't even remember seeing him today.

"I'm sorry. I guess I've just been so focused on my workshops and everything," I admit.

"I've heard some great feedback from the guests about you," he says. "They're already asking if we're going to do another of these next year."

"That's great," I reply with a smile. "I know you're happy to hear that people are enjoying themselves."

"I am. But I can't stop thinking about Jared and Sarah."

"Sarah is the server who didn't come to her shift this morning?" I ask.

A cluster of guests scurry past us and we go silent, pressing against the side of the staircase to keep out of their way.

"Yes. The same one who was late getting to the reception. She's fairly new at the resort. I'm not familiar with her, but like I told you, I know Jared well. This isn't like him."

"You did say you know him well. How often have you come here?" I ask.

"For the last six years my company has come here at least once a quarter for team-building and once a year for a larger networking event. We also hold our holiday parties here. Chelsea and I visit at least twice a year for personal vacations as well," he tells me.

It sounds like more than he told me before, but when I try to remember exactly what he told me the first time he said he comes to this resort frequently, I find myself struggling to recall it. The conversation is right there at the edge of my memory, but the best I can do is feel like I'm watching it through a pane of glass.

"That is certainly a lot," I say.

He shrugs. "Can you blame me? The first time I came here it was so beautiful I fell in love with it. The service is impeccable and they always go above and beyond to make everything perfect. I've never been anywhere like this and every time I come, I just want to be here more."

I understand what he's saying. It's the same draw I feel, only he seems not to sense the disquieting energy just beneath the surface.

The lobby has gone quiet and there are only a couple of people filtering in and out of the lounge. I glance at my watch.

"I need to get back to my seminar," I say. "Can we talk later?"

"Of course. I'll see you at dinner." I start up the stairs, but his voice stops me. "Emma. This isn't…"

His voice trails off and he shakes his head like he has rethought what he was going to say.

"What?" I ask. "This isn't what?"

Dan shakes his head again. "Never mind. I'll see you at dinner."

He rushes down the steps. I expect him to go to the other set of steps to one of the workshop rooms, but instead he heads for the sunroom and out toward the grounds.

CHAPTER TWENTY-EIGHT

"**D**ID YOU ENJOY YOUR BREAK?" I ASK AS I WALK INTO THE already-full room. I see the pile of folded pieces of paper on the table. "I see you didn't hesitate with the questions. That's great. Let's jump in so we can get as many of these answered as we can in the time we have left."

They're all looking at me with expressions that say that want some sort of explanation for why I'm coming in several minutes after the rest of them had already settled into their seats, but I don't offer any. Instead, I reach into the pile and pull out one of the pieces of paper at random.

"Do you ever get scared when you are on your cases?" I read. I look up. "Yes."

Tossing the paper aside, I reach for another one. Giggles erupt through the room and I look back at them. "Seriously, though, yes. Of course, I get scared. I feel like if I didn't get scared at least occasionally, it would mean I wasn't actually doing my job the way I'm supposed to. I mean, I'm dealing with mass murderers here. Of course, I'm scared. I'm getting right there in their faces, and that's not something they take to kindly. I'm always very aware of the fact that they could choose to eliminate me at any given moment. And many have tried.

"So, yes. I get scared. But I still do it. Fear has never stopped me. It never will. When I know there's something I need to do, a person I need to pursue, a lead I need to chase, it doesn't matter how scared I am. I do it. I recognize the challenge and possible danger ahead of me, but I don't let it stand in my way. I can't afford to."

I open the second piece of paper I picked up.

"Can you recommend a good sports bra?" I laugh. "Priorities."

For the next forty-five minutes I read out questions and answered them, sometimes just tossing out a simple response and others getting into longer conversations with the group. A few of the papers get discarded without acknowledgement. There are certain things I'm not going to entertain.

"Alright, it's looking like we're getting close to the end of our time here, so this is going to be the last question. For all the ones that are left, I'll read through them tonight and see if I can address any of them in my talks for the rest of the week." I swirl my hand around in the remaining papers to add some playful drama to selecting the last question. My hand falls on one that has been folded several times, making it harder and more noticeable than the others. I pick it up and open it. "Do you believe in the perfect crime?"

"That's a good one," someone says in that kind of hushed tone that says they wished they'd been the one to come up with it.

"It certainly is an appropriate one to end the session on," I say. I think about my answer for a few beats. It's not that I don't know how I feel about it because there isn't a single doubt in my mind. I just need to choose the words. "No. There is no such thing as the perfect crime. There are only crimes that haven't been solved yet because they haven't been seen by the right person. Now, I will admit that is from the perspective of an FBI agent. The answer is probably far different if somebody asked that question of a criminal.

"That's one of the most important elements of being an effective FBI agent. To understand that the criminals we are pursuing don't think in the same way that we do. And while I can stand here in front of you and say I do not believe there is such a thing as a perfect crime because there will always be evidence, even if it isn't obvious right from the beginning, not all criminals think that way. In fact, I would venture to say most criminals who have long criminal careers don't think that way.

THE GIRL ON THE RETREAT

"Criminals—except for the petty thief types—are conniving, detail-oriented, and almost without exception very proud of what they do. They go into their crimes with a plan, a specific vision for what they want out of that individual venture. Whether it's an art museum heist, string of bank robberies, or a complex murder, they know what they want out of it. And if they get what they want out of it, if it turns out exactly how they envisioned it, then it is likely they would consider that the perfect crime."

"And not being caught," Cory Mellon says from the audience. "That's an important part of it being the perfect crime."

I shake my head. "Not necessarily. For many of these perpetrators, it is the act itself that matters to them more than what happens afterward. They aren't committing a crime as some sort of game with the authorities. They don't go into it with a strict need to get away with it. Instead, their priority is just making sure they get what they want out of that incident.

"If that was the case, Mark Chapman would have run after shooting those four bullets into John Lennon's back. But he didn't. He sat down on the sidewalk right where he had been standing and started reading *Catcher in the Rye*. That's because his motivation was the killing itself. He saw himself as an analog of Holden Caulfield and killing Lennon was his way to punish and eliminate hypocrisy. He accomplished that without a shadow of a doubt. And so, in that way, it was a perfect crime. It didn't require he get away with it."

"So, you think there are people sitting in prison for horrible crimes who still think that what they did was perfect?" Cory asks.

"Yes," I say without hesitation. "Absolutely."

"Doesn't that bother you?" he asks. "You go through so much to get those people out of society and punish them, yet they still sit there satisfied with themselves because they did something well. They still consider themselves to be a perfect criminal."

"Someone who has committed their version of a perfect crime," I clarify. "Not a perfect criminal. And I suppose I have to say yes. That does bother me to a degree. I'm not immune to thoughts of vengeance any more than anyone else. It's just part of who and what we are as human beings. There's a little part of us, a big part in some, that wants people to suffer for their actions when they've done something to harm another person. We can admit that, right? When we see someone who has caused damage, whether it's through murder, abuse, sexual assault, theft… whatever it is that they've done to another person, there's that part of us that wants to see them face serious consequences and be punished for it.

"Thinking about them sitting there in their prison cell still feeling good about themselves and what they did is a blow to that. It makes it easy to become bitter, angry, and resentful. Which is why it's important to keep in mind that vengeance doesn't have to be the primary goal for putting a criminal away. Rather than thinking of it being about punishing that person's deeds, we have to think about it as taking them out of society and stopping them from hurting anyone else. When we think of it that way, it doesn't matter if they are happy with themselves and feel absolutely no guilt or remorse for what they did. What matters is they are no longer able to do the same thing to more people. I've put a bullet into a man who did unspeakable things to countless victims. Literally countless because their bones are still being unearthed. I took his life, but it wasn't a punishment. I didn't execute him. I saved people."

CHAPTER TWENTY-NINE

THE DOOR TO THE ROOM FULL OF CRIME SCENE PHOTOS I VISITED the first night I arrived is standing slightly open this time. I walk up to it carefully and peek through the gap in the door. I can hear people talking inside so I know the workshop that overlapped with my seminar is still active.

"Agent Griffin?"

I've been spotted. I push the door open a little further and look in. Kyle is standing to the side of the display of pictures while the group sitting around him in a circle lean in toward each other in smaller groups, talking eagerly about something. I'd noticed he wasn't there for the second half of the seminar and was reminded this workshop had started during the lunch break for my track.

The murder being discussed in the workshop hasn't left my mind since I saw the pictures and read through the details on the reports. I'm drawn to the image of the brutalized woman and the unexplained photographs found near her and in the area. I want to know what happened to her.

Kyle gestures with a sweep of his hand, inviting me to come in. I'd wanted to slip in without being noticed and hang around listening, but that's apparently not an option.

I offer a tight smile as I go the rest of the way in.

"Hello," I say. "I didn't mean to interrupt. I just thought I'd slip in and see what was going on in here."

"Don't be silly. You're not interrupting. We're glad to have you. I am sure everybody here would be thrilled to get the opinion of a real FBI agent on this case," Kyle says.

I glance around. "I thought you said the detective that was in charge of the case was going to be a part of the workshop. Facilitating it and making sure that things were kept confidential."

I hope the emphasis in my voice reminds him of the conversation we had the night I arrived and the concerns that are still lingering in the back of my mind about civilians poking around in a crime as recent and fresh as this one. Kyle smiles. It's a familiar kind of smile, like he finds my concern amusing.

"He is. He went to get a cup of coffee. As it turns out, Detective White doesn't eat breakfast and is somewhat particular about his lunch, so he's running on an empty tank right now. Fortunately, I told him that this resort has the best coffee in the world. As far as I know, anyway. I'm sure he'll be back any minute. Fueled up and ready to keep talking us through this case. The case he chose to present to the group, by the way," he says.

There's no aggression in his voice. He's not trying to embarrass me or show me up. He wants to make sure I understand he isn't the one who decided the group should discuss this particular case. He's covering his own rear end, so to speak.

"Excuse me," I say as I walk through two chairs to get to the display.

Kyle hasn't moved since I came in, but he reaches a hand out to me as I approach. "Good to see you again."

I laugh. "Since before lunch?"

"Yes. How did the rest of the seminar go? Did you get any good questions?"

"I did," I say. "It's always interesting to get a glimpse into the minds of other people. I like finding out what they are thinking when they look at me. Well, most of the time. Some of those questions were definitely not things I needed to know people were thinking. But, for the most part, it was a good discussion."

THE GIRL ON THE RETREAT

"Since I had to come here and moderate this workshop, I didn't get a chance to ask you a question," he says.

"Do you have one?" I ask.

"Yes."

"Go ahead," I say.

"How does it feel when you want so much to know what happened and not be able to figure it out?" he asks.

The question sends a chill along my spine. I meet his eyes and search for the thoughts behind his words. There's something there. A depth less like an ocean than a tunnel. I feel like I could walk down it, find something at the end. He blinks slowly and the tunnel closes. The question repeats itself through my mind.

"Motivated," I reply.

A smile slowly curves his lips.

"Well, hello there."

The voice sounds like it's coming out of my past. I wonder for a brief flash of a moment if Kyle can hear it. His eyes lift up over my head in reaction, showing me he does, and I stand, turning around to face Noah White. A smile breaks over my face and I let out a shocked laugh.

"Noah," I say.

"If it isn't Agent Emma Griffin. Or is it Mrs. Emma Johnson?"

I laugh. "Yes. To both of them."

He opens his arms and I take him into a hug.

"It's good to see you. It's been a long time," he says.

"Yes, it has," I say. "Have you seen Ava?"

He nods. "Some. She's a busy one."

"She definitely is. I can't even tell you the last time I actually saw her. She seems to constantly be on the move," I say. "But I've heard nothing but good things about her team and the work they've done. But actually, I ran into Dean recently."

"Huh, he didn't tell me that."

"Yeah, he came and asked my help on a case a couple months ago."

"They've been spending a lot of time in Sherwood," I tell him. "Sam and I moved into the house his parents left him and I gave Dean our grandparents'. I figured he should have more of a connection to the family and somewhere to stay while he's there that wasn't just my house."

Noah seems pleased to hear it. "I'm sure he's enjoying that. He always speaks kindly about Sherwood and you. It's good to see you're still close."

That means more than it might seem from the outside. It wasn't always a guarantee that Dean and I would form a close bond.

I realize Kyle has been listening to the conversation, his eyes flashing back and forth between us.

"You two know each other?" he asks.

"Agent Griffin and I have worked together on a couple of cases," Noah says.

"He serves the town where my very dear friend Xavier and my cousin Dean live. But it's been a while since we've gotten a chance to catch up. This is quite the surprise. I didn't see your name on the schedule."

"I have to admit, it's not that much of a surprise to me. When I first agreed to do this, you weren't a part of it, but I found out a couple of days ago. Work kept me too busy to be here for the opening reception, but I was hoping to get a chance to come to one of your talks. I didn't think you'd beat me to it. But, then again, I should probably expect that of you," Noah comments with a gruff laugh.

"Probably," I say with a grin. Getting slightly more serious, I point at the display. "Alright. What's the deal with this? This murder just happened. Do you really think it's a good idea to get other people involved in it?"

"I told her you weren't going to talk about anything that could compromise the case," Kyle says. It's obvious he can't handle not being the center of attention.

"He's right," Noah says. "I'm using this case as an example to talk about how cases are investigated, but I'm protecting its integrity. Have you heard of it at all?"

"Some," I say. "The Bureau isn't involved, as you know. I heard that some photographs were found near the body? And others somewhere else that might have been this victim? What's going on with that?"

"Stick around," Noah tells me. "The workshop is almost over. I'll give you a better overview afterward."

I agree and stand back while they get the attention of the participants. I find out they'd asked them to split into small groups and talk about the individual pieces of evidence they believed they saw in the initial crime scene photos, what they thought that evidence might mean, and how they would proceed with the investigation if they were at the head of it.

Knowing Noah is the one leading the conversation makes me feel much more comfortable with the concept. I know he's going to fiercely protect the case because he has the same kind of intense drive to solve crimes and bring perpetrators to justice that I do. He wouldn't do anything that could put the case at risk.

THE GIRL ON THE RETREAT

It's fascinating to listen to the people in the workshop talk through their thoughts and how they perceive each piece of evidence. Some of it is outlandish, so far off the mark of what would really matter in an investigation it almost seems like they're doing it on purpose just to get a rise out of the others. But some theories are well thought-out and even thought-provoking. These people may actually have a future in law enforcement if it's something that truly interests them.

When the workshop is over, some of the participants linger to talk to Kyle and Noah but finally drift out to head to their own lunch break. I stay and laugh at Noah as he takes a deep swig of the coffee he brought into the room with him.

"I hear you don't eat breakfast," I say.

"Nope. Waste of time."

"Says the man who left the workshop to go get coffee because he didn't eat and couldn't stay awake," I counter.

"The detective diet," he says.

"Clearly." I walk over to the display and look over it again. "So, what can you tell me?"

Noah comes up beside me. "Vicki Freeman. She was found like this a month ago by a bird watcher."

"That's unfortunate," I say.

"Truly an understatement. There was very little evidence. The only thing that seemed like it could be a lead at all is the photographs found near her. They aren't of her. It's an unidentified female who I doubt will ever be identified."

"Why is that?" I ask.

"Her face was completely demolished. It looked like it had been beaten by a claw hammer. She was blonde, but that's the only identifying feature. No tattoos. No scars."

I furrow my brow and add that to my consideration. "Have there been any other developments in the case?"

"A couple weeks ago a piece of another photograph was found near evidence of another crime."

"Evidence of another crime? What do you mean?" I ask.

"There was a considerable amount of blood and some hair. The medical examiner couldn't determine for sure whether the quantity of blood was enough to indicate death, but it definitely didn't look good. The partial photograph was found in brush a few yards away."

"What's in the partial photograph? What does it have to do with this case?" I ask.

"It appears to be Vicki's face while she was still alive," Noah says.

"Oh," I say. "Wow."

"Yeah. It's both a really exciting lead and absolutely nothing to go on."

"Do you have more of the pictures from this scene?" I ask. "Things you didn't show the workshop?"

"Yeah," he replies. "There are some."

"Can I see those? And the photographs found near the body?" I ask.

"Sure. I actually brought the entire file with me," he says.

He takes out a manila envelope and sifts through the contents before pulling out a few images. He sets them in front of me. My breath steams from my lungs. He wasn't exaggerating when he described the brutality of the images. Vicki's murder was horrific. Her body was mangled, and obvious great pleasure was taken in her torture prior to finally killing her.

But the woman in the photographs found near her had her face removed. Not just removed. Beaten into nothingness.

"What about the partial picture?" I ask.

He hands me another sheet of paper. It's a photocopy of the partial picture set against a piece of white paper to stabilize it. The woman in it is clearly alive. The terror and desperation in her eyes cuts through me. The picture captures her on the ground among a mound of dead leaves. Her position is odd. Something about her body is twisted like she's not sitting there on her own. The part of the picture that was torn away removed one of her legs and the corresponding hand. I look more closely and see something at the very edge near the torn piece.

"What do you see?" Noah asks.

"This," I say, tracing my finger across something black just visible among the leaves. "Is that a cord? Is she tied to something?"

"Possibly," Noah says. "The medical examiner noted some damage to her wrists and ankle that could have been restraints."

I keep staring at the picture. There's something about it that's standing out to me, but I'm not exactly positive what it is.

"There's more of the picture missing than is here," I say. "Look at the dimensions."

Noah nods. "It was torn in two different places. It's harder to see on this copy, but on the original you can see the fibers of the photo paper going different ways."

I go back to the display board to look over the pictures there. One of them in particular draws my attention and I stare at it, trying to figure out why. It finally pops out.

THE GIRL ON THE RETREAT

"Look," I say, running my finger along the edge of one of the pictures of Vicki's body. "Do you see this?"

"What?" he asks.

I hold one of the pictures of the unidentified woman up beside it. "She's lying on grass. It looks like it's spring or summer. It's all bright green around her. Now look at Vicki when she's alive."

"She's on leaves," Noah says.

"Yes. So it looks like fall or winter."

"Yeah."

"Okay, but look here." I trace my finger along the edge again. "It's green. She's lying on dry leaves, but there's a clearing of grass right beside her. And if you look really closely, what do you see right there?"

He leans toward the picture to look at what I'm indicating.

"Blue," he says. "There's something blue at the very edge."

I gesture back toward the unidentified woman. The picture focuses intently on her face and the blood that poured from her extensive wounds soaked most of her clothing, rendering nearly all of it a dark mottled crimson and purple. But at the very bottom of the image is a flash of the aqua shade visible on the green at the edge of Vicki's picture.

"It looks like this woman's shirt," I say. "I think Vicki is tied to her."

CHAPTER THIRTY

Him

H E WAS USED TO CONTROL. TO THINGS WORKING OUT THE WAY he envisioned them. His world was of his crafting and all things in it were at the movement of his hand.

Until now.

His feet fell loudly as he went down the steps into the Dark Wing. He flung open the door and stormed inside, his head racing and his stomach heavy like it never was when he came here. This was a place of enjoyment, of pleasure. That wasn't what he was feeling now.

It wasn't supposed to be happening yet.

He had three more days of plans in place. Three more days of entertainment for the VIP clients he'd invited for this indulgent experience. It had only just begun the night before and he'd planned for it to stretch on luxuriously, each phase unfolding with perfect timing to heighten the immersion and keep the level of energy at a constant roll. There were meant to be moments of greater intensity and rush, and others that were designed to be calmer, cleansing in a way to prevent his clients from becoming jaded.

But something had gone wrong. Someone had made a mistake. He didn't tolerate mistakes.

Those links shouldn't have been made. The photographs shouldn't have been mishandled. Now everything was in jeopardy. There was still so much they didn't know, he understood that, but with one detail often came more. One tiny shift, one change, and it could crumble.

They knew what they were signing up for. They knew the consequences.

He wouldn't let the work he'd put into all of this be destroyed. Not because of two careless people. Things would have to change. He'd have to take the plans he had and alter them to suit a new schedule and new circumstances, but he could do that. None of the select group of clients knew about the surprise he had in store for them. He hadn't told anyone about those plans. They were meant to be the pinnacle of the week, to offer the trophy game of his elite hunt.

She still would be.

It wouldn't be exactly the way he planned. He didn't like that. Things should be the way he wanted them to be. The way he planned them to be.

But he could adapt.

The hunt had already begun. And he would have the trophy he wanted. The ultimate kill.

He opened a cabinet and pulled out a shotgun.

But first, there was a matter that needed to be settled.

CHAPTER THIRTY-ONE

I DON'T LEAD ANOTHER WORKSHOP TODAY AND THERE ARE STILL A few hours before dinner. I'm certainly feeling the lunch I left sitting barely touched on the table in the sunroom and I suggest to Noah we go to the lounge for some coffee and a snack. I've heard several people mention how nicely the weather has warmed up. We could find a place to sit outside and talk more.

But Noah has another session for the afternoon and then tomorrow has to get back on the road. He was only able to get away for this small portion of the retreat and now he has to go back to Harlan to keep working the case as well as others that have piled up on his desk in the last several weeks. When he tells me this, I can see the years in his eyes. It hasn't been that long since we last worked together, but he seemed younger then. So much more so than the years that have passed should have changed him.

I can see how the pressure of all the cases he's handled is affecting him. He's achieved what he always aspired to. Now he carries the burden of that being his life. He'll do well. I see it in him. I always have. I just hope he's able to cope and keep going.

We agree to meet at dinner and I head to the lounge alone. It's empty as I get coffee and browse the new assortment of snacks and sweets available. I grab a few and am about to leave when Gordon comes in. He shoots me a smile from the other side of the room where a display of teabags, sugar cubes, and various types of honey stand apart from the coffee as if it would besmirch either if the two should mingle at all.

I bring a plate that probably contains far too much food but looks delicious over to the tea station and watch him pour water from an electric kettle over two teabags in a cup.

"Mixing different flavors of tea," I note. "That's some high-level technique."

"Not for beginners," he says. "I've been a tea drinker from way back." He cringes a little. "That didn't come across nearly as cool as it sounded in my head."

"It sounded cool in your head?" I ask.

He shrugs. "More or less. How has your day been? I've heard people talking about your workshops. They sound amazing."

"Thank you. It's been… eye-opening. How is Daisy? I haven't seen her all day," I say.

He glances over at me, then looks back to the cup he's stirring a long drizzle of honey into.

"She's good. She would be thrilled to know you're asking after her. She's been getting jealous because Chrissy and Sabrina have seen more of you than her," he says with a bit of a laugh.

"Well, you can tell her that she and I will always have the front porch," I say.

My smile only earns a confused look in return.

"The front porch?" he asks.

"From last night. We got locked out and stood on the front porch in the cold waiting to get back in," I explain. "When she went for her walk because she couldn't sleep. Didn't she tell you?"

He looks down into his tea again and his face suddenly shifts to a smile that doesn't look as genuine as the one that was there just a few moments ago.

"Oh, that. Yeah, of course. She has a lot of trouble sleeping sometimes and she likes to take long walks when it happens. She's always had problems like that, but growing up in the city she could never walk because it was too dangerous. So now she does it a lot. She's always so sweet making sure not to wake me up," he says.

Something about that explanation ticks something in my brain, but I hold my tongue. "So, I hear you are a photographer," I say. "That's how you got close with the Omnia Group."

"I am a photographer," he confirms. "I got to know Dan through some other work I was doing and he got me into photographing events for Omnia. Apparently it's easier to just be a philanthropist than it is to be a philanthropist *and* the one photographing all the good deeds you're doing."

"And now Daisy is a part of it, too," I say.

"It's perfect." He glances up at the clock above my head. "Well, I've got to get going. We'll probably see you at dinner?"

"I'll be there," I say.

He nods and leaves with his tea. I watch him walk away, then head straight for the front desk. I no longer care how pissed off to see me Stanford looks.

"Yes, Agent Griffin," he says. "What can I do for you?"

"Has there been any word about Sarah and Jared?" I ask. He looks up at me with slightly raised eyebrows. "From the kitchen. The two staff who are missing."

"I know who are you are talking about," he replies sharply, his voice starting loud and then lowering as he continues until he's almost talking through gritted teeth. "I would thank you to lower your voice. We don't need other guests to overhear you and think there's something wrong."

"There is something wrong," I counter. "Two people are unaccounted for. Unless you've heard something and you're just not telling me, no one has seen or heard from them since yesterday. That is cause for concern."

"Not yours, Agent Griffin. I can assure you, we are capable of managing our staff without your intervention. The situation is well under control."

"So they've both been accounted for? Safe and well?" I ask.

His mouth purses just slightly and I know he's trying hard to divert the conversation. "I won't be providing any further details. This is a private matter, and I won't offer information to you that you have no reason to know."

"I'm with law enforcement," I say. "That's reason."

"You're with the FBI," he says. "And the Bureau is not involved in this situation in any way. You don't have jurisdiction. Two people who skipped out on their shifts at work are hardly federal law territory. Now, if you'll excuse me, I have work I need to tend to."

THE GIRL ON THE RETREAT

"If I believe certain types of crime are being committed, or that have been recently, I have special jurisdiction to place the person under arrest. And, yes, Stanford, people going missing without explanation is federal law territory. Whether it makes you uncomfortable or not," I say.

Without another word or waiting for him to respond, I walk out of the lobby and into the warmth-softened afternoon. Several people are roaming around the grounds or sitting on the grass eating and reading in the beautiful warmth and sunshine. I avoid making eye contact with any of them so they won't try to stop me for a conversation and instead walk at a brisk pace toward the stable.

The doors are standing open like they were the first time I saw them and when I walk in, some of the horses are in their stalls. I walk through, looking for Grant, but don't see him. Leaving the barn, I go to the field where I'd ridden Bentley. The other horses are divided between the corral and this field, but I don't see Bentley or Grant. The hair on the back of my neck is standing up as I continue along the edge of the rail fence, checking every inch of the fields and still can't find either of them.

On my way back toward the main building, I see someone coming toward me. Her head is tucked down and her arms are tight around her, but I recognize her immediately.

"Daisy," I say.

She looks up with a startled expression and her cheekbones flush pink.

"Hey, Emma," she says.

"Taking another walk?" I ask. "It is really nice out this way. Though, I thought you might prefer the maze since that's where I first saw you the other night."

"The maze? Oh, right. Yes. I went through it, but it was a little much for me. I prefer just being able to walk around the open grounds like this. What are you doing out here?" she asks.

"I was looking for Grant."

"Grant? Are you taking a break from the retreat to take a quick ride?" she asks with a slight laugh.

"Even if I wanted to, I can't find him," I say.

Her face drops. "You can't find him?" Her expression rebounds as she seems to realize how she looks. "I'm sure he's just out doing something with the horses or the grounds or something. That's what he does, right? He can't just carry around hay and pat the horses all day."

She laughs awkwardly and I give a partial smile.

"Why didn't you tell Gordon about us getting locked out last night?" I ask.

"What do you mean?" she asks.

"I mentioned it to him as a joke and he looked at me like he had no idea what I was talking about, then said he did. But something he said was a little strange. He said you walk around so much because you grew up in the city. But the other day you mentioned that you grew up on a farm."

She holds her arms tighter against her body, her jaw tight. "Right. Gordon doesn't know about my childhood. I don't usually talk about it. I slipped when I was talking to you, but he thinks I grew up in a city and went to private schools."

"Why would you tell him that?" I ask.

She huffs. "Because he comes from a different world than I do, Emma. One I could have never even imagined before I met him. I didn't want him to think I was a piece of uneducated trash, so I lied. I'm not exactly proud of it, but it's not like I'm the only woman to ever lie about my background. Right?" she asks.

"That's true," I say.

She sighs, blinking back tears. "I need to go."

She turns on her heel to head back for the main building. I take a step toward her. "Wait, sorry. I need a favor."

She turns back to me, irritation in her eyes.

"I'm sorry about earlier. I guess I was just curious. I won't mention it to Grant."

"Thank you," she mumbles. "What's your favor?"

"Gordon photographed the fundraising run a couple weeks ago, didn't he?" I ask. She nods. "When he sent the pictures out, he sent me one of somebody else. I don't know who it is. If he lets me know where to send it, I'll send it back so he can get it to her."

Daisy shakes her head slightly. "Gordon doesn't send out the pictures. He didn't even develop the ones from the run. He just gives them to the Omnia guys."

CHAPTER THIRTY-TWO

I spend a few more minutes walking the grounds, hoping to find Grant. I'm glad to have seen Daisy, but that still leaves three people unaccounted for. I start toward the main building but change my mind and retrace my steps to Chelsea's cottage. She and Dan had mentioned that she wasn't interested in any of the retreat activities, so she would be spending her time relaxing at the cottage. I want to check on her and make sure she's feeling better.

What happened to her at dinner is still bothering me. With both her and her husband insisting she doesn't drink enough alcohol to get even close to that level of intoxication, I'm wondering what other explanation there could be. There was clearly something going on with her and it was far more than getting a little bit tipsy or being anxious and acting out a bit. Something was seriously affecting her.

She's sitting on the top step of the cottage, turned with her back leaned against the support beam and her bare feet propped on the other. A book is open in her lap and she's twirling her hair absently with one finger like a woman much younger than her years. Chelsea looks up as I approach. She smiles and I return it.

"Hi, Emma," she says. "Isn't it gorgeous out today?"

"It is," I agree. "You definitely look like you're enjoying it. And feeling much better."

She looks down at the book in her lap. "Sometimes there's nothing like just relaxing with a good book. I've read this one about a dozen times and I still never get tired of it."

"What is it?" I ask.

"Oh, just a sappy romance. Nothing of real substance," she says almost apologetically.

"It has substance if you enjoy it," I opine. "Doesn't matter what anybody else thinks."

She tilts her head to the side in consideration. "That's right."

"What can you tell me about Daisy?" I ask, the phrase making me think of her.

"Daisy?" Chelsea repeats. "Why do you ask?"

"I'm just curious. The way people were talking about her and then some of the interactions I've had. I just wanted to know kind of who she is and how she got involved in all this," I say.

I want to know if what Chelsea tells me is any different from her friends. So far, Chrissy and Sabrina are the only people who have expressed any kind of concern over her relationship with Gordon. They seem to know her the best, so I trust their impressions, but it's also possible there is more to the whole dynamic than they are aware of.

"Well, she and I aren't close or anything. It's not that I dislike her. She's perfectly pleasant. She can be quite a talker. But she's sweet and kind. There's something about her that's… refreshing? I don't know if that's the right word. I feel like her name suits her," Chelsea says.

"But?" I ask, sensing that transition in the statement.

"But like…" She hedges for a moment. "Maybe she's out of place. Not because anybody makes her out of place necessarily, just that this isn't exactly her world. I don't really know how else to describe it. Her fiancé, Gordon, has known Dan for a while doing photography for Omnia." She looks confused for a second. "Didn't I already tell you all of this? That he worked for Dan's company and then Tom thought his photography skills would be a good addition to the events for Omnia?"

"I think you did mention that." The details she's sharing have stayed consistent, which I find reassuring considering the variations I've been finding elsewhere. "Dan told me he comes here a lot with his company and the two of you come here for vacations pretty frequently. Did Gordon ever photograph events here?"

Chelsea nods. "Yeah. That's actually how all of us met Daisy. He introduced us during one of the business trips."

I lean toward her with a little smile like I want to share a secret with her. "Can I ask you something?"

"Sure."

"The gift basket I got after doing the run and the one waiting for me in the room when I checked in… did you plan those? They seem to have a bit of a woman's touch to them; they are so thoughtful."

She smiles but shakes her head. "Nope. That's all Dan. He's always been really great at things like that. Ever since we were dating, he's been amazing at picking out gifts for holidays and anniversaries, making sure people feel acknowledged on their birthdays. Thank yous. He's just one of those guys."

"Lucky girl," I comment with a grin. "Alright. I think I'm going to head back to up to the main building and take a little rest before getting ready for dinner. Are you joining us?"

"Absolutely. Dan promised nothing scary or sad at dinner," Chelsea says.

I chuckle along with her bubbly giggle and wave. "Enjoy your reading. I'm glad to see you feeling so much better."

"Thanks. Me, too. I'll see you down there!"

"Bye."

I go back to the main building but avoid my room for the moment. Instead, I make a direct line for the room where Noah was conducting the workshop. It's empty now, the other workshop he's conducting in a different area of the resort. I'm assuming that one isn't as graphic as this one. But that's exactly what I'm here for.

Reading through the file notes posted on the display board again, I find the detail I needed. It's just a reference, not even something concrete, but I can't believe Noah didn't mention it when we were going over the case. The photographs. They weren't just a random thing. According to the one-line statement buried deep in the file, it's a link, albeit the only link, to another case. I dig in my bag for my notepad and pen so I can jot down a few notes.

I'm headed down the steps toward the lobby when I hear someone say my name behind me. It's too soft and muffled by the other sounds echoing through the space for me to fully recognize it, but it sounds familiar. I turn around. There's no one behind me. Glancing around the lobby, I don't see anyone looking at me like they were the one who said it. I must have heard something else.

Halfway across the lobby I feel a touch on my back. I do not like being suddenly touched on the back. Whipping around, I face a startled-looking young man I recognize as being one of the people in my seminar earlier.

"I'm sorry," he says quickly. "I didn't mean to… I was calling for you and I guess you didn't hear me."

His is definitely not the voice I thought I heard. That was clearly a woman, and his voice is young but deep and smooth. If he did call me, I didn't hear him.

"No, it's fine. I'm sorry. I must just be a bit distracted. You were in my seminar earlier, weren't you?" I ask.

His face lights up a little when he hears I recognize him. "Yeah, I was. It was great."

"I'm glad you enjoyed it. What can I do for you? Did you have a question I didn't get to answer?"

"No. Actually, you answered mine. I realized I couldn't find my notebook and I went back to the room to see if I left it there. While I was in there, I found this. There wasn't anything in that room after your seminar, so I figured it had to be yours."

He holds out a black notebook with a piece of elastic holding the cover in place. I don't recognize it, but I take it from his hand.

"Where was it?" I ask.

"On the table. I've got to hurry, but I'm looking forward to your next workshop."

"Thanks for this," I say, holding up the notebook.

He nods and waves before jogging off. I look down at the notebook. I know it wasn't sitting on the table when I was in the room. I wonder if it might belong to someone else who took the seminar and it was put on the table when the room was cleaned. There's only one person I can ask.

Turning around, I head for the front desk. To my surprise, it isn't Stanford standing there. The woman in his place seems to notice the way my eyebrows shot up when I saw her. She smiles.

"Expecting Stanford?" she asks.

"I had started thinking he was the only person who works at the desk."

"Almost. But there are a couple more of us," she says with a smile. "Can I help you?"

"Yes. Well, maybe. Can you tell me if the rooms are cleaned after the workshops are over for the day?" I ask.

THE GIRL ON THE RETREAT

She looks at me quizzically. "Is there something wrong with one of the rooms?"

"No. No, not at all. I was just wondering if after the retreat activities are finished for the day, if someone goes in and cleans the individual rooms."

She shakes her head. "No. All cleaning and maintenance are done either in the early morning or after guests have gone to bed for the night. We try not to intrude on daily activities."

That gives me the same uncomfortable, queasy vibes as the back staircases and hidden elevator, but I smile anyway.

"Okay. Thank you."

I walk away from the desk, nearly reaching the steps leading upstairs before I release the elastic band and open the notebook. The first page is empty. I turn it and find another empty page. Then another. Flipping through, I see all the pages are blank. But at the center, something pushes the pages apart just slightly. I open it and find a playing card. The ace of spades.

Tossing the notebook and the card on the bed, I pick up the phone and call Eric.

"Noah referenced a photograph-selling ring in his report?" Eric asks after I've told him everything. "He thinks the cases are related?"

"There was one line in the case file that suggested a possible link between the murders of those women and a case that was developing. There aren't any details and he doesn't give much of an explanation. He has to go back to Harlan in the morning, but I'll ask him about it at dinner tonight. I just wanted to find out if you knew anything about that case," I say.

"Actually, yes. We were just called to get involved because it crossed state lines. Right now the details are still slim. What we know is someone is selling photographs of murder victims."

"Crime scene photos?" I ask.

"No. Those are pictures taken by the investigators that got leaked. These are gruesome, horrific pictures of the immediate aftermath of the murders. Sometimes right before. Sometimes during. They have to be taken by the killer. Or by someone who got a really shit side job."

"Could they be fake?" I ask.

"No. Some of them have been verified after the bodies were found. The others are simply far too realistic to not be real. There are some things that can't be faked. This is… torture porn, Emma. The people receiving them are getting off on the blood and the violence."

"How was the ring found?" I ask.

"A couple of pictures were turned in to the police by a dumpster diver who found them in an alley behind an abandoned apartment building. Some others were found in seized property during a raid. From there, several more photos have been found. They now cross three states with suspicion of them being in at least two more. This is a serial killer. Possibly more than one."

CHAPTER THIRTY-THREE

I GIVE ERIC A LIST OF THINGS I WANT HIM TO LOOK UP FOR ME AND tell him I'll call him back after dinner. One of the benefits of having one of my dearest friends be a supervisor in the FBI is having the resources of the Bureau at my disposal and him knowing me well enough to not have to ask a lot of questions. I don't take advantage of the research capabilities available through the Bureau in anything but the most pressing of circumstances. And that's exactly what I'm facing right now.

The longer I'm here, the more I feel like something is off. I find myself unable to remember the name of the resort. Or the faces of the people in my seminars. But I can remember Sarah's eyes. They only met mine for a brief second when she left the bathroom, but I can remember the flecks of gold against a green background, and the sheen of tears over them. I thought Grant seemed almost unreal when I first encountered him, like he was a prop or an actor put into place to make his surroundings seem real. And now no one seems to notice he is no longer around. Only me. And Daisy.

I feel separated from this place, like it's happening around me and I'm just hovering here somewhere between its plane of existence and my own. And at the same time, I'm gradually becoming more and more a part of it. Like it's seeping into me. Or I'm seeping into it. The colors. The opulence. The gritty underbelly. It's dizzying, and yet I find myself wanting to close the door and lock myself away within it forever.

Changing clothes, I splash my face with water again and stare into the mirror at myself. Water droplets glide down my face and drip from my lips. I look pale. The light coming from the bulbs over the mirror is much too bright. What the hell is wrong with me?

Dan is standing outside the dining room when I get to the lobby. He leaves the small group he's talking to and comes toward me.

"Where's Chelsea?" I ask. "Is she alright?"

"Of course, she's alright," he says. "She went to get a drink." I lift an eyebrow at him. "Coke. Her stomach started feeling a little queasy and the bubbles always help settle it down."

"Is she sick?" I ask.

"She says it's not bad. She's probably just eating a lot more rich food than she's used to."

"Have you seen Noah?" I ask.

"Noah?"

"Noah White. The detective," I say.

Dan looks confused for a second, then tilts his head back in remembrance. "That's right. You've worked with him. That cult. I didn't even think to mention he was going to be here."

"He's supposed to meet with us to talk over dinner," I say.

"I haven't seen him since an hour or so ago when he finished his last workshop. I know he can't stay all week," he says.

I shake my head. "No, he's leaving in the morning. That's why we need to talk tonight."

"Let's go find a table. He'll find us."

I make eye contact with Chelsea standing in line at the bar as we walk through the dining room. She smiles, then steps up to the bartender to order her soda. I watch him add ice to the glass, then fill it from a soda spigot before handing it to her. Dan finds us a table and she quickly crosses the room to join us. Almost as soon as we sit down, a tired-looking waiter comes to the table with a breadbasket and asks for our drink orders. His eyes drift over to the glass in front of Chelsea and his expression sags slightly, like it's a condemnation of his efforts for her to have a drink she got from the bar because she had to wait for him for so long.

I feel for the staff that are having to pick up the slack for the missing members of their team. A kitchen and waitstaff like this are designed to operate with a specific number of people, every element choreographed for optimal efficiency and service. When there's a gap, the entire thing starts to fall apart and the others have to work harder to make sure that their own role doesn't suffer while filling the one that's been left empty. But as much as I feel bad for them, I'm even more worried about Sarah and Jared. We order our drinks and as soon as the server walks away, I look at Dan.

"What I was trying to tell you earlier—the night of the reception, after I left the cottage, I ran into Daisy outside and we were locked out. We came around to the front and had to use the intercom to get Stanford. But before he came down, someone came to the door and let us in. When Stanford got there, the guy said he'd forgotten something in the kitchen. It was Jared. He went off to the kitchen, Daisy and I went to our rooms. He was gone the next morning," I say.

"And you don't know what he could have left?" Dan frowns. "Or if he came out of the kitchen?"

I shake my head. "No. He was still in the kitchen when I went upstairs. Nobody's seen him or Sarah since. No one knows where they went or what they were doing after. I know Stanford says they went out partying... but where are they now? By now they would have gotten in touch with someone."

"Emma."

I look up and see Noah coming toward the table. The relief that comes over me is disquieting. I don't want to have a reason to be relieved just to see him where he is supposed to be. Dan stands up as he approaches and holds out his hand.

"Detective White, good to see you again."

Noah reaches out and accepts his hand. "Dan. Chelsea." He looks at me. "I'm going up to the bar to grab a drink. Want to come with me?"

It's not an invitation to get a drink. It's a diversion.

"Sure. Can I get anything for either of you?" I ask.

They shake their heads and I get up to join Noah. When we're away from the table, Noah leans his head over toward me so he can talk without raising his voice loudly enough for the people around us hearing him.

"What did you find out about the case?" he asks. "I know you talked to Eric."

There's no lead up. No attempt to be subtle or give me the benefit of the doubt that I wouldn't immediately involve myself. He knows me well enough to know there's no way I could see that kind of evidence and not want to know what happened.

"I might not have," I protest. He gives me a doubtful look. "But I did."

I tell him everything Eric told me about the investigation into the photography ring and its possible connection to the murders of Vicki Freeman and the unidentified woman.

"He thinks there's a possibility they really are connected," Noah says, less a question than an acknowledgement, a sense of validation of what he was already thinking.

"Yes. There's strong indicators. Which brings me to a question I need to ask you," I say.

We step up to the bar and Noah orders a whiskey. I opt to stay away from alcohol tonight and get one of the brightly colored virgin drinks Chelsea had at the reception. I barely even think about it as I'm ordering. I realize once the glass is in my hand and I'm staring into the ocean-colored liquid, I'm curious about her reaction to her drinks. I want to know if the same will happen to me.

We thank the bartender and step to the side.

"What question?" Noah asks.

"How did you end up presenting at the retreat and why did you choose this case for your workshop?" I ask.

"That's two questions."

"Answer both of them," I say.

"I met Dan Vreeland and Kyle Harris when they were first starting Omnia. They were piecing together this idea and weren't sure how to make it happen. The grapevine of contacts eventually led them to me, and I helped them out with some questions they had and also connected them with some other people. When they started planning this retreat, I contacted them and asked if they'd be interested in me running a workshop for them," he says.

"Before this case started?" I ask.

It would make sense if he had already made the commitment before the intense case arose. He's the kind of man who wouldn't go back on his word if it wasn't absolutely necessary.

THE GIRL ON THE RETREAT

"No. I was already working the case when I asked them," he says.

That makes me frown. "I don't understand. You are obviously being stretched thin with this situation. You're stressed and so busy you have to leave the retreat early to get back to the work. Why would you go through all that voluntarily?"

I think I already know the answer. It's been simmering right at the base of my skull, just low enough beneath my awareness that I haven't latched on to all the details yet. But they're there. I just need confirmation from him.

He takes a quick glance around to confirm we're alone. "I think either the members of Omnia or people around them are being targeted. I'm not officially investigating the photography ring, so I don't have access to all the information. But I've been doing my own investigation as much as I can, and they led me to some very dark, grimy corners of the internet I didn't even know existed. I read a lot of things I wish I never did. That's saying a lot coming from a detective, but it's not even just the horrific things they were talking about, but the fact that I can't do anything about them. Does that make sense?" Noah asks.

"Yes," I say. "It definitely does."

"On one of those message boards, I found people talking about this person who sells high-quality morbid collectibles, including torture and murder imagery. They have all kinds of cutesy code names for it but it's easy to figure out what they're talking about. I've been following those boards and trying to find anything I could that would lead me to the head of the ring. I haven't been able to. But a few months ago, I started seeing mentions of this retreat and the people running it.

"They were talking about different motives for murder and their individual preferences for collectibles and memorabilia. They talked about how certain victims may be worth more than others. And the value of the victims increases depending on the circumstances of the murder."

I don't often cringe at hearing the details of something so gruesome but I can't help myself. "Jesus."

"Someone killed out in the middle of nowhere can be satisfying but not as thrilling as somebody targeted out in public, especially if they are already a prominent figure or there's a story behind it in some way. Then they started talking about choosing their targets. About their fantasies that could be fulfilled by this collectibles dealer. They go into some pretty intense detail about the kinds of pictures they want. Getting custom orders. But then one of them mentioned taking it to the next level and being a part of the entire process. Not as just an idle fantasy but like it was something real. Something they could achieve."

"Personalized fulfillment of murder fantasies," I say. "Not just pictures but the killing itself."

"The conversation just kept swirling around this retreat. Like they were hoping something would happen here," Noah says. "I haven't had any other concrete leads or anything that has given me any direction, so I figured the worst that can happen is I come here, do my workshops, and nothing untoward happens and all that has really unfolded is I have wasted a little bit of time. But even then, teaching people how to protect themselves isn't a waste of time."

I know that isn't the worst that could happen. I feel like Noah knows that, too, but he doesn't want to acknowledge it. Saying it will make it real and he wants to stay focused.

"I came here to try to find any other links and identify any danger that could be here. I hate that I have to go back in the morning. I should be here. If something happens…"

"If something else happens, I'm here," I tell him.

"And I'll get back here as fast as I can."

"The thing is, something *has* already happened. Two people are missing. And somebody was following me last night," I say. "I don't know who it was or what their intentions might have been, but I was able to scare them away with my gun. That doesn't mean they won't try again. I think you're right. I think someone here is connected to those murders and the photographs."

"Who?" Noah asks.

"I'm not positive yet. But I'm unraveling it. Now that I know about the photography ring, I think I'm a little closer. Dan says that his company has come here for business trips a lot. Which means that this place has to have a business center."

"I'm sure it does. Why?"

"I want you to show me these message boards," I say.

CHAPTER THIRTY-FOUR

"Hey, Dan," I say as we get back to the table. "Remind me when I get back to Sherwood to send you back the pictures that were in my welcome basket."

He gives me a strange look. "Why? Is there something wrong with them?"

"I mean, no, not in terms of the quality of the picture. You just sent me pictures of somebody else."

"Somebody else?" Chelsea asks.

I let myself chuckle just a little to make sure Dan knows I'm not mad about the situation as I reach for one of the rolls in the breadbasket and cut a pat of butter from a larger chunk beside it to put on my plate.

"Not all of them. There's just one, possibly two, of a different woman running. You must have just glanced at them and seen her hair and thought it was me."

Dan shakes his head. "I didn't choose the pictures. I put together the rest of the basket, but I'm not the one who deals with any of that kind of stuff. I don't have an eye for it."

"Gordon said he doesn't choose pictures for anything. He just takes them and then hands them over to you guys."

"He does," Dan says. "That's because Tom likes control. He wants to be able to look at every one of the pictures and select the ones he likes rather than trusting somebody else to choose. I knew Gordon was at the run taking some promotional pictures, and I thought it would be a fun addition to your basket to have some commemorative photos. I told Tom and let him choose them."

"He fancies himself a bit of a photographer, too," Chelsea explains. "But it's more of a hobby for him compared to Gordon."

The server returns with our drinks, this time eyeing the ones that Noah and I got from the bar. I feel a little bit bad about getting them. But I can understand why Noah wanted the distraction to pull me away from the table to talk to me about the case. I realize I haven't even looked at the dinner menu, but I don't want to keep the server delayed anymore, so I quickly scan my eyes over the options and choose the one that stands out to me the quickest.

"And knowing Tom, he probably got distracted by the picture and just grabbed it up with yours," Dan says.

There's a slight edge of significance in his voice but I'm not following it.

"Distracted?" I ask.

"Tom is not exactly known for his… monogamy skills," Dan says.

"Ah," I say, not really surprised by the revelation. "Well, I'm not sure if I should take that as a compliment or a slight, but either way, I'll make sure he gets the picture of the mystery girl back."

Chelsea has finished off her coke and is looking at my virgin cocktail. I meet her eyes.

"Is that…?" she asks, letting the words trail off as if she knows I'm going to catch onto what she's saying.

I nod. "Yep. It's delicious."

It's mostly sweet, but I can tell she wants one and doesn't want anyone questioning her for it.

"I'm going to go get one," she says.

"Just ask the server," Dan says. "He'll bring it to you."

"I know, but I don't want to bother him anymore. He already looks like he's being pushed right to his edge. I'm just going to go up to the bar. I'll be right back," she says.

"Do you want me to get it for you?" he asks.

Chelsea grins and leans down to kiss him. "No. Thank you, though. You stay here and talk."

She walks away and I turn to Dan.

"Is there a business center in the resort?" I ask.

"Mmhmm," he mouths as he takes a sip of his own drink. "A really nice one. It's down near the primary seminar room. Just down the hall and toward the back. Are you already missing work that much?"

He laughs a little but the sound doesn't go all the way to his eyes. He knows if I'm working, it means something has gone wrong.

"And it has internet, right?" I ask.

"It has what now?"

Out of the corner of my eye, I see Gordon coming toward the table. His eyebrows are tight together and his eyes dart back and forth across the room.

"Hey," he says as he gets to us.

"Evening, Gordon," Dan says. "Want to join us?"

"Thanks, but I can't. Have you seen Daisy?"

My stomach drops. "I saw her a couple of hours ago. She was outside taking a walk when I was."

"Taking a walk?" Dan asks.

"I went to check on Chelsea and was just enjoying the weather a bit. It seemed like that was what she was doing, too. But she came back toward the main building right after we talked for a second."

"I haven't seen her since this afternoon," Gordon says. "We were going to meet up in our suite before dinner. I've looked around for her but can't find her."

"Does she have a pager?" Noah asks.

Gordon shakes his head. "Not that she has with her. She only carries it when she's out working. I'm going to see if I can find Chrissy and Sabrina. She might have hooked up with them and just lost track of time. They might have ended up back in the hot tubs. She was talking about how she needed to relax her muscles and that she'd been thinking about getting in that hot tub again."

"If we see her, we'll let her know you're looking for her," I tell him.

He nods and walks away, headed for the doors to the dining room.

"Why wouldn't he have looked for her with her friends before coming in here?" Noah asks. "If he thinks that's where she is, why would he ask other people first?"

I shake my head. "There's something going on here, Noah. There are two members of the staff who have been unaccounted for since last night. I wasn't able to find Grant, who works in the stable, when I was out there today. Now Daisy."

"That many can't be a coincidence. And I already know what you're going to say," Noah says.

I don't even need to finish the line: I don't believe in coincidences.

"I want to know if anyone has contacted their families or if they have roommates," I say. "They should have emergency contacts listed in their employee records. Someone needs to be covering all the bases trying to find them."

"Stanford told me he did call their emergency numbers," Dan tells me. "But they didn't have any information about them. As for Grant… if it's only been a couple of hours I don't think Stanford is going to do anything."

"Do you know which of the cottages he lives in?" I ask. "I'll go check on him myself."

"I'll go with you," Noah says.

"Eat first," Dan insists.

"I can't. I need to know if he's alright. Can you ask them to pack it up and send it to my room?"

"Mine, too," Noah adds.

Chelsea is back, sipping her drink. She looks sad as she realizes we're leaving. "Where are you going?"

"To check on Grant," I say. "Which cottage is his?"

"Number eight," Dan says. "But I'm sure he's fine. He's upset about his horse being missing, so he's probably still out searching for it."

"I want to make sure," I say.

As Noah and I cross the lobby, I shift to the side. "Can we run up to my room really fast and grab my coat? I'm sure the temperature has dropped out there and I've had my fill of the cold."

"Absolutely."

We get up to my room and I grab my coat, then go to the bedroom and get the card from the flowers and the notebook. I bring them out to Noah and show them to him.

"Does this mean anything to you?" I ask.

He looks at them. "Ace of spades." He shakes his head. "No."

I explain how I got both of them. "It can't be a coincidence either."

He chuckles at the second invocation of my mantra in the last few minutes. "Of course."

I shrug into my coat and head back down and out into the evening. Just like I thought, the temperature has gotten much cooler and I'm thankful for the extra layer. We walk quickly down the drive to the cottages and search for the one marked number eight. When we find it, I hop up onto the porch and knock on the door. There's no light coming from inside and he doesn't come to the door. I knock harder, calling in to Grant, but the cottage remains quiet.

"Not there?" Noah asks.

"No," I reply as I come back down the steps. Come on, let's go to the business center. I want to see those message boards."

We're nearly to the entrance of the tiny village of cottages, when something pops into my head. I hesitate and Noah looks back at me.

"What's wrong?" he asks.

"I need to check something. I'll be right back," I say.

I turn and jog back toward Chelsea and Dan's cottage. Walking around the side the direction whoever made the shadow across their room would have gone, I head deeper into the grounds. Ahead of me I see a small shed. It's locked, but walking around it, I find a burn pit several feet away. I crouch down next to it, wishing I'd brought some light with me.

"Noah?" I call. "Do you have a flashlight?"

There's something in the burn pit. It reminds me of the chunk of melted plastic I found on the step, just larger. I use a swipe of my hand to flip it over. I hear footsteps coming toward me but realize at the last second they are coming from the opposite direction Noah would have come. A hand clamps over my mouth and an arm wraps around my body, trying to pin my arms to my sides.

I wrench back, able to move just enough to plunge my elbow into the person's ribs. His hands grab me and we tumble to the ground. I land on my back on top of him and twist my body until I break the grip around me. His hands claw at my chest and I feel something cut into my skin.

"What the hell are you doing?" Noah's voice bellows.

I'm shoved forcefully to the ground and the person scrambles on the ground for an instant before he stands and plunges into the woods. Noah comes running up and starts in after him but comes back a few moments later.

"I couldn't catch up. I'm sorry."

I blow out a long breath, slowing my heartrate. "It's okay." Getting up to my feet, I lean over, my hands pressed to my thighs. "Shit."

"Are you alright?" he asks.

"Yeah. I'm fine." I press my hand to my chest where I felt the sharp pain and realize the retreat pin is missing from my shirt. "My pin. He ripped it off."

Noah looks around and then scoops down to pick something up. "Here. I don't see the back."

"It's in my shirt," I say, shaking the small piece of metal loose.

The red pin is covered in dirt and I shove it and the back into my pocket.

"You wanted this," Noah says, handing me a small flashlight.

"Thanks." I shine it on the burn pit and see the melted plastic container. The label is gone, but there's still a partial impression of a word up near where the neck of the bottle was. I realize the plastic I found was likely the lid. "Premixed." I think about it for a second. "Antifreeze. Why would someone put this in a burn pile?"

Noah shrugs as he huffs out a breath. "Come on. Let's get inside."

CHAPTER THIRTY-FIVE

NOAH TRIES TO CONVINCE ME TO GO TO MY ROOM AND CHANGE when we get inside but I refuse. I want to see the message boards he was talking about. He reluctantly agrees and we go through the lobby and find the staircase to the refurbished basement level area.

For the next couple of hours we dig through the message boards, my blood running colder with every new message I read. I want to say I can't believe what I'm reading but that's not true. It's an unfortunate reality that I'm rarely shocked or surprised by anything anymore. I've seen far too much to ever question the potential for cruelty and barbarism among humans.

"Emma, you really should call the police about the attack," he says.

I brush him off. "They can't do anything. I didn't see who it was and we weren't able to catch him."

"Alright. But I need to get some rest. I have to leave early. Can I walk you back to your room?" he asks.

I shake my head. "No. I'm going to stay here for a bit longer. There's still a lot for me to read."

"Promise me you're going to get some sleep tonight," he insists.

"I will. And I'll see you before you leave. Meet me for coffee in the lounge."

He nods and leaves. I go back to the message boards. I don't know how much time has passed before I leave the business center. Rather than going back to my room directly, I weave back through the path I took the first night I came down here, retracing my steps to the places I first felt the strange atmosphere of the resort. As I do, the memory of the conversation that night trickles back into my mind.

It was Sarah.

The suggestive, flirtatious conversation I overheard near the seminar room was the now-missing server and a man.

Walking down the dim back hallway, my heart pounds in my chest. I can hear voices ahead of me. I get to the door of the unused kitchen and realize the voices are coming from inside. I open the door and see Stanford, Tom, Kyle, Cory, and two men I don't recognize sitting around the table in the center of the room. Cory is holding a deck of cards and doling them out. They all look up at me in surprise.

"Emma, what are you doing here?" Kyle asks.

"This area is for staff use only," Stanford snaps.

"I wasn't aware that Mr. Murphy, Harris, and Mellon worked for the resort."

His face flushes bright red and Cory opens his hands over the table like he's putting everything on it on display to show none of them are hiding anything.

"Nothing to be concerned about, Emma. Just a friendly game of cards. Join us?" he asks.

Kyle seems to notice my condition and starts to stand up.

"Are you okay? What happened?"

"I'm fine. Just being clumsy outside. No thanks, on the game. I appreciate the offer. I think I'm just going to take a shower and get some sleep," I say.

I leave the kitchen and go back to the lobby. I'm almost to the steps when I hear Dan behind me.

"Emma, Emma."

I turn around and see him running toward me frantically. "Emma, it's Chelsea. She's sick again."

"Sick?" I ask.

THE GIRL ON THE RETREAT

"Like the other night. It's like she's drunk, but she didn't drink anything tonight. Not even one cocktail."

"Call an ambulance," I tell him. "I need to go make a phone call and take a shower, then I'll meet you at the closest hospital. Do not let *anyone* near her room. No one but the medical team."

He sighs. "Thank you."

I run up the stairs and take the fastest shower I can. While I'm getting dressed, I call Eric to see if he's found out anything. As soon as I hear what he has to tell me, I know what's wrong with Chelsea. And that things are about to get much worse.

"Call Sam," I tell him. "I'll let you know what's happening when I can."

I put my coat on and run downstairs and out to the parking area. I'm almost to my car when the headlights of a nearby car pop on, blinding me. I step back, lifting my hand to cover my eyes, and hear the engine rev.

Him

This was worth it.

All the hassle. All the planning.

This was worth every bit of it.

He leaned back in his chair, watching the video on the screen in front of him. In front of him, his elite clients sat in their own plush chairs, their rapt attention on individual monitors.

This was his greatest innovation. He called it The Park. Designed for large-scale hunts like this one, the expansive stretch of land was filled with treacherous obstacles, traps, weapons, and lethal games for the targets to try to survive. And for them to enjoy watching.

It wasn't unfair. Not completely.

He hadn't designed it to be entirely hopeless. They did have a chance of survival. If they did it right.

If they paid attention and completed each puzzle correctly. If they didn't let their primal instincts take over.

Though, he hoped they would. It was so much more fun that way.

One of the men in front of him let out a cheer as his chosen target broke through the tangled branches of a stand of trees and stepped directly into the fearsome steel jaws of a bear trap. Her tortured scream reverberated through the viewing room, and he used the controls of the closest camera to zoom in closer to the carnage. Blood ran down her leg from where the teeth of the trap dug through her skin and snapped the bones. Her back arched in agony as she tried to fight her way out of the trap. All that would do was make her bleed out faster.

Which was exactly what they wanted. They groaned and laughed with joy at the flood of red spilling over her skin and discoloring the clothes she had left. This part they anticipated. It was a special request of the man who'd chosen her. He'd wanted to see her trapped and allowed to suffer before death, and he made it so.

They didn't know what was coming next. Not everyone brought to play in The Park was chosen by one of the elite clients. That wouldn't have been nearly enough fun to fill the several days he wanted this to last. He added several others to keep things interesting. That was his specialty.

There was tremendous, twisted pleasure in watching people who knew each other barely hang on as the others around them ripped each other apart. And the sickening realization that they'd have to fight each other to the death for survival. But it was a new, fresh kind of excitement when the people *didn't* know each other and were far more ready to brutalize and betray the others for their own salvation.

But it wasn't the fights that gave him the greatest pleasure. His favorite part of any experience was watching them struggle with themselves. The moment of hesitation before ending the life of another. The war they had to wage within their own minds and souls was enthralling to witness. They had to break themselves open and face what was really inside. Everyone has darkness in them. It is a simple reality of birth. They may try to deny it or suppress it but that can only last for so long.

Eventually something would force them to look into that darkness and reveal it to the world. They would become that darkness if it meant another moment of survival.

CHAPTER THIRTY-SIX

The Park

"WHERE IS SARAH?" JARED ASKED IN A HUSHED WHISPER, crouched at the base of a tree, his back pressing into the coarse bark. "I don't see her."

"That was her," Alyssa said from the bush nearby where she was hiding. "I heard her scream."

"It was coming from this direction," a man Jared didn't know and whose name he hadn't yet caught, agreed.

There were four of them in this group, and he knew at least another four were in The Park, not including Sarah. They hadn't seen them for hours, but they'd heard the screams. Each one was more gut-wrenching, and Jared was starting to lose his grip on reality. He didn't know how he got here or who'd brought him, only that he had been in the kitchen to get the apron he'd forgotten and heard somebody there with him.

He'd thought it was Stanford. He'd known the resort manager was going to be angry with him for coming back after hours, even though it wasn't ever expressly forbidden. He would probably be angrier for letting those women in through the front door. He had obviously gotten out of bed to come down and let them in, but Jared wasn't going to allow guests to just stand out on the porch in the freezing temperatures just so Stanford could take his sweet time putting on a suit.

But nobody had answered when Jared called out into the main area of the kitchen. He hadn't seen anyone when he walked out of the storeroom where he had accidentally left his apron. Everything was dark and still. Everything was quiet. Then suddenly there was a chain around his neck, tape over his eyes, and a gag so far down his throat he didn't know if he would survive being dragged out of the building and tossed into the back of a vehicle. After that, he knew nothing but The Park.

He hated the sound of that from the first time he heard it coming through an unseen speaker. The man's voice who said it was altered so it almost sounded mechanical, like the surroundings themselves were speaking to him rather than another person. Jared knew this place couldn't be anything like the bucolic, beautiful green spaces he thought of when he heard that word. From the moment he opened his eyes and was welcomed into The Park, he was surrounded by horror.

The first thing he saw when he opened his eyes was a man tied to a nearby tree. Bright yellow ropes strapped his chest, his stomach, and his hips in place so he dangled several feet above the ground. But even though he looked like he was completely secured there, a trail of blood and bits of flesh embedded in the bark above him proved he had gradually slid down by the force of his own bodyweight. His head was hanging down, his chin on his chest, and Jared couldn't tell if he was dead or had simply given up to the pain and the weakness from blood loss.

That began the endless stretch of horrors Jared had experienced in what he estimated to be nearly twenty-four hours since being brought here. He quickly learned the rules of The Park: no one here knew who'd brought them or how they had come. Their only goal was to stay alive. They were surrounded by traps and weaponry, sometimes finding obstacles and puzzles they had to overcome in order to avoid brutal backlash from unseen gamemasters.

There was more than one. Though they heard the mechanical voice of the first man most often, occasionally someone else's voice would come through the speakers, instructing them of what they were to do next, warning them of what would happen if they didn't. He'd already witnessed one girl refuse to partake in one of the games, and instantly a large blade rigged into a nearby tree was triggered to swing down and bury itself in the center of her skull. Jared decided not to argue after that.

They were promised there was an end to this. There was a way to get out. If they made it through the obstacles, completed the puzzles, and won the games, they could find the one and only exit from the park. Because none of them knew how they got there or who'd brought them, there could be no consequences. They would never be able to bring the police here or tell them who had done this to them. But they could live. And right now, that was all Jared could think about to keep putting one foot in front of the other. He didn't truly believe he could trust the voices but he had to. He had to try.

He was bruised and cut from what he had already gone through, but he'd managed to avoid some of the most horrifying threats waiting for them. It had only been a day, but he could barely remember how the group of them had pulled together. Alyssa told him she'd already been there for three days. A man was there when she got there, but she hadn't seen him in more than a day when she found Jared.

The Park had to be massive. They had no real way of knowing how big it was or how to navigate it. The only thing they'd learned was to listen for the voices and follow marked trails when they found them. They knew there would be something horrible down that trail, but at the end of each, when they'd made it through, they were rewarded. It felt pathetic to even consider finding scraps of food or bottles of water rewards, but it was all there was. Sometimes there would be a sign or a note telling them which way to go next. They obeyed. He hated the feeling of being trailed along blindly, knowing in the pit of his soul that he was following the Devil and relying on him to tell the truth.

There was no other way. It was either follow the path and be a part of whatever gruesome sport awaited them, or venture off into the open unknown without any clue of what could be waiting there or even which direction to head. There would be no more food or water. No more directions. Nothing to keep him alive long enough to even dare hope he would find the exit. And he knew that even if he was the luckiest person to have ever lived and he happened to stumble on the exit, they wouldn't let him out.

Whoever was hovering above them, hidden away somewhere so they could only hear and never see them, wouldn't just have an open gate somewhere. Jared wouldn't be able to just walk through it and try to go back to his life. They would have total control over who got out and when. Those who didn't do as they were told would never make it out.

Sarah had been with them up until a couple of hours before, when one of the games sent her down a different trail then them. Though when they reached the end of the trail and saw that the end of the one she went down connected with theirs, they didn't see her. They called for her and ventured up her trail but saw no trace of her.

Then they heard her screams. He recognized her voice. He knew it was her. But they couldn't find her. From their hiding spots they were trying to figure out where to go next. They wanted to look for her, but they also wanted to keep moving ahead.

They lingered for a little while longer, then ventured out in what they thought was the direction of Sarah's screams of pain and terror. Jared didn't want to contemplate what had happened to her. He could only hope she was still alive. That somehow they would find her and be able to take her with them.

They walked through an open clearing and into another set of trees. To either side of them were several trails. The man stopped and pointed ahead.

"There's a marker."

Rushing toward it, they saw an arrow pointing them down a trail. Jared let the man go down first, following right behind to keep Alyssa and Molly behind them. Fear and anticipation got more and more intense as they walked down the narrow path without anything happening. He expected the mechanical voice but it didn't come. He waited for an obstacle or a pile of weapons, a temptation for them to kill each other to increase their chances of survival. But it was just a path.

They walked on for what felt like an hour or more, the only light in the night around them coming from small bulbs strung up in the trees and the occasional light embedded in the ground. Finally, ahead of them, they saw a brightly lit clearing open out from the end of the path. They hurried toward it, some hope starting to spark inside them, but stopped when they saw the tables set up in the center.

Jared walked toward them feeling like a burning rock was sitting in his gut. He knew what this was. He'd seen it before. The first table held a display board with a picture of a cow, the outline of its body divided up into different sections to demonstrate the cuts of meat. The other table was empty except for a large knife. This was for him specifically.

He was expected to break a primal cut down into the different pieces. Only there was no animal to use.

"What are you supposed to do?" Alyssa asked.

"There's no animal to break down," the man said.

THE GIRL ON THE RETREAT

A loud sound cut through the silence and a bullet passed just by Jared's head. That was intentional. It wasn't meant to hit him. It was a warning. He had to do this, whatever it took.

He looked around the clearing. Maybe he had to hunt down something lurking in the woods. He caught sight of a blue marker on one of the trees, leading him to the end of a path he hadn't noticed. He ran toward it as another bullet nearly hit Alyssa and she screamed, dropping to the ground.

Jared ran down the trail, looking to either side of him for something to try to kill. Then he saw it. He knew what they expected him to do. His feet skidded to a stop and he nearly threw up. The knife dropped from his hand and the other hand flew up to cover his mouth. Ahead of him, buried in the thick undergrowth, was a massive bear trap.

And caught in it was Sarah.

She wasn't moving. Her leg was snapped and blood poured around her. Her head hung back, her hair over her face. Alyssa and Molly ran up behind Jared, stopping behind him.

"Oh, my god," Molly whispered, turning her back sharply.

"Is she alive?" Alyssa asked.

"I don't know," Jared said.

Another bullet came and then the voice.

"You know what you have to do."

"What does that mean?" the man asked, coming up behind them. "What do you have to do?"

Jared shook his head, unable to speak past the stinging ball of bile in his throat.

"He has to butcher her," Alyssa says.

He shook his head again, his knees going weak beneath him. "I—I can't."

This time, the bullet found its home in Molly's leg. Her cry of pain and seeing her hit the ground shot Jared into action. He picked up the knife and went over to the trap. His stomach turned and his heart dropped when he saw her chest rising and falling irregularly.

"She's still alive," he said. "She's still alive, I can't do this."

Molly screamed again as another bullet cut into her.

"Jared, you have to," Alyssa said. "She's not going to survive that trap. You know that. But they'll kill the rest of us."

The man snatched the knife from Jared's hand. "I'll do it."

He took one step toward the trap and his head shattered, blood and brain matter spraying over them as a bullet passed through him. His body dropped to the dirt in front of Jared, who stumbled back as the voice came over the speakers again.

"It has to be you."

CHAPTER THIRTY-SEVEN

I WAKE UP TO THE SOUND OF GUNFIRE.
    I know that sound well. I can tell exactly what kind of gun it is. I know what it takes to fire it.

I also know what it does when it hits a living being.

It feels like I'm lying down, but also like there's nothing solid under me. I try to move and feel myself shift, my hand go through something and into nothingness. As my eyes adjust to the darkness and to the pain pounding in my head, I realize I'm in a rope net, suspended above the ground. There's some moonlight, but very little. I don't know where I am or how I got here.

All I remember is the car headlights and trying to get out of the way as the vehicle lurched toward me. I don't feel any injuries severe enough to indicate I actually got hit by the car, but I can't really tell. As my eyes adjust, I can see ahead of me and note lights in the darkness.

I shout for whomever might hear me. Immediately the net lifts up a little higher and then drops down, slamming me into the ground. I cry out in pain and the net pulls me up slowly again. In that second, I learn my first rule: there is no calling for help.

I instinctively touch my hip to check for my gun. It's not there. Whoever brought me here must've taken it from me.

Using what little light is coming from the moon, I try to figure out how big the net is and where I am in the tree. Hitting the ground was painful, but I wasn't up high enough to break any bones. Which means it was only a few feet. Grabbing onto the rope on the side closest to the tree, I pull myself up and try to feel for the branch near where I'm suspended. It's a couple of feet above my head, so I am able to push against the trunk and launch myself upward to grab onto it with one arm. It pulls the net up in a way that crushes against the side of my face and makes my foot go through one of the holes, leaving me in pain and with little mobility, but it's what I can do for now.

I can feel the band of my bra against my rib cage and I know my knife is still there. No one would know to look for it and the fact that it hasn't been moved tells me that whoever took me only thought about my gun and didn't think to search me more thoroughly. I'm thankful for that as I pull the small blade out of place and use it to cut through the rope of the net. It only takes me a few seconds but much longer to disentangle myself and scramble up onto the branch. I've managed to free myself, but now I don't know what to do next.

"Impressive, Agent Griffin," an unrecognizable voice says from somewhere around me. It's metallic, robotic, twisted, but I can hear the very human malice in it still. "But don't think your visit to The Park is going to stay that simple. We have far more in store for you. You are our trophy, our prize target. But we have integrity. We like to keep things fair. Prove yourself and the worth everyone seems to place on you, and you have a chance of survival. But in order to get out of The Park alive, you have to play our game… and win."

Scrambling down the trunk of the tree, I jump down onto the ground and orient myself. I don't know where I am or which direction the voice wants me to go, but I know I'm going toward those lights. I set off at a run. I pay close attention to the ground in front of me, waiting for any type of obstacle that might get in my way. I've been lowered into games before. I remember the train ride from hell that nearly ended the lives of hundreds of people. I won't let it happen again.

I get close to the lights and realize they are surrounding a clearing in the forest. There are other people there. Remembering what happened the first time I shouted out, I don't call out to them. Instead, I make as much noise as I can as I approach so that they will know I'm there.

If they are here in this place with me, they are likely being tormented in the same way. They have likely been here longer and have been put through things I don't know about. I know they're going to be scared and reactive. The last thing I want is to startle them.

"Someone's coming," I hear one of them say.

"Agent Emma Griffin, FBI," I announce when I am nearly to the edge of the clearing.

"Is it really you?"

I know that voice. It's Jared.

"Yes," I say. "It's really me."

I walk out into the clearing with my hands up so they know I am not armed and not one of the people posing a threat to them. I don't know what to expect, but the scene that unfolds in front of me is unlike anything I could have imagined. Jared walks toward me with wide, blank eyes. He's covered in blood and he grips a knife in his shaking hand.

"Agent Griffin," he manages to get out before dropping to his knees in front of me.

"Jared, what happened?" I ask. He doesn't answer and I raise my voice. "What happened?"

He shakes his head back and forth. "Sarah."

The name barely croaks out of his throat and I know she's not safe. I look behind him at the tables in the center of the clearing and my stomach turns. The pieces of meat on display on one of the tables don't look like they came from the cow pictured beside them. The head on the ground behind it belongs to the young server I saw run from the bathroom and heard pleading for her job.

"Come on," I say, going back to Jared and picking him up by one arm. "We're getting out of here."

"How?" he asks.

"We do what they say."

"That's your answer?" a man I don't recognize asks angrily. "We just *comply*? Do you see what he had to do? I just found them. I don't even know what else they've gone through, but I did see a man with no head on that path and watched *him* butcher a human." He jabs an angry finger at Jared. "You want to go along with what these people say?"

I turn to him. "Who are you?"

"Austin Taylor," he says.

"What do you do?"

"Career military. Retired."

"Then I would hope that you have more respect for human life than to argue with me right now. I see very well what he did. And I know what we're facing. You may have seen war, and I respect that. But I walk through battlefields every day. This is the type of enemy I fight. You choose to do whatever it is that you want to do. If you want to lay down your life for these people, that's on you. I'm not doing it. I'm not sacrificing anyone else. I'm getting out of here. And if that means that they want me to play their fucking game, that's what we're going to do."

"What about Molly?"

I leave Jared and walk over to the woman I didn't notice lying on the ground. She's barely conscious and the woman who is holding her across her lap looks terrified.

"What happened to her?" I ask.

"She was shot."

Blood is gushing from Molly's leg at a tremendous rate. I look over at Austin.

"Give me your shirt."

He looks for a second like he wants to argue with me just for the sake of doing it but finally gives in. He strips off what's left of a tattered, stained t-shirt and hands it over to me. I find what bits of it have the least amount of mud and dried blood on them and tear them into bandages. I cover the bullet wounds with them, then tie the rest tight around the scraps. It's not perfect but it will have to do.

"She can't walk," the woman says.

"You're going to have to carry her," I tell her.

Austin picks her up and puts her over his shoulders in a fireman's carry. I don't know which direction to go, so I choose the path I was already on and start toward it.

"That was a very inspirational speech, Agent Griffin," the voice says, making all of us stop and look around. "We are impressed by your willingness to be a part of our fun. Though, I'll admit I did expect a bit more resistance from you. It takes some of the excitement away when you are so happy to simply do as we say. But don't worry. There's plenty ahead of you. We will make sure this is worth your time. We will even let you keep your knife. After all, we've already provided plenty of… shall we say, toys for all of our guests. Remember, you aren't in this together. The fewer of you there are, the greater your chance of getting out alive. Play nicely. We are watching."

CHAPTER THIRTY-EIGHT

"There," Jared says, pointing in front of him. I see a blue arrow pointing to the side. We've gone all the way down the path that I was on when I woke up and reached a fork. He indicated the marker, telling me that these are what have directed them through the park so far. With nothing else to go on, I turn down the trail and follow it. It isn't far before we reach another clearing. This one is much larger, the size of a small meadow rather than just a clear area among the trees.

It takes a second before I see that it isn't completely empty. Instead, there's a shadowy shape in the distance.

"What is that?" Alyssa asks.

"It's a horse. It's Bentley," I say.

I can't see the animal's markings and I don't know for absolutely sure that it is Bentley, but something inside me says this is the missing horse. He was released from his paddock and brought here. And as we approach, I know why.

Bentley is wearing a harness and attached to it is a large metal hook with a chain through it. The chain stretches up and attaches to a pole several feet behind him. It's deeper in the shadows of the field so I wasn't able to see it when I was first approaching, but now that I am close, I can see Grant standing on a very small platform high above the field. A loop of chain around his neck is tight enough that he's struggling to breathe. He makes a few desperate noises but doesn't say any words.

"We have to get him down," Jared says.

I see two large wheels almost like gears positioned a few yards away, attached to the chain like a pulley system.

"That's exactly what we have to do," I say. "Those wheels are attached to the chain. One of them is going to release him. One of them will probably do something that startles Bentley and make him run. If that happens, Grant's neck will snap."

"Which one is which?" Alyssa asks.

Lights suddenly pop on to the side of the field like they were waiting for someone to ask that question. If I wasn't right in the midst of this and was watching it on a movie, I would almost cringe at the theatricality of it all. Instead, I run for the lights. A white picket fence surrounds a chaotic-looking flower bed. Rather than being planted with any sort of organization or color scheme, various types of flowers press right up against each other without any rhyme or reason. Green and blue paint on a small wooden sign almost like a garden marker plunged in the front of the bed reads: *Go with the majority.*

There's nothing else. No explanation. No other instructions. I try to process it. I'm trying to figure out exactly what this is supposed to mean. It's not random. It's not just there to confuse us. I know it means something. If it didn't, it wouldn't be amusing to the people watching us. But Alyssa is not as patient. She runs forward, dropping to her knees next to the flower bed and reaches out for them.

"What are you doing?"

"There has to be something buried in here," she says.

She grabs for the nearest flowers and screams, falling back and holding her hand up. Blood trickles down from puncture wounds in her palm. I lean closer and see that each of the flowers has tiny sharp points along their stems.

"We aren't supposed to pull them. There's something about the flowers. Go with the majority. That means something," I say. "What are the flowers? Can anybody identify them?"

Jared comes up to me and looks out over the flowers. He points to one of them. "That's a hyacinth. That one over there is a petunia. I think that is a hydrangea, but I'm not sure. These aren't naturally growing. They've been cut and just put into the ground."

"That one is a daisy," I say, pointing to a white bloom nearby.

"So is that," Alyssa says, indicating a pink flower nearby. "Transvaal. They come in all kinds of colors, not just white."

My brain sparks. "Show me the rest of them. How many of these flowers are daisies?"

She gets up, cradling her injured hand in front of her, and looks at the flowers. She points out more than a dozen flowers in a variety of shades. I count the other different kinds.

"Daisies," I say. "There are more daisies than any other type of flowers."

"Alright, so daisies are the majority. What does that mean?" Jared asks.

Behind us a creaking sound makes us turn. The chain has pulled up and now Grant is barely on the tips of his toes on the platform. None of us saw which of the wheels turned, but we know what it means. This is a warning. We're not going fast enough.

"Daisies. Daisy, as in the aerobics instructor."

As soon as I say it, I know exactly what it means. I run back to the wheels and choose the one on the right. I push on it but I'm not strong enough to move it on my own. I yell for the others and they run up behind me, adding their own force to turn the wheel. Grant lowers down, his feet finally touching the platform, and then it brings him down closer to the ground. Austin has lowered Molly to the grass and runs over to release the chain from Grant's neck. He collapses, coughing and desperately trying to get air. I've been trying to hold myself together throughout this, but the anger is starting to bubble up and more intense inside of me. I have to keep it together. I have to hold it in. Count the time. Know the minutes are passing. It's almost over.

"Who else is here?" I ask. "Do you know everybody who is inside here?"

"Keep going, Agent Griffin. There's more fun to be had," the mechanical voice says.

This time, I ignore it. "Who else is here?"

"It was us," Jared says. "The other man, he was shot. Sarah."

He swallows hard and Alyssa continues the list. By the time she's finished, we know that everyone they were aware of who had been put in The Park is accounted for, either alive or dead. This is exactly what I wanted. I have them all together. Now we get out.

"We're done," I say loudly. "The game is over."

"What are you doing?" Alyssa hisses. "You're going to get us killed."

"No, I'm not. They aren't going to hurt anyone else."

"Stop, Emma," Jared says. "Let's just keep going. We've gotten this far."

"And it's as far as we're going to go," I say.

"Listen to them, Emma. You don't want to do this," the voice says.

"It's Emma now?" I ask. "Are we friends?"

The voice laughs. "Maybe. Too bad you don't know what to call me."

"I think I do," I say. "Which is why you're going to let these people go."

"And why would I do that and ruin my fun?"

"Because I haven't told them who you are. I haven't said a single word even though I know. I know who you are, and I know who is there with you," I say. "And if you let them out now, they won't know. And you'll have me. I'll keep playing your game. You can have your prize."

"Emma, you can't do this," Jared says.

"You would sacrifice yourself for them?" the voice asks.

"You said you have your integrity. I am taking you at your word that you mean you would treat this as a fair hunt," I say.

"Of course. There would be no fun in just executing you."

"Then, yes. You let them go and I will continue on with whatever you have planned for me. And if I survive and get out, I do. If I don't, at least they will have lived. Do we have a deal?"

There's a pause and I can imagine the men wherever they have posted themselves talking about my offer. I know this is an incredible risk. But it's one I have to take. I need to know the others will be safe. No matter what it means for me.

"Agent Griffin, get on your knees where you are. Jared, blindfold her."

He blanches, but I shake my head.

"Go ahead," I tell Jared. "It's going to be fine. Just do what they ask."

With trembling hands, Jared tears off a piece of his shirt and wraps it tightly over my eyes.

"I'm sorry," he whispers.

"Don't be. Just go. Get out as fast as you can. Don't stop," I tell him. "Everything will be fine."

"Follow the lights," the mechanical voice says. "Say nothing to anyone. Take the horse. I'm tired of caring for it."

I stay on my knees for a long time. I can only hope they have the integrity they say they do and that the group will be released. I also hope Jared and the others know well enough not to listen to the warn-

THE GIRL ON THE RETREAT

ing of not saying anything to anyone. It doesn't really matter. It won't be long now.

CHAPTER THIRTY-NINE

"They're gone," the mechanical voice tells me. "Get up."

I climb to my feet and take off the blindfold.

"What now?" I ask.

I only need a few more minutes. Just to convince them that I really am being compliant with them. If I can get through the next few minutes, I can end this. But they need to believe I've given myself over to them.

"Go to the edge of the field. You'll see a sign with instructions to follow."

A single pinpoint of light appears at the edge of the field and I go to it. Just as the voice told me, there is a sign attached to one of the trees. In the same combination of paint colors as on the sign in the flower bed, the sign tells me to find the maze and make my way to the end. I'm sure the wording is meant to be poetic, but it comes across as awkward and pretentious. Not surprising but enough to make me cringe.

THE GIRL ON THE RETREAT

I follow the path and lights appear as I go until I reach the opening for a maze. It looks like a thrown-together Halloween attraction made of a wooden frame and black tarps. I stand at the mouth staring into the darkness for a second, then walk in. It's absolute blackness as I make my way along the corridor. I reach out to my sides to touch the walls and feel blades slide through my fingertips. Hissing, I wrench them back.

Taking a breath, I continue forward. I glance up and see tiny pricks of light. That's where the cameras are. I pretend like I don't see them, like I'm still searching, but use them to follow my way along. Occasionally I purposely make a wrong turn so they don't catch on to what I'm doing. After one turn, something hard pops out of the wall and hits me in the side, taking my breath away and cracking my rib. After another, a gush of freezing water comes down onto my head, chilling me to the bone.

After another hard impact sends me to the ground. I count the minutes. I count the seconds. I'm finished.

"I'm done," I call out. "Let me out."

The mechanical voice laughs. "So soon? You think we're going to make it that easy for you?"

"Yes," I say.

"Don't flatter yourself. You don't scare us," he says.

"I can," I say. "Face me for yourself. Enough of the games. You really want to make me your prize, do it. Get me out of the maze and face me for yourself. I know who you are already. You're not keeping secrets."

"You think we believe you? I know you're lying. You don't know who I am," he says.

I reach into my pocket and pull out the green pin. I hold it up above my head, then look up at the camera.

"Look familiar?" I ask.

"So, you know I'm from the retreat. Everyone there has one of those," he says. "That one is yours."

"Everyone else has their own. This one is yours. You have mine," I say.

"How would you know that?" he asks.

"Because you grabbed mine off the ground when you attacked me, and you didn't realize it because you don't know that the colors are wrong. You're colorblind, Tom."

There's a long pause. "What are you talking about?"

He's forgotten to put the voice modulator on and now I hear his real voice.

"You're colorblind. The pictures of the dead women, the paint on the signs, the picture you sent to me of the wrong woman in the run. You can't tell the difference between certain colors. You told me once you do things for fun. And you think that's what you're doing now. You're giving these people an experience, something to indulge themselves, to collect. But they have their reasons. Grant and Daisy are lovers. They have been since they grew up together. Eric found their hometown and the yearbooks that prove it. Gordon, I know you're hurt and that's why you wanted to punish him. I'm sure there are explanations for the others. But the one that interests me the most is Chelsea.

"You didn't put her in here after you poisoned her with antifreeze to make it look like she's drunk because you wanted to watch her torment and humiliate herself in front of people. You wanted to punish her for killing her girlfriend in the same drunk driving accident that killed her sister."

"Don't you dare," he growls.

"Come face me. Enough of the drama. Enough of the tired, re-used games. This has been done. You know it is. The cards, the flowers. They were all to throw me off. You were trying to toy with me before you got me here, but here's the thing. You don't know who you're dealing with. Let me out and find out for yourself."

Bright lights burst on around me and I'm able to see to walk through the rest of the maze. I walk out into the gradually rising sunrise and see Tom Murphy striding toward me with my gun in his hand.

"Oh, hell no," I mutter and launch myself at him.

A shot rings out, reverberating in the air, and I hear the whistle of the bullet as it passes just outside of my cheek. A slice of white-hot pain sears over my earlobe, but I barely have time to register it before my shoulder makes contact with his stomach.

The breath leaves his body in one heavy whoosh and we crumple to the ground, me rolling to the right at impact to get to my feet quicker. I hear a clattering that can only be the sound of my gun falling away from him.

He clearly didn't expect me to hit him so hard. My ribs have gone from a dull ache to a roaring fire in my chest and side, but I push through them. This has to end now.

I dive at him, the adrenaline giving me the extra energy I need to slam my fist into his jaw hard enough to rock his head sideways. His eyes are glassy as I hit him again and again. I think I have him. I think it's done.

Suddenly, he shifts hard to the right, and I tumble. He kicks directly into my ribs, and it sends me rolling away in pain. I struggle to my knees

THE GIRL ON THE RETREAT

and see him shaking off the cobwebs. Then he looks off to the side, between us and several yards away.

It's my gun.

He looks to me as I look at him, our eyes meeting in a glare of determination and hatred. It's him or me. One of us will get the gun. If it's him, I am as good as dead.

He lunges and I dive, my hand arm stretching out as far as I can despite the screaming pain in my ribs. Desperation drives me.

We touch the gun at the same time, but my hand swats it away. My back is to him and he grasps at me, trying to wrap his arm around my throat. I throw my elbow back and hit him in the stomach, which loosens his grip before he can really seal it in.

I claw at the ground toward the gun, and as I reach it, wrapping my fingers around it, I spin on my back and point up into his shocked face.

"This is mine," I grumble.

His chest is heaving as he breathes hard. He smirks. Blood trickles from the lip where my knuckles had split his skin.

"Shoot me if you must," he says. "But I have more on the way."

Keeping the gun pointed on him, I stand. It's my turn to smirk.

"See these?" I asked, turning my shoe sideways so he could see it. "Xavier designed a GPS tracker for my boot. You should have checked me better."

An explosion of sound fills the air as a group of officers rush in, Sam at the lead. Their guns are drawn. Cuffs are pulled out. Tom is thrown to the ground, his eyes never leaving me. The smirk has vanished and replaced with a shocked expression.

"Emma?"

I turn to see Sam, his face a mask of concern.

"Emma?"

I want to respond to him, but the world is going gray. Suddenly, I feel myself falling. Exhaustion and pain have overwhelmed me, and the only thing that saves me from hitting the floor is Sam's quick reflexes. He scoops me up and pulls me toward him, and I collapse into his arms.

"Come on," he says. "Let's get out of here. We can go somewhere else for the night."

"Debrief," I mutter. "We have to do exit..."

"They can do that at the hotel," he says. "Let's go."

The next hour or so is a blur. The car is piled with our stuff, and I am in the passenger seat, bandaged, exhausted, and curled up with a pillow against the window. Sam gets in and turns on the car, sweeping the radio over for a few stations before giving up and spinning the knob to turn it off. We drive in silence until we reach the new hotel, and he goes in to check in for us.

In a daze, I follow him to the room, Sam insisting that I shouldn't carry anything, that he has it all. The cold air of the A/C hits me and it sends a shiver over my body. The adrenaline full and well gone, I just want to go to bed. Sam pulls back the covers and I slide in to the tightly tucked sheets that I enjoy so much. Sam slips in behind me and curls around me, one arm under a pillow under my head and the other draped over my stomach. His breath on my skin soothes the chill, and I feel my whole body relax.

The window is almost closed all the way, but a small slip of the night sky is visible. A thick, heavy fog is rolling in. It nearly blankets the sky with a curling, gray wall. Gradually, my eyes close, and I listen to Sam's heartbeat as I drift off to sleep, knowing that it's finally over.

EPILOGUE

I don't know why Sam set the alarm for so early. Neither of us is going to work today. We're going to drive home and spend some time together. But the high-pitched beeping is dragging me up into consciousness. I try to tell him to turn it off but can't make the words form in my mouth.

Something sounds strange about the alarm. The beeping is too short. it's not loud enough, even if it's enough to set me on edge. I hear something else. Voices. A lot of them, actually, saying things that don't make sense. Why would anybody be in the hotel with Sam and me? But I can hear them getting more distinct as my awareness returns.

"I can't eat any more of this food. I'm going to order something. Anybody else in the mood for Thai?"

It sounds like Dean. Why is he here?

"Grab my phone," Sam says. "I should have Joe's number saved in there. He's doing grabs from most of the restaurants in town. I can see if he's doing the Thai restaurant."

His voice doesn't sound like it's coming from beside me in bed the way it should. Why would he get up and hang out with Dean while I'm lying here asleep? I try to reach beside me to feel on the mattress for him, to search for the warmth in the sheets that would tell me he'd gotten up recently. But I can't seem to make my arm move.

That beeping has to stop. I can't think straight listening to it.

Did he say Joe? Why would he ask Joe to drive an hour from Sherwood to bring food to us? Why are everyone's voices so muffled?

"What do they have?" Xavier asks.

"Thai food," Sam answers, sounding exhausted.

"I have a menu," Dean says. "Just scroll through and see if you can find anything that sounds good." There's a pause and his voice comes again, only this time it's lower, heavy. "Are you okay?"

"No," Sam says.

Nothing else. It makes my heart ache and I want to touch him. I reach a hand out, but my body still won't move. Why won't it move? I try to reach again and feel the tips of my fingers tingle.

"Did you see that?" Xavier suddenly asks.

"What?" Sam responds.

"Her fingers. They moved."

"What?" Dean gasps.

"Her fingers," Xavier says again. "Only a little, but they moved."

"Emma?" Sam asks, his voice lifting a little. "Emma, can you hear me?"

The beeping gets a little faster and someone takes a sharp intake of breath. I want to open my mouth and say, "yes, I can hear you, you idiot, what's going on," but I can't open my mouth. I can't even open my eyes.

"The prevailing theory is that hearing isn't necessarily the issue," Xavier says. I hear what sounds like a couple of steps coming closer. "Emma, are your cognitive faculties returning so you are capable of effectively processing what we are saying to you?" A brief pause. "That doesn't have the same zip."

I try to reach again. Nothing.

"I saw it that time," Sam says. "Dean, get the nurse."

Nurse?

"Emma. Babe, can you look at me?"

I feel his hands touch the sides of my face and run back through my hair. I'm suddenly aware of the cold on my arms and the sharp smell in the air. My eyelids seem to glow as awareness of light around me increases. They are impossibly heavy as I start to open them.

"Her eyes," Xavier says.

THE GIRL ON THE RETREAT

"I saw," Sam responds with a touch of excitement in his voice. "Come on, honey. Look at me. Open your eyes."

Everything is a bit hazy as my eyelids part and gradually open. But what I can see makes my heart fill. Sam's face is right above me, his eyes locked on mine. The light above his head is bright and embedded in a fiber panel ceiling. Not a nightstand lamp. Not a hotel ceiling. A hospital ceiling.

"She's awake," Xavier calls. "Dean. Dean, come back, she's awake!"

Footsteps pound back toward the room and a hand touches my arm. There's someone else beside me, but I'm just focused on Sam.

"I'm going to text Eric and Bellamy," Dean says.

"Tell them to be careful driving over," Xavier tells him. "Look outside. The fog is getting thick."

"I'm so happy you're awake," Sam whispers. "I was so worried. I missed you so much."

I don't know how but I'm able to barely wrench my mouth open.

"What—where is—" I start, but I can hear my words fade into blurry nonsense and my brain can't even process how to say what I'm trying to. What happened to Jared and the others? Did they make it out okay? Did they arrest Tom and everyone involved?

"Shh, shh," he whispers, tears filling his face. "Just rest. It's okay. You're okay."

"It may be some time before her motor functions are optimal again," Xavier rattles off.

"Not now, X," Dean gripes. "They're on their way. Emma, we're so glad you're awake."

This time, I'm able to get my mouth a little wider open. I try to sit upright, but everyone freaks out and immediately urges me to lie back down.

"Wha—what about the case? The resort and... the... the park..."

"I thought she might be experiencing that," Xavier tells Dean. "All the brain activity..."

But his words float off somewhere else in my consciousness as Sam takes my hand and squeezes it tightly. "Emma, you've been asleep. For a long time."

AUTHOR'S NOTE

Dear Reader,

Thank you for choosing to read *The Girl on the Retreat*, the final installment of the *Emma Griffin® FBI Mystery Retro - Limited Series*. It has been a joy to explore the 80s, to dive into the nostalgia of the time period, and to bring that era to life through the eyes of Emma Griffin and the other characters in this series. From the neon lights to the cassette tapes, it was a blast to immerse myself in that unique time period. I hope that this book provided a satisfying conclusion to this limited series and that it has left you wanting more. Now, back to regular Emma series and any questions you might have will be answered there!

This series was a special project for me, and I am grateful for the opportunity to share it with you, my dear reader. It has been an incredible journey, and I couldn't have done it without your support and enthusiasm. If you can please continue to leave your reviews for these books, I would appreciate that enormously. Your reviews allow me to get the validation I need to keep on writing as an indie author. Just a moment of your time is all that is needed.

My promise to you is to always do my best to bring you thrilling adventures. I can't wait for you to read all the books I have in store for you!

Yours,
A.J. Rivers

P.S. If for some reason you didn't like this book or found typos or other errors, please let me know personally. I do my best to read and respond to every email at mailto:aj@riversthrillers.com

ALSO BY
A.J. RIVERS

Emma Griffin FBI Mysteries

Season One

Book One—The Girl in Cabin 13*
Book Two—The Girl Who Vanished*
Book Three—The Girl in the Manor*
Book Four—The Girl Next Door*
Book Five—The Girl and the Deadly Express*
Book Six—The Girl and the Hunt*
Book Seven—The Girl and the Deadly End*

Season Two

Book Eight—The Girl in Dangerous Waters*
Book Nine—The Girl and Secret Society*
Book Ten—The Girl and the Field of Bones*
Book Eleven—The Girl and the Black Christmas*
Book Twelve—The Girl and the Cursed Lake*
Book Thirteen—The Girl and The Unlucky 13*
Book Fourteen—The Girl and the Dragon's Island*

Season Three

Book Fifteen—The Girl in the Woods *
Book Sixteen —The Girl and the Midnight Murder *
Book Seventeen— The Girl and the Silent Night *
Book Eighteen — The Girl and the Last Sleepover*
Book Nineteen — The Girl and the 7 Deadly Sins*
Book Twenty — The Girl in Apartment 9*
Book Twenty-One — The Girl and the Twisted End*

Ava James FBI Mysteries

Book One—The Woman at the Masked Gala*
Book Two—Ava James and the Forgotten Bones*
Book Three—The Couple Next Door*
Book Four — The Cabin on Willow Lake*
Book Five — The Lake House
Book Six — The Ghost of Christmas

Dean Steele FBI Mysteries

Book One—The Woman in the Woods

Emma Griffin FBI Mysteries Retro - Limited Series

Book One— The Girl in the Mist*
Book Two— The Girl on Hallow's Eve*
Book Three— The Girl and the Christmas Past*
Book Four— The Girl and the Winter Bones
Book Five— The Girl on the Retreat

Other Standalone Novels

Gone Woman
* Also available in audio

Printed in Dunstable, United Kingdom